cafe

FRASER BEATH MCEWING

Horizon Publishing Group™

First published in 2008
Horizon Publishing Group
PO Box 275
Cherrybrook NSW 2126
Australia
www.horizonpg.net
Email: orders@horizonpg.net
         info@horizonpg.net

2nd edition published by Horizon Publishing Group in 2018.

The moral right of the author has been asserted

National Library of Australia Cataloguing-in-Publication data:

Author: McEwing, Fraser Beath
Title: cafe / author, Fraser Beath McEwing.
Edition: 2nd. ed.
ISBN: 9781922238764 (pbk.)

 A catalogue record for this
book is available from the
NATIONAL
LIBRARY   National Library of Australia
OF AUSTRALIA

Cover by Damian Vuleta.
Typesetting & Page Design by Inception Press.

Disclaimer

*****

"For Michelle
and the path we took together

*****

Chapter One

My job at Lead Balloon was teetering.

I knew the way Felix Crouch and Wesley Crowe worked. They were leaving me in my comfortable office with its view across terracotta tiles and distant harbour, but giving me work I loathed. I'd seen them do it before to people they wanted out of the agency at low cost.

Okay, so I'd had no opportunity to even dislike my new pet-food account, but the signs were all there. I didn't have to meet the client to know that his outfit would be even more loaded with death by boredom than Dempster Family Funerals and Awayaway Bus Holidays that had recently crash-landed on my desk.

Only four years earlier, at forty-eight, I would have told them to stick the job up their arses and marched out laughing. But now, I realised, fifty-two in the advertising business was twice as old as forty-eight. If I resigned I would be walking into an employment desert with no water, no food and not even a fucking hat.

I re-read the briefing notes Felix had given me. In ten minutes I'd have to play image therapist to a pet-food company and its vice-president.

'His name's Morton Whitbread, an American,' Felix had told me. 'Squared-off type from Utah. Probably Mormon. No coffee and seven kids. Anyway, I don't care about his religion. He's got a pet-food line that needs a change of identity. Just the sort of thing you can manage these days.'

'Who have you got in mind for the team?' I'd asked, ignoring his reference to my sagging reputation.

'No team,' Felix had said. 'He hasn't mentioned a budget.'

'How do we put together a media plan then?'

'No media either. Look, he only wants names, logos, packaging, and maybe some point of sale. You might be able to talk him into media and some other stuff. But if it had been up to me we wouldn't be bothering at all. Wesley's wife Enid met him at a dog show somewhere and offered our help, thinking he'd be a good account.'

'So you want me to knock out a few ideas and get rid of him.'

'Without taking the piss out of him,' Felix said. 'Just help if you can, but don't waste too much time on it. Any graphics you need can come from young Andy down in the art room.'

The choice of young Andy ranked as even more of a putdown than the assignment to a non-spending, non-future, bible-brandishing American pet-food manufacturer. Andy wasn't long out of graphic art school, and knew everything about everything. The only client he'd clicked with was Downheaval, a new pop group we'd taken on. In my state of pessimism I saw Andy and I together on this new account like the unborn tethered to the dead.

Whitbread's need was obvious. He couldn't use Good Fortune

Dog and Good Fortune Cat in Australia without being sued for passing off an established brand. But why would an American pet-food company waste its time on the small Australian market anyway?

Donna called from reception to announce the arrival of Mr Whitbread. I told her to send him up to the top floor and to arrange coffee, biscuits and a big jug of our caffeine-free Sydney water for him. I checked the boardroom again. All in place: the long grey granite table and leather-covered chairs with the springy backs that could set off a bout of involuntary nodding when the occupant moved. I straightened my client contact pad, automatically pulled my tie to just short of choke, and went to wait by the elevator.

The twin mirror doors opened, splitting me in two, and Morton Whitbread stood there, tall and flat, with broad shoulders. An abundance of greying hair waved precisely away from a rectangular forehead. He smiled up a set of well-made crowns as he stepped forward for the multi-pump American handshake.

'Ed, so good to meet you,' he said with a clergyman's enthusiasm. Then he moved aside to reveal another man. 'I'd like you to meet Nat Cohen.'

His companion made an immediate visual statement with his stubbly black and white beard which covered generous jowls that were visually balanced by large, perfectly round spectacles. He offered a flaccid fillet for me to knead. 'Nat is what we call an independent distributor,' Whitbread continued, maintaining his smile as I led them into the boardroom. 'That won't make much sense to you until we get around to explaining the Good Fortune pet-food marketing system. It's all in the brief I'll leave with you later. I must say,' he chuckled, 'I just love the name of your advertising agency. Lead Balloon brings a smile to everybody who hears it.'

'We're all used to it by now,' I spoke the familiar lines, 'but we're always aware of the reverse symbolism.'

I seated us at the far end of the table where they could enjoy the view while I concentrated on them, a positioning trick I'd picked up from Felix. I called reception and increased the morning tea order to three before I leaned back in my chair at the head of the table.

'So you're in pet-food,' I began, taking up my pen and hovering it over the pad in front of me.

'Yes indeed, but there's a lot more to it than that,' Whitbread said, pinning me with his God-innocent blue eyes. 'The product is only part of it.' He picked up the grained leather briefcase he'd brought with him and laid it on the table. 'There's a revolution in here,' he said, patting it like you would a child.

'Let me ask you a question.' Cohen suddenly spoke up in a husky voice that matched the loose folds of his black suit, black shirt and black tie. 'You got a dog or a cat?' His New York accent drew out 'dawg' to make it sound as though it should be a dachshund.

'We've got a labrador and a moggy cat.'

'Good, good,' Cohen continued. 'Tell me something else, Ed. What's the worst thing about your puppy dog and your pussy cat?'

I pondered. I could only think of good things, like Jessica's tail thumping with welcome against the door of my Karmann Ghia when I arrived home, or the peace of Muffin's purring in my lap when I watched television.

'The vet bills,' I volunteered, although they wouldn't know that my veterinary friend Sid Willis refused to charge me for anything but the medicines he used.

'Go worse,' Cohen said.

'That's difficult, Mr Cohen. I suppose fleas, but I think we've beaten that problem with ...'

'We're off the track here, Ed. Please call me Nat, incidentally. What I want to hear is shit.'

I wrote 'shit' on my pad.

'Droppings, pavement foul, doggie doos, excrement, faeces, the nice words go on and on, but what we're talking about here, Ed, is shit.' Nat's voice rose with a passion that lifted his heavy face and transformed his eyes into shining peat ponds. 'Ever think about how many dogs and cats there are, and how much shit comes out of their arseholes? It's the curse of neighbourhoods and cities throughout the world.'

I wrote down on my pad 'coiss of neighbourhoods and cities'.

'I'll have to ask Nat to hold it there,' Whitbread interrupted, 'and likewise, please call me Morton. Nat gets excited about the end benefits, if you'll pardon the pun. Let's go back a little.' He opened his briefcase and lifted out two containers. They could have been soup cans but they were not made of metal and they carried no stickers.

'I took off the labels for a good reason,' he said. 'I wanted you to have a clear run at this. In any case, the brand we use in the States would be illegal here.' He slid one of the cans across the table to me. When I picked it up it was heavier than I'd expected. I also noticed that it had a screw top that fitted flush with the side of the can.

'Nice container,' I commented.

'Even nicer than you yet know,' Morton said. 'This can doesn't need an opener. It unscrews at the top, which breaks the seal and gives you about two weeks to use the contents. And there's more. This can is biodegradable. In twelve months the polymer's self-triggering memory cuts in and the can destroys itself in about a week.'

'What happens to the contents?' I asked.

'All over the place,' Nat cut in. 'But believe me, people who buy the stuff never leave it around long enough to see that happen. They put the new cans at the back of the shelf and move the old ones forward.'

'Ed, premature container breakdown just isn't an issue,' Morton confirmed. 'The big benefit is that the can turns into plant food wherever it's dumped. Some people break up the empty cans and dig them into their gardens. It's an environmental enhancement.'

A knock on the door and the sight of Elsa's reversing bony buttocks announced the arrival of morning tea. She set the tray down on the bar cabinet and placed a plate of chocolate biscuits between us. A second plate offered slices of apple, long slivers of carrot and cherry tomatoes.

'We kind of celebrate the end of the week with chocolate biscuits,' I explained, 'but this month we're celebrating our new fresh food account by offering fruit and vegetables to the staff and visitors.'

Nat's puffy but surprisingly mobile fingers reached for the first of what would become a succession of chocolate biscuits, while Morton, with a faint cough of pleasure, took some carrot and apple. I noticed that Nat had some words tattooed on the back of his right hand, but I couldn't read them.

'Well, it looks as though you could sell your container and not worry about the contents,' I said over my coffee cup.

'If you think the container is good, wait 'til you hear what's in it,' Morton said, striking an icy chord as he hard-landed his glass of water on the granite table. 'Let me take you back in time a little. In 1988 a couple of postgraduate students working in the food nutrition lab at the University of Salt Lake City were doing a study on pet-food. They were particularly interested in what happened to the food in the digestive system of the animals – mostly dogs and cats. They found that only a small part of the nutritional value of the food was turned into energy. Most of it was excreted. Even when they improved the food quality it didn't help digestive efficiency very much. They reasoned that if they could combine the right amount of essential nutrients with an inert, neutral carrier, the animal might be able to absorb all of the nutrients and excrete the carrier.'

'Yeah, that's how it started,' Nat interjected, as he quickly rounded up another biscuit.

'I won't go into the scientific details, I'll leave those with you, but after three years the kids got it right,' Morton continued. 'They had to do a few tricks with getting the animals to like the food and go on liking it. One way was to provide six different flavours. You might love smoked salmon, but if you have it every day you grow very tired of it. Are you with me Ed?

'The two students, Ellis Sommerville and Sally Ness, never finished their doctorates. They went into business, selling their pet-food from a kiosk on Ellis's daddy's fruit farm. That was in 1991.'

'And then they formed a corporation,' I prompted.

'I'm coming to that,' Morton said, to which Nat murmured around his latest biscuit that we were about to hear the best part of the story.

'Their pet-food was too dear to sell if it had to carry a normal retail profit margin, plus advertising and promotion. You know how much money goes into advertising pet-food here? It's worse in America. And you know who pays for it? The pet owner who buys it. Good Fortune had to be promoted by word of mouth. You see Ed, it has only good ingredients in it. There are none of the cheap fillers like jelly and gravy and ground-up gristle that you find in commercial pet-food. It was pure nutrient and carrier, a true meeting of science and nature.'

Nat swallowed quickly and took up the story uninvited. 'Obviously they had to go the network marketing route,' he said. 'They had a friend, Gerry Silver, who did the marketing plan for them. They gave him twenty per cent to come on board. What a *metziah* that was for Gerry! Now the three of them run the fastest-growing pet-food company in the world. Could be the fastest-growing food company in the world, period.'

'We called ourselves the Good Fortune Pet-food Corporation,' Morton continued, 'with Good Fortune Dog and Good Fortune Cat as our brands. We're doing over two hundred million dollars annual turnover in America and now we're going on our global expansion program. We've opened in Canada and Mexico. Australia is next.'

'Why Australia?' I asked on cue.

'I'm glad you asked that Ed,' Morton replied. 'You speak American English. You're a strong dog- and cat-loving society. You're well off enough to afford the products and, most important of all, you probably have the biggest mix of cultures of any country in the whole world. This means that if we get networks established here, they will have immediate access through family and friends to other countries we're going to open. Everybody here knows somebody who knows somebody in England or Europe or Asia. You'd be surprised how isolated we Americans have become. It's like the generations have covered our roots.'

After many years, the acrid smell of network marketing suddenly curled up my nose again. I remembered the night Mat Occleshaw from the yacht club asked for my advice on a new business. Flattered at his confidence in my acumen, I took Clarice to his house for what we thought was a friendly chat after dinner with his wife Pat, only to be rushed off to a meeting hall full of bemused people. When the doors were closed an intense, grinning man on the dais revealed that we were all going to be told about **Prodmasters.** Clarice and I felt betrayed. We came away from the meeting determined not to use the products or be duped like that again.

I still felt angry about it, even though it had happened fifteen years ago. Since then, I'd been approached by a stream of people, a lot of them family or friends, each trying to get Clarice and me involved in network marketing. We were offered discount telephone calls, car maintenance systems, wine syndicates, jewellery, gold coins, management seminars and a variety of personal care products. We liked some of the stuff enough to buy it but we never wanted to become part of an army of hypnotised consumers and evangelical business builders. We hated selling and we feared rejection and we weren't so desperate to earn money that we would re-engineer our personalities to get it.

Now the phantom of network marketing had returned in the guise of Morton Whitbread and Nathan Cohen. Felix and Wesley had surely set me up. I'd been served a rotten egg which had set off a round of sniggering in the kitchen while they waited for me to break it open.

I considered showing these two men to the door and then marching in to tackle Felix and Wesley together. But maybe that's how they wanted it. A dummy-spit from me would be far cheaper for the company than a dismissal after twenty-two years – with all the financial jewellery they'd have to hang on it.

I looked across the table at my two clients. I couldn't blame them. I even had to admit a growing liking for them. They were believers in the upswing of an enterprise that would deliver them riches, maybe fame. I decided to play along – for the time being at least – until I could think it through and discuss my career with Clarice.

'So what do you see Lead Balloon Advertising doing for you?' I asked with a smile I had to paste on.

'See Ed, we need another brand name and logo for Australia,' Morton said. 'And then I guess we should get new labels for the cans. I can give you all the information you'll need on ingredients. We have to reveal those in the US, by law. And then we might need some corporate stuff like letterheads. That might lead on to posters, show cards and so on down the turnpike.

'Now I'm not making any promises, but there's a chance we might take up the new name – and the other work you do for us – to use overseas. If Gerry, Ellis and Sally like it, they just might use it in the States too. They don't believe that "Good Fortune" is appropriate for the company now.'

The egg may not have been as rotten as those fuckers in the kitchen had thought. The dollars for all this creative work could mount up. That would at least buy me some employment planning time.

'Morton,' I said, returning his candid eye contact, 'normally an account director would ask you this, but I have to. I might as well be frank. Does your company have the funds to pay for the work you want us to do?'

Before Morton could reply, Nat gave a hooting laugh.

'I'm glad you brought that up,' Morton said. 'I'll leave you with credit references. We have the highest credit rating that Dun & Bradstreet ever gives. We've built the business entirely debt free. Our profit for last year could easily buy this advertising agency. Oh, and I should mention, we don't quibble over fees. Felix has quoted your fees to me and we'll pay twenty per cent more if you come up with a brand and logo that we decide to use. There will be a lot more again, of course, if we use it outside Australia.'

'Does Felix know about the extra fees?' I asked.

'Not at this point in time,' Morton answered. 'Why, should I tell him?'

'No,' I said quickly. 'Absolutely no need. Leave that all to me.'

'I thought that may be the case,' Morton said, letting his blank expression wink for him. 'Now, we've got to get along. Here's the brief and the product details. You have a week to come up with something.' He reached into his case again. 'And here's a couple of cans for your dog and cat. Try them and you'll see how well the product works.' He returned to his formal American persona and shook hands. 'Ed, it has been a real joy spending this time with you today,' he said.

He left the boardroom. Nat followed, the rhythm of his walk giving a separate life to his clothes as fat and muscle competed for the limited space.

***

Chapter Two

I had to wait until Sunday afternoon before I could get to work on the brief Morton Whitbread had given me. I'd had the more pressing matter of Dempster Funerals to finish first. The roughs were okay but the copy needed a heading.

'Your moment in time' was the heading Horace Dempster liked, although I didn't think it said enough. In fact, it didn't say anything at all. The heading I wanted him to choose was 'The last thing you can do well'.

I never would have been game to pitch old Dempster the press ad I really wanted to run. There would be a line of black funeral cars, computer-multiplied into the distance, and in old English type above them: 'We've got hearsepower!'

That was the trouble. Wesley and Felix were strangling me with accounts that left me no creative room. They'd obviously decided that my well of ideas had dried up. Maybe this new pet-food account might put me back on the winners' podium when they least expected it.

I happily abandoned the nap I'd recently been taking after Sunday lunch, and instead went to my study. Clarice had taken Sibyl and Taya to see their grandmother for a birthday afternoon tea, a visitation that may well have included me, were it not for Good Fortune.

'Oh, the slings and arrows of outrageous fortune,' I muttered as I sat down at my old oak desk and opened the file.

My study, for all the painful thinking it had hosted, was still my solace. As I sat facing the creeper-draped window I realised how long it had been since I'd dealt with anything more than household matters at this desk. Here was another sign that I was sliding as a creative writer at Lead Balloon. I no longer needed to bring work home.

While we all acknowledged Clarice as the minister for home affairs, that stopped at my study door. Working on briefs at home had won me the sovereignty of this room, where chaos or order or stupidity or obscenity could rampage when I wanted them to. If for nothing else, I welcomed the need to work on the Good Fortune account because it re-marked the boundary of my small kingdom.

Immediately I opened the brief, I concluded that Lead Balloon was not the only advertising agency that had been given the task of coming up with a new name and logo for the Good Fortune Pet-food Corporation. The material seemed too well prepared, like the package you found on your chair at a management seminar. It included a potted history of the company, some press clippings, ingredient details and glossy photographs of the striking company buildings in Salt Lake City, along with pictures of the partners trying to look like regular guys. But the product brochure really lifted my eyebrows.

'What goes in must come out' it boldly announced in rushing italics, and then traced the digestive process of a dog and a cat, finishing with a picture of each, and a thick arrow, carrying the word 'challenge' pointing to their arses. A similar arrow, carrying the word 'solution' pointed to cans of Good Fortune dog and cat food.

I expected the ingredients to be good for the animal but I didn't expect the claim that their shit didn't stink or, to put it in their terms, 'odourless excreta'. Moreover it would, when dry, turn into harmless powder which would blow away in the wind to become part of the regenerative dust of the planet. It didn't even look offensive. One close-up showed it to be the colour of beach sand, while in another, a dear old granny smiled down at a lump of it she'd squeezed in her hand.

Another booklet explained Good Fortune's 'unique system of network marketing'. It seemed that everybody who became a distributor and put in a reasonable amount of time recruiting other distributors would make a substantial income – which would continue as long as the consuming beasts continued their liking for Good Fortune. Of course, I'd heard those sorts of network marketing claims before, supported by statistics and graphs. I remembered the bulging bags of gold coins, and families running up paths of the mansions they had just bought, complete with the new Mercedes' nose poking out of the garage. This is not pyramid selling, the folder claimed in bold print, it is rectangular selling. Everybody formed their own rectangle which was part of somebody else's rectangle. More than half the cost of every can of Good Fortune found its way into the pockets of the networkers relaxing in their rectangles.

I understood the need for Gerry, Ellis and Sally to change the brand name. They might have seen themselves as fortunate to own such a good business but, after that, the idea of good fortune was counter-productive. If you allowed good fortune, then you had to allow misfortune. The concept of the laws of chance was at odds with the inevitable success that would come to earnest distributors. With an annual turnover now at two hundred million dollars, I imagined that the term 'good fortune' would have become an embarrassment to them, so much so that they now had a squadron of advertising agencies working on the case. Here in my peaceful little study I would probably have to compete against some of the best creative brains in the world.

I stood up and gazed through the creepers into the garden below. The swimming pool lay in the arms of shadows thrown by old trees. An occasional wink of harbour water broke through their branches whenever the wind moved them. I closed my eyes and called up The Channel. There was a lot riding on this one. Not only trying to impress Crouch and Crowe, I was out there in cyberspace, playing against other minds of unknown capacity for a prize of galactic proportions. I should have known The Channel well enough to remember it to be a contrary bastard. The best ideas arrived unbidden, but if I really needed something world-beating, as I did now, it would just as likely shut down, or at best send through gravel when I needed nuggets. Not even gravel came to me as I opened my eyes and stared first into the garden and then the glass-fronted cabinet where my dusty creative awards stared mockingly back through my own reflection.

I leaned back in the balding green velvet office chair once owned by my grandfather. It groaned in keeping with its age. I closed my eyes again and went mind-walking on the ordered streets of Mosman, looking for dogs bearing ideas. Cats were not a pavement problem; they dug holes and elegantly hid their shit.

I realised what a taboo subject shit was. People talked endlessly about food but never about its destination. Shit only ever came up in the media when governments discussed sewage disposal or fouled public places. Sometimes they managed, holding their metaphorical noses, to utter the words: 'untreated solids'. Yet shit was more likely to overwhelm mankind than most other stuff. There seemed too much of it to handle. Every day billions of sphincters disengaged – to the private pleasure of their owners – and released millions of tons of shit, maybe billions. Every sweet child, every gorgeous model, every nun, every derelict, every athlete, every prime minister – they all took a shit.

Somewhere in the United Nations there had to be an agency dealing specifically with the facts about shit. There would be studies on how much shit there was on a daily, monthly and yearly basis. It would also have calculated how long the human race could last before it drowned in its own shit. Some future generation would have to build spaceships for mankind to escape the Earth because it had turned into a huge, rotating ball of shit. But the United Nations wouldn't dare publish its findings because the problem could not be solved and, much more to the point, decent people couldn't bear to be confronted with it. Decent people could talk about global warming, AIDS, weapons of mass destruction, the big bang, the mind of God, orgasms, but not about shit.

It was feasible that the Good Fortune Corporation might eventually develop a product called 'Good Fortune for People', being food to nourish the body but produce omni-friendly shit. How about that as a campaign for my best creative talents?

I had to stop at this point as I felt myself falling into the trap of thinking up campaigns for non-existent products. I pulled a pencil from the anniversary yacht club mug on my desk. I needed a name first. Everything else would follow. The Channel released some gravel. Dog & Cat Phood. Doofood. Friendly Pet-food. Cleansquat. Kleenafood. Rearguard Action. Exitpong. Envirofood for Pets. That one wasn't bad. The Channel was warming up. Next I wrote down K9 Kontribution. That had a good ring to it but it was too subtle for the average pet owner and it excluded cats. It did, however, lead me to canine and feline. The solution might be hidden somewhere there. I began to think too hard, and The Channel departed in a huff.

***

I didn't usually pull Clarice and the girls into my creative dilemmas, but I couldn't help introducing the subject of cats and dogs during dinner that night. The subject never failed to extract anecdotes, even from people who didn't own a pet. But the girls, both needing to finish weekend homework, left the table without throwing any sparks.

'Do you want coffee in front of tele?' Clarice asked as she stood up and began to gather plates.

'I'll make it while you load the dishwasher,' I said.

With my mind still wandering about in dog and cat land, I took the packet of ground coffee from the refrigerator and set up the percolator on the green granite bench. If this was a can of pet-food, what would be printed on it? What would I want to see?

As I listened to the dribbles and muffled pops of the percolator I decided not to go back to Morton with a fistful of ideas, knowing most of them were padding. Although time was short, I had to spend it doing the discarding myself. Those other creative brains working on this would fire one silver bullet. They would be prepared to walk away after that, with the conviction that the client would be insane if he didn't love it. That's how a young pro would do it, and that's how this seasoned pro would do it too.

I took Clarice her coffee. 'I'm going for a walk,' I said.

'Nothing you like the look of in the TV guide?' she said, looking up and smiling.

'I haven't even opened the guide,' I replied. 'I need to air the brain.'

'Do you want company?' she offered. 'You know I'll never knock back some exercise.'

'On this occasion, no. I need to go alone, like the foetus kangaroo crawling to its mother's pouch.'

***

Chapter Three

I left the house trying to think about pet-food but instead my mind fell into a furrow about Clarice. According to everybody else, she looked wonderful. She'd had her hair coloured a reddish tan and shortened to a lavish cup around her head. It suited her well-defined features, now even more prominent since she had driven the fat from her body. Almost overnight she'd become addicted to diet and exercise. She now worked out every week day and probably only rested from it on weekends when she focused her attention on the girls and me. She was fitter than any of us and slimmer as well. Most men would have been delighted with a wife like Clarice, who had shown such determined interest in improving her appearance. They would have shared her pleasure when they heard that hardly anybody recognised her at the school reunion the year she shed all that weight.

But I wasn't one of those men. I'd married Clarice with a secret, one that I'd never shared with anybody except my therapist. I had a passion for fat women. They aroused me sexually. At twenty-three Clarice had been a fat bride, and I had been a husband who came to bed with an expectant angle in his pyjamas almost every night.

Here was a parable, a comment on the self-deceiving society into which fate had cast me. People didn't want to discuss shit, and men didn't want to admit the pleasure of sex with fat women. The required reaction to fat women among the blokes had to be one of dismissal. You'd be an outcast if you said that bulk gave you a boner. There was a stereotype woman you had to groan with lust over if you wanted to be in the blokes' club. She had a small arse and big tits. I asked Dr Greenstrum, my therapist, about this. He'd worked up a conclusive theory to explain my love for fat women, but he couldn't explain the popular enthusiasm for small arses and big tits. He suggested that maybe men, Australian men at any rate, didn't like to admit what really turned them on. Statistically, he reassured me, men ejaculated more semen into fat women than thin ones.

I couldn't help thinking that Greenstrum got a kick out of my case. His questions and his notes and his tapes of our twenty or so consultations over six months actually reached a logical conclusion. I'll bet he wrote 'cured' on my file entirely for his own satisfaction. Most people in therapy, he admitted to me at our last session, gave up with either half cures or decided to live with the stubborn twist in their personalities. Many simply ran out of energy; they grew tired of the continual inward examination. Some older patients died during the long process, bringing about a total cure at 'their moment in time' as Horace Dempster would have liked it expressed.

Once I'd begun to unburden my secret to Greenstrum I could relax and enjoy watching his tangled eyebrows travel up and down his long forehead like bookies' odds. I thought he'd lose them altogether when I told him about my gay father, by that time deceased.

My mother had died when I was two, and after that my father had given in to his true sexuality. That hadn't made him a bad father. Quite the opposite. He became mother and father rolled into one. He had a friend, Uncle Billy, who spent a lot of time with us, but never once did I see my father show emotional affection towards him. That went on after I had gone to bed, I later discovered, but as a little child I was simply a boy who'd lost his mother, and whose father had not re-partnered.

Eventually my father had to decide on a compromise that would allow him to follow his heart, and for me to grow up away from a situation he didn't know how to handle. He sent me to a Christian boarding school for boys when I was eight. I came home for holidays, and he devoted himself to my enjoyment and wellbeing. One Christmas – I was thirteen by then – he poured me what he thought was my first glass of beer. As the froth rose up in the glass so did tears in his eyes. This was going to be his moment of sexual confession. I put my arms around him and told him I already knew he was gay and, more importantly, this was not my first glass of beer. After that, he invited Uncle Billy back into the house, where they had lived together for years between school holidays. Uncle Billy returned to his own bedroom next to my father's.

Dr Greenstrum probed doggedly for sexual abuse in my childhood home, but found only love and care. What sexual abuse there had been had occurred at school. A house master was well known among the borders as a nocturnal wanderer. Every week or so he would walk the dorm after lights out to check the boys' bedding, and would run a random check on their genitals at the same time. Nobody took it very seriously. If you were awake you simply rolled over on your stomach and he would go away. If you were asleep you didn't know it was happening. Groper Kennedy ran the boarding house for as long as I could remember, and he was never brought to heel. I suppose if he were here now he'd be in prison, and my classmates, settling down for their run into old age, would be blubbering on television while money changed hands in lawyers' offices.

Greenstrum diagnosed that I'd been deprived of the closeness of women when I'd needed it in my formative years, and this had set up over-compensation which I expressed in my adult sexuality. I saw curves, and therefore flesh and weight, as the female identity. My subconscious decided that thin women resembled men. When Clarice began her diet and exercise regimen on Taya's third birthday, I progressively lost my libido. When she hit her target weight I bottomed out at impotence in our marital bed.

'You have a few treatment alternatives,' Greenstrum had said. 'First, I don't suggest you try to reverse your wife's weight-loss behaviour. That would put your relationship under extraordinary strain. You'd both probably have to go into intensive counselling to save the marriage. And you'd have to tell her about your strong sexual preferences.

'You could seek an extramarital relationship with a fat woman, but that wouldn't help the situation at home. Remember that you came to me because you thought your wife was missing intercourse as much as you were. In any case, I don't think an extramarital relationship would suit you. It would confuse your strong loyalties.

'I suggest you work at positive fantasy,' he concluded, with the same conviction I used when presenting a campaign idea. 'You must imagine the woman that turns you on, and superimpose her over your wife.'

'Don't you think I've tried that?' I replied.

'Ah, you didn't listen to me. I said positive fantasy. That other one is a negative fantasy in which you feel guilt because you feel disloyalty. Positive fantasy is giving yourself permission. It's for the good of all concerned. What I suggest you do is create a woman that doesn't currently exist. That will make her acceptable and far more useful to you.'

It took some effort but it worked. I began an affair with a woman I'd built from the soft soles of her feet. She had olive, baby-texture skin, mid-length dark hair, full lips, deep green eyes and a small, straight nose. She was not gross like those women in fat-porn magazines who seem to be carrying around a payload of independent lard bags attached to them by slings of stretched skin. My woman was rounded, with high, generous breasts, and buttocks like two big party balloons pressed lightly together.

Clarice accepted the steady change without question. She welcomed back my hard-ons and treated them with the same pleasure I remembered from early in our marriage. We restarted our sexual partnership as though my cock had returned from a beneficial stay on a health farm – which I suppose it had.

But sex has a perversity of its own. It seemed as though once Clarice had seen us through the change, she slowly began to lose her own libido. She would apologise for being dry even after I'd done all the things I knew she liked. When I introduced KY jelly into the sequence she admitted that although she loved me as much as ever, I no longer aroused her – but that she would accommodate my 'needs'. There was no pleasure for me under those circumstances. After a while I grew accustomed to spending time with the KY jelly tube and my fantasy woman without bothering Clarice.

***

Chapter Four

I re-ran this familiar documentary in my mind's theatre as I sauntered around the Mosman shops, their windows bright with display lights but their doors and cash registers darkened and locked.

Unconsciously I'd given myself a break from pet-food for a while so that I could come at it from a fresh angle.

Because I'd taken Jessica with me on the walk I had to stop every so often while she conducted a forensic analysis of posts where other dogs had left their encoded messages.

'You know the answer,' I told her at one point, as she frowningly stared, tail thrashing, at the brick wall below the newsagent's window. She growled at the departed depositor. Was it the noise animals made that I should use? Growl Grub? Woofeow? No, that was far worse than Good Fortune. I was staring blankly across the road into the real estate agent's patch-worked window when The Channel suddenly flung a nugget at me. 'Canine - feline' began to pulse. Then it broke into parts, leaving 'ca' and 'fe'. I joined them up. Café! '*Cafe* for pets!' I shouted at Jessica, who, thinking she'd misbehaved, sank down on to her haunches.

'Come here, you beautiful dog,' I said, bending down to hug her. 'Daddy has hit the fucking jackpot.'

The journey home turned euphoric. I floated down the quiet streets leading in the direction of the harbour. A breeze had set the April trees around me sighing with salty nostalgia. I felt like a young man on a first date, the girl of great promise deposited safely behind her front door, the taste of the final kiss still on my mouth, and now the fragrance of damp gardens my companion as I went to catch the last train.

When I reached home I wanted to burst into the house, turning on lights as I went, and call everybody together to recount my epiphany. But instead, I opened the heavily lead-lighted wooden door as quietly as I could, and crept down the hallway without disturbing the light seeping from beneath Sibyl's door.

Clarice, her legs tucked up beneath her, had gone to sleep in front of television. I crossed the room and turned off the set, then returned to caress her forehead. She awoke slowly, reaching up to draw my face down for a sleepy kiss.

'Did the walk do the trick?' she asked as she stretched and arched like a cat.

'It did,' I replied cautiously, knowing from past experience that to parade an infant idea at home often killed it before it had learned to walk. 'The important thing is that I discovered I can still think up good ideas. All I've got to do now is convince these Americans to buy it.'

***

Andy was in no hurry to respond to my request for a meeting about the Good Fortune Pet-food Corporation. Felix hadn't bothered to tell him about the new account, probably on the assumption that it would peter out before ever needing the art department. Andy wasn't a good morning person in any case, so it was just as well that he could only disengage himself from his high chair to see me shortly before midday.

By the time we met I'd been thinking about *cafe* for a few hours. I knew exactly what I wanted. The can label background would be dark brown, almost black, with the brand name reversed out in white. I'd studied the ingredient details Morton had left with me and found there was not enough room to fit it all on the label and still leave room for the brand name. I'd need Sid's advice on what I could leave out. I considered the possibility of Sid becoming the company spokesperson in Australia. If *Cafe* was recommended by a practising vet it would be a powerful endorsement.

I hadn't forgotten that the flavours had to be displayed. They would be at the base of the can directly beneath the brand logo, probably written in a bright colour. So far, I'd been given only numbers for the six flavours each for dogs and cats. I scribbled a note to ask Morton whether they had names like 'rabbit sidewinder' or 'bazooka beef' that we could use.

Andy entered without knocking and sat down opposite me. He stared through big pale blue eyes under partly-closed lids at the material on my desk while he slowly scratched the side of his head, taking care not to disturb the apparently random pinnacles of his blond-tipped hair.

'What's the product again?' he asked in a monotone.

'Pet-food,' I replied, telling myself that I had to remain calm and patient if I was going to avoid standing up and shaking Andy. 'A special kind of pet-food.' I emphasised the consonants.

'How do you mean?'

'Well, for a start, it's synthetic. No animals get slaughtered to make it. And it's entirely nutritious. No fillers or waste stuff. The result is, to put it frankly, that the animal's shit doesn't stink.'

Andy laughed, revealing surprisingly good teeth. 'Doesn't stink?' he said, pulling at a couple of the dull silver earrings that hung like a row of coathangers from his narrow lobe. 'I oughta feed it to Hanna.'

'What kind of dog is Hanna?'

'Hanna's not a dog. She's my girlfriend. And when she goes to the crapper ...' He let his screwed-up face finish the sentence.

'They haven't perfected it for human consumption,' I said dryly, 'but if they do I'll get you some wholesale. Now, let's get down to looking at what we've got to work with. The name of the product is *Cafe*.'

I wanted to move on but I couldn't help pausing to see his reaction. Apart from my inspirational outburst to Jessica, this was the first time I'd uttered the name to a living creature. Andy just blinked and waited for me to continue.

'It's a word I built from "ca" for canine and "fe" for feline. You know, dogs and cats.'

'Cool, cool,' he said, nodding approvingly.

'We need some roughs,' I continued quickly to hide my pleasure at this flattery. 'First a logo, then using it on a label for this.' I pulled one of the Good Fortune cans from my drawer, reminding myself to take them home for a trial on Jessica and Muffin. 'I've roughed out my idea of how the logo and the label should look, but I know you'll tidy it up.' I passed across my sketches and some typed copy.

'Yes, I'll tidy this up all right,' he said looking at my work with distain. 'What are these colours you've got marked in here?'

'I want the can label in dark brown, a kind of espresso colour.'

'Dunno about that,' he said. 'I think you got *Nescafé* mixed in there somewhere.'

'Look Andy,' I said breezily, 'just go away and work on it. Give me what I want, and you can give me what you want as well, and we'll decide between them from there.'

As he gathered the papers and stood up, he looked directly at me for the first time. 'This has got possibilities,' he said. 'I'll get on to it.'

***

Chapter Five

Lead Balloon suffered the dilemma of all advertising agencies over how to bill its clients. Most of the profit came from taking a percentage of media budgets, but that didn't always cover the creative costs in getting a campaign to the point where the client liked it. Some clients, hooked on flattery, could go on knocking back one concept after another as they gorged themselves on the praise of expensive, creative people. So, where it could, Lead Balloon settled on an hourly creative charge, sometimes balanced by reducing the media percentage.

In the case of Good Fortune, charging out was easier. We simply billed for creative work by the hour, although Felix would never tell anybody what that hourly rate was. It was company practice for each creative employee to keep a record of how much time he spent on each account. For me, that was becoming an exercise of growing discomfort. There were many time periods where I had done nothing, not because I was lazy, but because the bastards had given me nothing to do. The time sheets were designed for everybody to fill in the hours they spent on each account and to block in, using a fat red marker pen, time periods that were not specifically chargeable to any account. My time sheets were suffering the worst attack of red plague I'd ever seen at Lead Balloon. They looked as though they were being knifed to death. I was therefore relieved, on Monday afternoon, to be able to fill in 'research, Good Fortune Pet-food' for a three o'clock departure from the office, with no return for the rest of the day.

I'd called Sid that morning and asked him to see me at short notice. I might have to wait if there was a busy surgery, he'd warned, but there would be a beer later by way of consolation.

Leaving the office brought me the childish pleasure of playing hooky, especially when it was to visit Sid Willis. My red Karmann Ghia, with its noisy dak-dak engine, seemed to enjoy the trip up the Pacific Highway past the expensive pseudo-English residences of the North Shore. I was headed for Hornsby where old money met new. Beyond, the houses were smaller and more densely packed. Hornsby was the perfect place for a veterinary clinic. From one side Sid and his wife Stacey saw long-haired, snobbish dogs and pedigreed cats, while from the other came animals of mixed breed, generally smaller, and included the occasional guinea pig, rabbit, or illegally detained possum.

Sid and Stacey should have moved their veterinary practice years before, and separated the business from home – but now it was too late. They had grown used to being part of a commune of transient creatures. Some stayed in the hospital building at the back, and when that was full they took the least threatening into the house with them.

The brightly-painted waiting room, more like a kindergarten than a veterinary clinic, smelled powerfully of disinfectant underlaid by the remnants of incontinence. I imagined a *Cafe* show card on the reception desk and, on the shelves behind, cans of *Cafe*. If fed to the patients, it would certainly improve the smell of the place.

Sid passed briefly behind the receptionist and waved to me, indicating that he had first to deal with the waiting owners. They were all occupied reassuring their inconsolable pets that being there was okay, and not to bother about the enemy sitting in cages and baskets within assault distance. As usual, Sid was dressed in his long white dustcoat. A once-white beanie covered his bald head, creating the impression of a giant stick of chalk with a discoloured tip.

Sid and I shared the ownership of *Three Oranges*, a twenty-four-foot Hood class yacht with the temperament of a cranky old stallion. We kicked and sailed it together in the summer, competing in races at the Mosman Sailing Club. After fifteen years we could still win a race or two on handicap, but now with cunning rather than courage.

My sailing reverie came to an end as the last cat was carried out singing a repetitious aria in its cage, and I found myself sitting in Sid's surgery at the side of the building.

'I envy you being so busy,' I said.

'You wouldn't want to be busy in this business,' he replied, stretching his long legs under the Formica cream desk. 'Every bugger I saw today grizzled about being overcharged. Anyway Ed, enough of that. You said you wanted me to take a look at something.'

I explained my meeting with the Good Fortune people and their product. Sid said he thought he'd read about it but couldn't remember details.

'And you want me to look through the specs,' he said.

'Yes I do, but only so I can cut out the stuff that isn't essential.

I've only got so much room on the back of the can. It's illegal to make the print too small to read without a magnifying glass.'

Sid took the sheets I handed him and put on his half-frame glasses. He read for a while and then went to his cabinet to get a reference book. Finally, he looked up at me.

'Pretty impressive technology,' he said. 'There's a lot of stuff here I'm frankly not familiar with. You say they're selling it okay?'

'To the tune of two hundred million dollars a year in America. Once it goes global it'll be a billion dollar company.'

'I wouldn't mind having shares in it,' he muttered, staring down at the pages in front of him and marking the essential information with a green highlighter.

'It's still a private company,' I said, 'but it'll have to go public if they want to grow it quickly. I'll keep you posted.'

A knock on the door was followed immediately by the appearance of Stacey. Like Sid, she was dressed in her white vet's outfit. She was a woman of quick movements and sharp features, which probably explained why she was seldom bitten by her patients. Sid, by contrast, was more trusting and had had the end of his left little finger squared off by a cockatoo. Stacey kissed the air near my left cheek, mechanically asked after the family and, without waiting for a reply said: 'Sid, you've taken in too many sicks and we're full up – yet again.'

'Okay,' Sid said, 'we'll have to use the spare room. We'll put the ferrets in there with a few cats. They should get on.'

***

I arrived at work earlier than usual the next morning, ready to scale down the number of words describing Good Fortune's ingredients and nutrition. Recommended servings, based on the weight of the pet being fed, had to be fitted in as well. I was making good progress using the lines from the brochure that Sid had highlighted for me, when my desk phone gurgled quietly.

'Ed, this is Andy Hope,' an unexpectedly bright voice greeted me. 'I've got a few roughs for *Cafe*. Can I bring 'em up?'

'As long as you make it quick,' I replied, trying not to sound eager. 'I've got Awayaway bus holidays at eleven.'

'On my bike,' Andy said.

This time when Andy arrived I noticed his eyelids had gone up like raised Holland blinds. He put two folders down on my desk and opened the top one.

'What you wanted,' he said.

He had indeed produced the one I had wanted, with the *cafe* logo in chunky white capitals on the rich brown background. I was pleased he had got it right.

'Good,' I said, sitting back with my head on one side to admire it from another angle.

'Not good,' Andy corrected me. 'Fucking bad. Nearly made me spew having to do it. I don't know why writers think they're artists. This is what I like.' He opened the second folder. The logo was styled ca-fe, the 'ca' in magenta and the 'fe' in process blue. A black hyphen separated them. The background was white.

'Looks like a lolly,' I commented sourly.

'No, that's what yours looks like,' he said, wrinkling his bony nose. 'Like shitty dark chocolate. It doesn't go with the product.'

'Listen Andy,' I said, 'do me a favour and stay out of the decision making.'

'But my reputation's on the line here too,' he said with unexpected passion. 'If this stuff takes off, somebody is going to ask who did the crappy logo and chose the fucking dreadful colours. You won't own up – even if you're still around.'

'What do you mean, still around?'

'You know what I mean, Ed. There aren't many old creative writers still at it. You'll probably be sitting on your arse in management by the time this campaign gets going.'

I dropped that line of conversation. If he'd heard something negative about my future, I didn't want to give him the satisfaction of battering me with it.

'Look, I'll tell you what I'll do,' I said. 'I'll submit both versions to the client. He can decide.'

'Yeah, and you'll talk him out of mine and into yours.'

I wanted to tell Andy to fuck off out of my territory, but I forced myself to be calm. 'No, I give you my word,' I said slowly. 'I won't do any persuading. I'll say they both came from the art department. He can make up his mind between them. And don't forget,' I slowed for dramatic effect, 'he may not choose either. He hasn't even approved the name, let alone how it is written.'

'I want to be at the meeting when he looks at these,' Andy pressed on.

'And you don't realise,' I continued on my tack, 'that we're almost certainly competing against other agencies, probably in the United States. Our odds of winning are pretty poor.'

'I don't give a rat's arse about that,' Andy replied, 'I just want to be at the meeting.'

My immediate reaction was to say no, but I could have been throwing away a chance to show off my professional judgement to Andy. In any case, the client wasn't getting much for his money with a wobbly writer and a raw artist to look after his two hundred million dollar name.

'Okay, you can be at the conference,' I said, 'but conditions apply. One, you have to shut up unless I invite you to speak, and two, you clear the time with Felix. Don't forget, he pays our wages.'

***

Two days later Andy and I were seated next to each other in the boardroom with Morton Whitbread and Nathan Cohen opposite us. Their smirking faces confirmed my suspicion that we were making just one of many submissions. While we served coffee, water, biscuits, and vegetables, three of us splashed around in the shallows of small talk while Andy kept to the battle plan and said nothing.

'So how'd your dog and your cat like our products?' Morton said, to reel us back to business.

'I know they're going to love them,' I said enthusiastically, 'but to be honest I haven't actually opened a can yet.'

'So your creative work hasn't been based on practical experience,' he said, pinning me with his holy stare.

'That's not strictly the case, Morton,' I replied. 'I've carried out some veterinary research which has been very valuable to the brief.'

He let my feeble reply hang in a smouldering silence until he said, 'Okay let's see what you've got.'

Suddenly I regretted not having taken the safer route of smothering the table in decoys. Why hadn't I told Andy to do ten roughs for each of ten names? I should have had enough material to use up at least an hour of presentation – along with a storyboard. Instead, two forlorn folders lay in front of us. They would probably die in a millisecond. As I looked at them they seemed to shrink away to the size of business cards.

I had a passing vision of Felix examining my time sheets heavy with red plague. I was suddenly angry with him. The flimsiness of this presentation was somehow his fault. Jaw set, I stood up and drew my professional persona like a sword.

'Before I show you what we're recommending,' I said a little too loudly as I walked to the window and back, 'let me tell you that we've market tested as many names as time allowed. One stood out so strongly that I'm not even going to waste your time with the others. As far as stylising the name goes, we've given you a couple of options and there may still be room for development. That's why I brought Andy into our meeting.'

I leaned over and opened both folders together.

'Coffee,' Nat muttered flatly.

'Another cup?' I offered with a tight smile.

'Na. This *Cafe* thing, what's it supposed to mean? Let me ask you a question, Ed. Are we all talking the same product here?'

'You've missed it Nat,' Morton said after a lengthy pause. He pointed to Andy's version of *Cafe*. 'It's a combination of canine and feline. Now that's darn clever. I can't say I like the black hyphen though, it breaks up the word. The two colours do the job just fine for me.'

I didn't have to look at Andy to know he was smirking.

'I thought the word needed character,' he said, having now awarded himself the right to speak. 'What about we keep the two colours, close it up, and put it in italics.'

From his pocket Andy pulled out a couple of crayon stumps and drew *cafe* on the rough. The colours were not accurate but they gave the effect.

Morton looked at the modified name then back at the original. 'Yes, the letters look fine, just fine, but I'm not sold on the white background.'

'What about we have it in a sandy colour, like the shit?' Nat suggested.

'I don't like the reference, Nat,' Morton replied curtly,' but the sandy colour could look mighty good. What do you say, Andy?'

'I'll do a few roughs,' he said, containing his exuberance.

'We go back to the States day after tomorrow,' Morton said.

'Then I'll do them this afternoon,' Andy replied immediately.

'We'll have them couriered in,' I added quietly.

'And we'll let you know how city hall likes them when we get back,' Morton concluded as he stood up.

***

Chapter Six

When I thought about the Good Fortune account and the meeting we'd just had, I gobbled up all the credit for it. I needed to. I was starved for encouragement. But when I arrived home to tell Clarice what a great creator I'd been, I found myself praising Andy Hope as well.

I felt a vague, growing connection to Andy. We met by accident at the sandwich shop a couple of times and I invited him to eat his lunch in my office. I can't say the conversation was easy or even enjoyable, but it was as though we had drawn each other as partners in a forthcoming Siamese race and needed to synchronise to avoid falling over.

Meanwhile my red plague worsened. That wasn't something I could share with Andy, although I would have liked to tell him what lay ahead in the creative advertising life. I would have described it as a ball thrown vertically into the air, and how it slowed to a dead stop before it began its fall back to earth. I was in the falling-back phase.

When Felix made a formal appointment to see me a week later, it was as though he'd booked me into the gallows. Looking around my office before I went to meet him, I was sure I'd be cleaning out my drawers when I returned.

I'd been over that meeting so many times in my mind that when I entered Felix's office it was already like a replay. I could see my time sheet poking out of the top of the folder sitting on his otherwise barren desk. He picked it up.

'Ed,' Felix said indulgently, 'time we had a talk. There's some sorting out to do.' He stood up and motioned for me to sit in one of the lounge chairs next to the coffee table by the window. Armed with my notice of execution, he walked across and sat in the chair opposite me. He looked better seated than he did walking about. He was a short man, and when he abandoned his diet, which he had recently, he reminded me of an inverted comma.

He opened the folder and glanced briefly at it through his Buddy Holly glasses.

I remained silent. I was going to make the bastard work for this.

'You're being drowned in the red plague,' he said, 'and now it's time to resolve it.'

The rope was around my neck. His hand was on the trap-door lever.

'I'd better get this over with,' he said, a hangman's farewell smile playing around the edges of his mouth, '*cafe* has hit the home run in Salt Lake City. Not only do they want to use the name in Australia but they're going global with it. They're going to change the name of their whole fucking company to *cafe* Pet-food International, logo included.'

'What about my red plague in that folder?' I asked, stupidly pointing.

'I just wanted to make sure you'd have the time for *cafe,* that's all. In your case, the red plague is the gold plague. Now, since the *cafe* people started dealing with you, and they like you, we'll leave you in charge of the campaign. There's still not much media spending but there's plenty on print and other stuff, and fucking lovely creative fees to go with it. We'll pass on some of the loot to you, incidentally, and get you a proper team, including a good graphic artist.'

'I'd prefer to stick with Andy,' I said distantly. I was still trying to grasp the idea of the reprieve. 'The Yanks like him too. And anyway, he designed the logo. If there's a bonus coming, push a bit across to him, would you Felix?'

'If you say so,' Felix said, his speckled granite-green eyes devouring me through the magnification of his glasses. He handed me a folder. 'Here's the correspondence and the agreement for you to look at. As usual, the fees are deleted, but rest assured there's enough to give you what you need in team talent. There'll be a few trips to the US as well.'

When I left Felix, I didn't go straight back to my own office. I took the elevator down to the art department and called Andy out into the passageway.

'I've just got news of the *cafe* account,' I said in a monotone.

Andy's Holland blinds rose slightly. 'What'd they say?'

'We got it!' I bellowed into his face.

After staring at me for a while he said, without expression, 'Radical,' but then, as the possibilities trickled into his mind he punched me lightly on the arm, and added, with a quick nod, 'fucking rad'.

***

Chapter Seven

Just as I hadn't dared to share my career fears with anybody at Lead Balloon, I couldn't share my elation at being saved from the sack either. Apart from what was now a professional link with Andy, I had to let the news about *cafe* percolate through to the rest of the Lead Balloon staff.

But at home it was different. Clarice would have mourned with me at the graveside of my career if Felix had fired me, and now it was Clarice with whom I wanted to share my jubilation. That night we let the girls phone for takeaway pizzas while we went out to The Four Winds at The Spit for dinner. I ordered a bottle of vintage Dom and toasted Clarice's warm brown eyes, fruit, vegetables, and shit.

We came home to a quiet house with two sleeping daughters, the faint smell of pizza still in the air around the television. In bed Clarice covered my face in kisses, before hugging me and then rolling on top of me.

'I'm so proud of you Ed,' she said close to my ear, and nibbled my lobe. 'I love being on the winning side with you. You're so clever.' She began to grind her pelvis across my stomach. She stopped to throw off her nightie and, as she did so, I touched her between the legs to find her already wet.

I summoned my fat girl, noting that it was high time I gave her a name. She entered the bedroom wearing a soft towelling robe, which she untied and let slip to the floor as she approached the bed. Clarice obligingly dissolved and my girl took her place on top of me. Where I had been hanging on to Clarice's soft, overtrained arse muscles, I now had my open palms around vast satin globes. Two heavy breasts hung down and buffeted my cheeks. Nipples tripped on my nose and rubbed against my closed eyelids. When I pushed my cock up between large, rounded thighs, my passion lifted off the runway. I was fucking the curves and weight and substance that my lust craved.

As Clarice reached her orgasm she called to God and Jesus in the pillow but my fat girl threw her head back and bellowed at the ceiling, catapulting me into mine. As I slowly returned to earth, my creation obligingly morphed back into Clarice.

**

I had been haunted by Morton Whitbread's accusing stare at our last meeting when I'd had to own up that I'd failed to feed our pets *cafe*. That had to be put right, and quickly too. I was likely to have contact with him quite soon and I knew he'd ask me if I'd carried out this simple act of faith. I told Clarice and the girls over breakfast not to feed Jessica or Muffin their evening meal until I arrived home, because I would.

'Why do you want to feed them?' Taya, our eleven-year-old,

asked over the top of the cereal packet.

'To try out a special pet-food,' I replied. 'I'm in charge of a new American account called *cafe*.'

'Funny name,' Taya said. 'So what's special about it?'

'Highly nutritious,' I replied. 'It's actually a synthetic food. We have to weigh Jessica and Muffin before we give it to them.'

'Why, are they supposed to get fatter or thinner?'

'Neither. It's done so the animal gets the right amount of food.'

'You'd better give her the full story,' Clarice said from the toaster.

'Well, this food, besides being very good for pets, also results in no smell when they go to the toilet,' I said, thinking that Taya was still three.

'You mean their shit doesn't stink,' Taya said.

'Something like that,' I said. 'Listen, won't you miss your bus?'

'I've got half an hour,' Taya replied. 'Tell me some more.'

'There's not much more to tell you until we try it out,' I said, feeling increasingly uncomfortable. 'There are different flavours, the can is biodegradable, it's sold through network marketing. I can't think of much else.'

'How are we going to tell whether the stink part works?' she pressed on. 'We won't know when Jessica does it, or if it's an old one or a new one.'

'The new one will be a pale colour,' I said wiping my mouth with a napkin and standing up to leave the table.

Taya laughed, showing her oversize adult teeth in their pristine pink gums. 'Make Sibyl pick it up,' she said.

***

Domestic animals are not pleased with changes to their feeding routine. When I arrived home that night at about six-thirty Jessica was gnawing and growling at her plastic bowl, and Muffin was pacing about with his tail up like an antenna, crying pitifully at anybody who would look at him.

I opened the dog food can first. It was a satisfying experience, screwing off the top and feeling the faint snap of the seal being broken inside. The food came in pale lumps of various sizes, no doubt computer designed to represent bravely felled prey to the dining animal. The lumps were held in suspension by a speckled paste offering up a faintly cooked-sausage smell.

Clarice, reading from Morton's brochure lying open on the kitchen bench, reminded me that I had to weigh Jessica before her first helping. From her tightly-folded arms I judged Clarice to be torn between wanting the test to succeed for my sake and wanting it to fail because it challenged her position as food provider for all living things in the house.

'How are you going to weigh her?' she asked, eyebrows comically high.

'On the bathroom scales, of course.'

'Does she have to take a shower first?' Taya sniggered.

Rather than get into a wisecracking contest I headed for the bathroom, pulling Jessica with me by her collar. She resisted entering the bathroom, thinking that no good could come of it, and I had to slide her on her haunches across the tiles to the scales. When she saw them she whined as though she'd been brutally attacked by them on some previous occasion. She acted like that too. I could get one pair of her legs on to the scales but not all four at once. I ignored the snorts of laughter from the doorway as I turned to lateral thinking. I first weighed myself and then tried to pick Jessica up to weigh both of us so I could deduct my weight and calculate hers. But picking up a fat Labrador that doesn't want to be picked up would have taken a stronger man than me. I finally abandoned the exercise and shouted at Jessica to get out of my sight. As she slunk quickly from the bathroom I had to listen to the laughter-punctuated admonishments of my wife and two daughters.

'I'm settling for forty kilos,' I said back in the laundry as I emptied about half the container into Jessica's bowl.

'You might get too much poo ' Taya remarked.

'You'll get poo in a minute,' I muttered, setting the bowl down.

Labradors have short memories and big, indiscriminate appetites. Jessica grinned up at me, her tail conducting happy music, and then demolished the contents of the bowl in a brief series of gulps and slaps of her tongue.

'Well, she seemed to like it,' Sibyl observed.

'I hope nothing happens to her,' Taya sniffed, going for pathos.

'So what will you do now darling?' Clarice asked. 'Follow Jessica around with a little spade and test tube?'

'We'll just keep her in the garden and wait for results,' I said. 'It shouldn't be too hard to spot.'

'What if she gets diarrhoea?' Taya asked.

'It'll be nice diarrhoea,' I replied tersely.

Muffin proved to be a much less stressful proposition. For the time being he could be a simple consumer rather than a test case. I wasn't going to follow him around with a pick and shovel like some instant archaeologist. As Taya picked him up and took him away for his bathroom scale weigh-in, I opened the second can. The cat variety of *cafe* was similar to the dog, except that the pieces were smaller and it gave off the delicate smell of seaweed. When I set down Muffin's bowl he did a lot of sniffing at it and stared up at me as though wanting reassurance. But suddenly he got to work, seeming, like all cats, to caress and clean the food rather than eat it. Nevertheless his bowl was empty in not much longer than it had taken Jessica with hers.

'Do you want Muffin to stay in my room with some litter in a box?' Taya offered.

'No, we'll concentrate on Jessica for the time being,' I replied.

***

'I suggest we all stop talking about this,' Clarice broke in. 'We'll be trying to eat our dinner in fifteen minutes. Go and get ready.'

As I went to the bathroom to wash away dogs and cats, I remembered the yacht club meeting I had to attend that evening. One of the reasons I'd agreed to go on the race committee, which set courses and rules during the racing season, was that I could stroll from home to the meetings. The committee met in the race room off the members' bar every Tuesday evening, but a rostering system broke the commitment down to once a fortnight. Race planning would never begin until everybody had a drink, and a long meeting would test the members' judgement under the influence of alcohol. Those who came and went on foot were more reckless with their intake than those who had to drive themselves home.

I was relieved to have an excuse to leave the dinner table early, because I knew that Clarice's embargo on the subject of animal excreta would expire during collecting the dishes and I'd be back under cross-examination from my daughters. They seemed to have developed a far greater curiosity about how *cafe* worked than I had.

With a sense of escape I set off down the hill for the kilometre walk to the club, basking in the belief that my life was in the ascendancy. Work was moving well and my family was functioning nicely, including Clarice's sparks of interest in sex. It occurred to me that these days she was turned on by success. Maybe she always had been. If this was the case, I could understand her loss of interest over the past couple of years as fear of losing my job had eaten into me. I saw a parallel with my loss of interest over her loss of weight. Maybe Greenstrum could help her create an imaginary winner, so that there would be four of us happily fornicating in the marital bed instead of the current three.

As I'd anticipated, the committee spent a lot of time that night in planning the end of season race day in May, when all the classes of yacht in the club would participate on handicap. After that, the club would function only on a social basis until racing resumed in November.

As a kind of acknowledgment that I owed my improved circumstances to Americans, I drank unfamiliar bourbon during the long meeting. It trickled down my throat with deceptive amiability until, with the course maps almost plotted, I couldn't find north on the blurred sheets of paper before us. North had vanished, but I had the good sense not to alert the other members of the committee to my discovery.

I kept a needful grip on the polished wooden rail as I finally descended the thickly carpeted stairs with my seven fellow committee members. Outside I bade them goodnight with a controlled wave and set off up the hill, beating into a fresh southerly – or was it a nor'-easterly? The streets seemed longer and steeper than usual. I undid the band that held my ponytail in place and let my hair fly in the salty wind, imagining myself King Lear, although my daughters hadn't stuffed me up the way his had. If I could have remembered some lines from the play – in which I'd appeared with some distinction at school – I would have shouted them into the wind. But in truth I needed to save my bourbon breath for climbing the hill.

There is a myth that says fresh air clears an inebriated head.

It doesn't. It only provides a contrast between the freedom of the surrounding air and the captivity of the brain in a slurry of alcohol. That is why, despite my refreshing walk, I tried to enter my garden via the wrong back gate, and was greeted by my neighbours' furious terrier. My mind had been taken up with a simple task that I had resolved to complete before I went to bed. At a second attempt I let myself in through my own gate and groped my way to the garden shed for a torch. Easy to comprehend by day, at night the contents of my shed were arranged by the Devil. I knocked over a tower of empty plastic pots and upset a bucket of something on my way to blundering into the row of gardening implements leaning against one wall. The torch only revealed itself after I'd strewn snail pellets on the brick tiled floor. When I switched it on the light was faint and flickering, like a small cylindrical animal about to die. I advanced into the garden and was greeted by the soft whacking of Jessica's tail against my legs as I searched the grass and flower beds for a vital sample of spent *cafe*.

Since part of Clarice's daily exercise routine comprised a run in Mosman Park accompanied by Jessica and a scoop bag, there was never much to clean up in our garden. That would make my search easier, I reasoned. But not so. The bourbon, the wind and the failing torch conspired against me. I lurched around this strange, vast and tilted garden, cursing as I fell into shrubs that sprang out at me from billowing quicksand. At one stage I took a piss and Jessica walked right through the line of fire. That demanded another trip to the shed where I groped about for some rags to dry her off. While I was searching I saw something funny in pissing on my own dog and I fell into shrieking spasms of laughter. The next-door neighbour's back light went on to frighten away the insane prowler he could hear, and I had to almost choke myself until he'd switched it off.

I'd decided to continue the search in the morning when I saw my quarry in the grass at the far end of the garden. I shone the weak light on to a glistening, massive, pale cigar. With a guffaw of pleasure I fell to my knees to pick it up and squeeze it in my hand the way granny had in the brochure. Like a presumptive wine judge I raised it to my nose for the test. Another truth: alcohol does nothing to dull the sense of smell. With a howl of disgust I flung as much of it as would detach from my hand into the garden.

Later, in bed, after I'd spent half an hour in the laundry using every household cleaner I could find, Clarice murmured: 'You didn't read the brochure thoroughly. It states the third stool rule. The first lot smells no different to what went before.'

**

Chapter Eight

My intuition about Morton Whitbread proved to be right. When he called me the next morning, his first question was whether I'd tried the products.

'Of course I have, Morton,' I replied.

'Tell me this Ed,' he said, 'and I want the absolute truth here, did you get caught with the third stool rule?'

'A handful,' I said, ruefully sniffing my fingers.

'Then you've graduated,' he laughed. 'It means that you're connected with the product. That's important for the work we're going to be doing together. Ellis, Sally and Gerry are so looking forward to meeting you. Ellis and Sally look upon you as a messenger of the Lord, and I do not blaspheme here. They truly believe that you were sent. That's why we want to give you and your agency as much of the change-over work as we can.'

'We're on the starting blocks and ready to race,' I said, trying to sound American without aping the accent.

'Glad to hear it. I sent Lead Balloon a parcel express delivery today. It's full of briefs. Felix will pass them on to you. We've also talked to him about security. See Ed, the pet-food industry doesn't want us around. Even though we don't have a significant market share yet, they can see where we're headed. They're scared, Ed, and folks can do some stir-crazy things when they're scared. If they got wind of our name change they'd try to block it. Are you with me?'

'I am still with you, Morton.'

'Australia suits us just fine for the development work,' he continued. 'If it was an agency in the States we'd have a lot more to worry about, but we still can't take any chances. Are you with me Ed?'

'I'm right up there with you, Morton,' I responded. 'I most surely am.'

'I've discussed some security ideas with Felix and we would value your input too,' he continued. 'What I'm trying to say here Ed, is that the going might be a little rough while you're working through. Do you work by beacons, Ed?'

'Beacons?'

'Yes, beacons. We work to the beacon management system here. Used to be called goals, but that doesn't go far enough in today's demanding market. Goals just kind of glow but beacons flash in both directions, beckoning and pointing. Every plan we make has to have beacons. They can be deadlines, dates, formulations, financial outcomes. We had a beacon on the new name. What I'm trying to say here Ed is that we now have a beacon on the announcement of the new name, and you'll note that I'm not using the new name on the telephone. This is the beginning of the blackout.

'But to get back to the specific beacon, we're going to blast the whole thing off at convention. We have a distributors court convention first of October every year. I'll explain later about the court, but at convention we always hit the distributors with a positive sidewinder. This one will be sensational: new name, new logo, new look and some new products.'

'I am with you,' I said automatically.

After I had put down the phone I thought about the security problem that all agencies had to deal with. Every campaign began with a tiny idea seed, swimming about in infinite thought-space with billions of other tiny idea seeds, one of which would penetrate the ovum of need to become a campaign foetus. It would grow inside the head of the creator to be born through the mouth or the fingers. At that stage there may not be any need to keep it secret, but if it found an adoptive client where secrecy was critical, it may have to be hidden away from the world until fully grown.

cafe was like that. I tried to think of who already knew about it, and who they might have told. There could be hundreds in the multiplier by now. Had it reached the ears of the wicked pet-food competitors' consortium? Assuming there were too many people to swear to secrecy, how could we cover the trail now?

Lead Balloon had faced that problem before, but there was no standard way to deal with it. What we needed was a decoy. I searched my computer until I found the original notes I'd made on Good Fortune. I looked at the stillborn ideas. 'Envirofood' looked the most promising. Felix and Wesley could put it around the agency that the client had rejected that other name and now we were full throttle on Envirofood for Pets. That might take a bit of shadow-boxing inside the agency but it could be done. We'd take some half-hearted security measures but leaks about Envirofood would be to our advantage. In the meantime I could be working quietly on *cafe*. I congratulated myself on inventing this tactic. I could feel control coming back to my side of the employment equation. I even roughed out the phoney team we'd announce as being in charge of Envirofood.

I was impatient to tell Felix. We should put the plan into operation even before the package arrived from Morton. I made myself a note: 'Any correspondence or packages that arrive from Utah in the future should only be opened by Felix or myself''. We didn't want the mailroom stumbling into the secret.

I called Felix's extension and I was pleased that he could see me immediately.

'Glad you dropped in, Ed, save me calling you,' Felix said, motioning me to the chair opposite the front panel of his self-designed six-sided desk.

'You've had a good chat to Morton?'

I nodded.

'So have I. And I managed to talk to Ellis too. They're moving fast. And they're petrified about security, not just about their competitors finding out, but more about the "court" finding out. I don't exactly know what they mean by the court, but it's a term used in their network marketing system. Basically, courtiers are distributors, I think.'

'I've got the solution to the security problem,' I said with relish.

'You have? Tell me about it.'

I delivered my plan, adding a few frills as The Channel prompted me.

'Not bad Ed,' Felix said, 'but we've been doing a bit of thinking too, and we've got a better idea.'

I waited.

'You're fired.'

'You ... I mean, that has to be ... For chrissakes Felix, don't talk bullshit.'

'No bullshit, Ed. I think you should clean your office out right away and be out of the building by midday. I'll go over your entitlements with Wesley, and believe me Ed, we'll be very generous. You've been a great member of the Lead Balloon team. In any case, we need to buy your silence, if you follow. I'll call you tomorrow and we can discuss severance details. I know you'll be pleased, Ed. We'll organise a farewell dinner for you too, next week. I know this is sudden but you know I always prefer the guillotine to crucifixion.'

'I'll have your balls for unfair dismissal,' I said, springing from the chair. 'You're crazy. You'll fuck up the whole *cafe* campaign – the one *you* said was going to bring in such huge fees.'

'Calm down Ed,' Felix said, remaining seated and leaning back. 'We thought about all that and we've got it covered. You must have known this was coming. Look at your red plague records. In this business they're the warning letters. I know you've got a promising new account but my attitude is: "One swallow doth not a summer make".'

'What about Dempster Funerals and Awayaway Buses?'

'They didn't cover expenses,' Felix said. 'You knew that.'

I had no more cards to play. I turned and left his office. Taking the elevator up was a death experience, rising away from my own corporate corpse. As I entered my office I remembered that I'd played this scene in my imagination many times, but in reality it was quite different. Everything in my office seemed to demand urgent attention, like baby birds in a nest. Going through drawers that held the dust and trivia of twenty-two years deserved hours or even days of pondering. My fingers ploughed between sheets of paper and business trinkets. I read the funny cards and picked up the crooked little figures from the Snow Black campaign, the trick corkscrew that collapsed when used; we'd given them away at the launch of the screw-top wine bottle. These should have been thrown out long ago but memories clung to them, and they begged not to be discarded.

I had the mailroom send me up some cardboard cartons. When I'd finished sorting I had three boxes of books and computer disks, one of memorabilia I wanted to keep and one of personal items like my shaver, toothbrushes and hair brushes and some rubber bands for my ponytail. The rest of the boxes were rubbish. I was astonished at the great pile of out-of-date reports and fact sheets, given to me at some time in the past with breathless urgency, but probably never read, and now on the other side of useless.

Felix was right about the guillotine. I loathed him for firing me but leaving the building before the word got around was a good idea. I didn't want fifty corridor stops to tell the same story, even if I could think of a good way to disguise my failure. I felt like the torch in my garden shed, except buying new batteries for me would take more than a simple visit to the supermarket.

With the help of the mailroom junior I moved my filled boxes down to the car park and into the trunk and back seat of my Karmann Ghia without being sprung. The junior, Danny, was the only person I shook hands with before I left Lead Balloon. I didn't want to face Wesley or Arnold Rich or Doc Sherlock. They could all fuck themselves. And I didn't want a farewell dinner so they could all be smug about their own jobs by seeing mine go.

I started the car and nosed it out into Nester Avenue. I hadn't gone fifty metres when I saw Andy Hope sauntering along wearing his fringed Indian leather jacket. His once-was-beige canvas bag was slung over his shoulder. I stopped and leaned across to wind down the passenger window.

'Taking an early lunch?' I inquired.

'And early fucking everything else,' he said, walking up to the open window.

'What do you mean?'

'Doc Sherlock just gave me the big heave, like I'd nicked something. The cunt told me to leave the place by lunchtime. I didn't even have time to finish the new Downheaval poster.' His eyes rested on the boxes visible through the back windows. 'You moving a bit of stuff?'

'You could say that,' I replied, realising that, for the time being at least, I'd prefer to talk to Andy rather than Clarice. 'Let's go and have a beer. I'll fill you in.'

We chose one of the North Sydney's budget pubs and sat behind tubs of plastic ferns in the beer garden where we wouldn't be found by nomadic advertising executives. Andy insisted on buying the first round of drinks.

'I can't say cheers,' I said, holding up my glass, 'but I can say good luck. We both need it.'

'Why you?' he asked after taking a drink that gave him a blond moustache of froth on his upper lip, to match his hair.

'I'm in the same boat,' I replied. 'Well, not really, because my boat's a lot older and leakier. It can't sail off in a new direction like yours.'

'What are you talking about?'

'I got the flick too,' I said, 'from Felix. I don't know what the pay-out deal is yet. I'll probably sue the bastards.'

'I won't be doing that, man,' Andy said. 'The only awesome thing was the money. Doc said as long as I didn't spew about leaving on the spot they'd give me six months pay. Said he'd contact me in a day or two about some freelance work. That's bullshit though. I might take Hanna down the coast for a while. Anyway, what's going to happen to *cafe*? '

'We'll never know,' I replied.

'Pity about that,' Andy said wistfully, 'it had fucking possibilities.'

Andy and I drank our way through a few glasses of beer that washed down a greasy lunch of calamari and chips. By half past three our conversation was becalmed. Without fuelling it with more personal history we couldn't go on. He stood up.

'For an older bloke you weren't bad to work with,' he said, his Holland blinds more than halfway down. He held out his hand. 'See ya, Ed.'

I watched him unsteadily leave the pub. We didn't exchange phone numbers. There was no point.

I ordered another coffee and resisted buying a packet of cigarettes to have my first smoke in ten years. Instead I fixed my mind on the question of what I'd do with the rest of my working life. I took out the little notebook I always carried in my wallet, a reminder of the stingray leather goods account I'd worked on. I began to make a list: write a Mills & Boon novel, travel through China on a black bicycle, open a delicatessen and specialise in pickles, become a boat broker. I didn't even consider looking for a job with another advertising agency. I'd done with that career. I admitted to myself that part of my growing misery at Lead Balloon had been the onset of boredom. The continuing change of client landscape had masked my weariness of briefs and art departments and budget overruns and endless creative meetings. I still liked working The Channel, but that was only a small part of it, like an orgasm compared to a long tedious foreplay with an unattractive woman. Mills & Boon sounded like a good place to start. It would make me busy but unaccountable. Every copywriter fancied himself as a novelist if only he had the time. I was no exception.

I looked at my watch. Four-thirty was too early to go home unless I wanted to give Clarice a hard landing with the news of an unemployed husband. If a winner turned her on, I didn't like to think what a loser might do – to the girls as well, for that matter. I assumed they liked having a successful advertising writer as a father. I needed to work out a plan of action. Maybe I'd pretend to go to work every day and eventually invent a situation where I seemed to make the decision to leave. I needed advice. I called Sid on my mobile.

'I'm in a North Sydney pub,' I told him, 'and I've just been fired. I don't know what to do about Clarice or a fucking job or anything.' I had to blow my nose. I was on the verge of tears.

'Lucky bugger,' Sid said. 'I wish Stacey would fire me with the settlement they'll have to give you. Anyway, you sound pretty low. Want to meet?'

'Yes please. Where?'

'The Greengate in Killara. That's about half way for both of us. Good excuse for me to get out of here. I'll leave now; Stacey loves being in charge.'

***

Chapter Nine

As soon as I arrived home and was safely parked in the garage with the door closed behind me, I quietly lifted the boxes from my car and stacked them on a high shelf where I covered them with an old rug. I entered the house at about seven o'clock, a time Clarice wouldn't think to query, but I had no clear plan of how or when to make my announcement. Sid told me to let providence guide me, that I would be shown when it was time to say my piece. I hoped that Clarice hadn't telephoned my office instead of calling my mobile. She was busy in the kitchen showing a severely disinterested Sibyl how to prepare a tuna casserole.

She slid the baking dish into the oven, rinsed her hands and came over to kiss me. 'Hello, darling,' she said smiling into my eyes. 'Feel like joining me in a Scotch?'

I nodded. 'Let me get them,' I said with forced brightness.

I went to the bar in the lounge and poured two doubles over ice.

'How was your day?' Clarice asked as I handed her the drink.

'I'm getting a bit fed up with the politics,' I said, leading vaguely in the direction of my dismissal. Sid and I had decided that I needed to invent a blow-up at work which led to me quitting. I had to appear the moral winner.

'Are you going searching in the garden tonight, Dad?' Taya inquired. 'Jessica's just started on her second can of that dog food.'

'I had to tell the kids about last night,' Clarice giggled. 'Sibyl was scared by the noise coming from the shed.'

'I might take a look around in the grass later,' I muttered, 'but we can't get any more cans for the time being, so there's not much point.'

'Daddy, that's a shame,' Taya said with disappointment in her voice. 'I told my friends at school about what we had, and they said they'd get their parents to buy some too.'

This was the moment Sid had said would come. I took a deep breath.

'I won't be going to work tomorrow,' I said. 'You see, I ...'

'Good idea, Ed,' Clarice cut in. 'You can concentrate so much better on that new account here where there's peace and quiet. I'm glad you took a stand. I'm on school tuckshop tomorrow so you'll have the place to yourself.'

The moment passed. Or rather, I let the window of opportunity slide shut. I'd take another run at it later.

The meal meandered along as usual, except that I was pregnant and couldn't give birth. We talked about what was on the news and Sibyl's mid-term party, and Clarice's mother's trip to England. I went into labour a couple of times but nothing came of it.

When we got into bed Clarice was as randy as a rabbit. She immediately pulled off my pyjama shorts and went down on me. It took some effort to summon my fat girl but eventually she arrived and took over with the enthusiasm I had built into her.

I slept late the next morning. A combination of emotional exhaustion and too much to drink the day before made me sleep through the girls leaving for school. It was only when Clarice leaned over to kiss me goodbye that I realised this was the first day of my membership of the unemployed.

'Got to rush, Ed,' she said softly. 'I've left a couple of pies in the fridge for you to heat up for lunch. See you about five. Remember that Taya gets home about half-past four, so don't get a fright when she lets herself in.'

I lay back on the pillow and listened to the muffled vibration of the Range Rover starting and the whirr of the garage door opening and then closing. After that cycle had finished there was silence. Muffin jumped up on the bed to examine me in this change of routine, then lost interest and disappeared. The silence pressed down on me like a heavy net.

'Florence Formby was fed up with men,' I said aloud. 'She craved love but hated the cruelty that always seemed to go with it. That's why she went to work on a fifty-foot dredge at the mouth of the Derwent River.' Easy. I'd get up and move straight from the unemployed to the self-employed.

I shaved, showered and ate breakfast while I read the business pages of *The Sydney Morning Herald*. All those stupid pricks would be snarling at each other today over money while I wrote a romance. I hummed to myself as I packed my dishes into the dishwasher. Instead of being dressed in a suit and hurrying to North Sydney I was in jeans and sloppy joe, sauntering to my study.

I turned on the computer and stared out of the window at the clear, lifting morning. I typed the heading 'Derwent Forbidden

Love'. Now what was the opening I had quoted to myself in bed? What was the beautiful woman's name? I called The Channel. Surely it would work for my romance story like it had on my advertising lines. Gravel will do to get me started, I said in my head. But not even a speck of dust arrived.

I sat fidgeting for more than two hours. I kept hearing Felix's feeble effort at justifying my sacking and Sid telling me to sue the bastards if they didn't drown me in money. I went over it all many times, always trying to get back to the woman and the Derwent River dredge. Finally, in frustration, I shut down the computer and left the house.

I walked up the street to the Mosman shops. I'd never wandered around them before on a weekday with no reason to be there. The shops were familiar enough, but not the mix of people. Young mothers practiced the art of public speaking as they made loud, long explanations to pram-trapped babies who couldn't understand them. And he was everywhere: the retiree. He wore long plain shorts in colours between brown and grey, a check short-sleeve shirt, pristine joggers with white socks to the knees, and a silly canvas hat. His glasses were oversize with aggressive frames. Squinting, with mouth agape, he was always two paces behind his purposeful wife. He was my destination if I didn't move heaven and earth to avoid it.

I sat in a coffee shop and ordered toasted sandwiches for lunch. Fuck Clarice's pies! They symbolised being stuck at home, unemployed. Other than mothers and retirees, the diners looked like salesmen or middle managers who'd taken a self-determined lunch break. There was the occasional singleted labourer too, who should have been told to leave because of his scruffy appearance, but retained his seat because of his threatening muscles. Apart from talking to myself, or an occasional solitary episode with my fat girl,

70

these people could become my daily companions. I didn't count Clarice. I was sure she didn't want any more of my company than she already had.

As I left the coffee shop I experienced a wave of panic that I thought must have been common to all people who had been suddenly fired and were facing their first day on the other side of employment. With no plan formed, they were islands surrounded by empty seas. Somebody had robbed them of forty or fifty hours of endeavour a week. Money wasn't the immediate issue: time and purpose were. No wonder so many of them got sick. They needed something to occupy their time. Heart disease or prostate cancer at least offered full-time occupations.

I began a slow walk in the direction of the zoo. In my mind I implored The Channel to give me at least a modest start to a Mills & Boon story. The lovers met at the zoo. They were animal feeders. She saved him from the gorilla's grip by stripping outside the cage on a Sunday afternoon in front of a crowd of adolescent boys. No, The Channel was having fun at my expense.

By the time I had arrived back home I was ready to abandon my Mills & Boon career in favour of something less dependent upon being creative. As I opened the front door I heard the telephone ringing. I hurried to the kitchen and just beat Taya to the handset. She glared at me and went back to her room.

'Been out job-hunting?' Felix's voice inquired.

'Not really,' I replied. 'More like deciding on jobs I don't want, like being a writer and an account director in an agency that treats people like they were turds.' I'd already wasted too many words on him. This was the arsehole who'd fired me and I wasn't going to be chatty with him. 'Anyway Felix, what do you want?'

'To come over to see you after dinner.'

'What, to my home, tonight?'

'If that's convenient. Could we make it, say, about eight o'clock?'

'You're bringing your cheque book?'

'Of course.'

'Okay, make it half-past. I'll try to get dinner over with by then.'

I punished the telephone with a crash landing. Why hadn't I told the bastard I didn't want him in my sight, let alone my home? I paced up and down the hallway, composing what I would say when I called him back to cancel his visit. I was well rehearsed and on final approach to the kitchen when Clarice arrived, pink-faced from the aerobic class she'd fitted in after tuck shop.

'Felix wants to come over tonight,' I said loudly, 'I Don't know why I agreed. I really don't want him here. I'm going to call him back and put him off.'

'Well, if he wants to come here Ed, it must be important, otherwise he'd talk to you at work,' she called over her shoulder as she hurried to the shower.

As I followed her I opened my mouth to explain why I didn't want to see Felix, but the prospect of shouting my news over the gush and splash of water begat another postponement. I decided to let the bastard come after all. It would serve to announce my jobless status to Clarice and the girls, and I could get in a few insults to Felix so that I could come out with a few points to my name.

At dinner I had no enthusiasm for Clarice's soy chicken, even though it was one of my favourites. From eight o'clock I began to listen for the arrival of Felix's Mercedes in the street. By the time it did arrive, I'd arranged the chairs in the lounge several different ways to achieve my best bargaining position.

When the bell rang I strode up the hallway ready to face my executioner. I swung open the front door to find Felix and Wesley both standing there. Reacting automatically, I shook hands with them and then regretted it as I led them to the lounge room where my chair layout was now obsolete.

Both of them were dressed casually. Felix was done up in a loose cream silk shirt and black trousers in an unsuccessful attempt to hide his hemispherical mid-section, while Wesley had on a deep green Armani sweatshirt and matching jeans that picked up the unintentional green tinge in his hair on its reluctant journey back from white to grey.

'Drink?' I offered.

'When we've done some talking,' Wesley answered for both of them. 'We'll all need something by then.'

I sank into the wrong leather chair and folded my arms. 'So let's have it,' I said.

'Ed, I'm sorry I was a bit brutal yesterday, but there was a reason,' Felix began. 'This *cafe* business is bigger than any of us dreamed, and their paranoia about security is unbelievable. They demanded we took the action we did. It was a case of do it their way or forget the account.'

'We don't like being dictated to,' Wesley took over, 'but on this occasion it was worth it; or will be. They've now thrown media buying our way. We prepare the name-change material and they book it in the countries where they're doing business. We get our creative fees and our media commission as well.'

'Why are you telling me this?' I asked.

'Because you're on the case,' Felix chortled. 'We didn't really fire you at all. It was a blind. As far as the staff at Lead Balloon is concerned, the account suddenly died and you had to go.'

'And Andy too?'

'Right,' Wesley said. 'Doc Sherlock nearly resigned himself

when I told him Andy had to go. He's got a lot of time for Andy, although I can't see why.'

'So Ed, you're still on the payroll,' Felix said, 'and so is Andy. We're seeing him tomorrow, at home too. You're both going to love the money we've got in the pipeline for you.'

'But there are conditions,' Wesley cut in with a wagging finger. 'You must work away from the office. The same applies to Andy. We'd like you to consider setting up here, at home, provided you can fit Andy in. We'll put you in direct touch with Ellis and Morton on the internet. That'll mean new computer gear for you. Huge memory capacity and a big mother of a monitor. Nothing must go in the mail or by fax. They insist the whole thing is electronic and encrypted until their October launch.'

'I'll bet you're relieved,' Felix said. 'You should have seen your face when I fired you. It was so hard not to laugh. When you left the office I nearly cacked myself.'

I caught sight of Clarice in the darkness of the archway leading to the dining room. I thought she was coming in to offer us coffee but she just hovered there.

'You might as well come in and hear this,' I called to her. As she entered both men stood up and greeted her indulgently. 'They fired me yesterday and they've come to re-hire me tonight,' I added.

'I know, darling,' she said with a smile she might have reserved for a patient who had just woken from a coma. 'Felix called me the minute he did the mock firing. I was to be your guardian angel until tonight. I felt so sorry for you, poor pet.'

'And the fun isn't over yet,' Felix said. 'We're still going ahead with your farewell dinner. We'll have a ball putting that on.'

'Well,' I said, easing back into the soft burgundy leather, 'you've certainly produced a clever pantomime. It's like a close friend dying and then suddenly sitting up in his coffin at the funeral.'

'That's very good,' Wesley laughed. 'Classical creative talent of Ed Sharock.'

'Thank you for the compliment,' I said, 'and now for the good part. The corpse isn't going to sit up.'

'What do you mean?' Felix asked with a quick snap of his head that made his glasses jump.

'You fired me, and I'm staying fired, with all the wrongful dismissal trimmings that go with it. The whole agency witnessed it.' I stood up. 'You can deal with my lawyer on a settlement, but let me warn you that it'll have to be fucking good if you want to stay out of court.' As I walked from the room I added: 'You might get a coffee out of your guardian angel here, but make sure you're gone when I get back in half an hour.'

'Ed, darling, where are you going?' Clarice said with an imploring, twitchy smile. 'Felix and Wesley had to do it this way.'

'And I have to do it a different way,' I called from the hallway as I opened the front door.

I merged with the sea-scented night. The harbour drew me like a balm, although I didn't really need one. My feet bounced along the pavement in time to a Mozart tune provided by The Channel. When I reached the yacht club I took a walk out along the marina pier where the moored boats nodded in the gloom. I sat down on the rough bleached wood and let my feet dangle over the black water gurgling against the encrusted piles beneath. I hadn't felt so good in a long time.

***

Chapter Ten

Clarice thumped about the bedroom the next morning while I clung to my pretence of sleep. Finally she palpated my shoulder.

'I'll get you some eggs,' she said.

'Bad for cholesterol,' I muttered from beneath the sheet.

'Ed, are you going to work or what?'

'Undoubtedly what,' I replied. 'And what can be roughly translated as calling Martin Gait, our trusted family lawyer.'

'You're not serious about knocking back Felix and Wesley.'

'As serious as they were about delivering a killer blow to my self-esteem.'

'But they didn't mean it like that. They had to do it.'

'No they didn't. They could have planned it with me instead of playing war games. It's like the judge telling the jury to disregard the last remark from the prosecutor. The damage is already done.'

'I think that's being a bit churlish, Ed. This is our future too, you know.'

'Go to gym and let me worry about our future,' I said as I turned over in search of sleep.

Clarice took a noisy shower, thinking perhaps the sound of running water in the ensuite bathroom might wash away my stupidity.

'If you're going to hang around the house today you'll have to put up with vacuum cleaners and things,' her raised voice echoed around the tiles. 'You know I clean on Thursdays.'

'I won't bother you,' I said. 'I'll be going out.'

'Really, Ed?' Her towel turbaned head appeared around the edge of the door. 'Where?'

'Martin Gait, and then sailing.'

By the time I got up and had a leisurely breakfast, the day had arranged itself as far more suitable for sailing than visiting our stuffy lawyer. I thought of trying to seduce Sid into meeting me at the yacht club. I think I would have succeeded if I'd described the gentle nor'-easter that was stippling the harbour, but I realised I wanted my own company. As I dressed in my blue cotton trousers and plain white sports-shirt I could feel Clarice trying to guess what I was planning. Twice the telephone rang and I ignored it until she answered. On both occasions it was Wesley Crowe. In spite of Clarice's mimed pleading, I refused to speak to him.

As I left the house Clarice ran after me for a kiss and to hand me my mobile phone which I had left behind. I accepted the kiss but refused the phone.

I drove down to The Spit yacht suppliers to pick up the nylon waterproofs I'd ordered the previous week and then stopped in at the sandwich shop to buy bread rolls and a Coke for lunch. It was eleven-thirty by the time I parked outside the yacht club. The main building and bar wouldn't be open until five o'clock when some members might call in for a homeward-bound drink, but the double doors of the boatshed were ajar.

Inside, the smell of salt dried on canvas, and seaweed, and the oil of small engines excited me. Once my eyes had adjusted to the gloom I greeted a few members toiling on their obstinate hulls before I crossed to our locker to change into my stained, sea-mouldy clothes. They were still waiting for the laundering I'd promised them six months before.

Three Oranges was ideally crewed by two, but both Sid and I knew her so well that we could sail single-handed. I jogged down the marina, jumped aboard and began rigging immediately. It was not long before I was heading slowly across the harbour under a slack mainsail, and feeling as though I'd broken free of life's gravitation.

I sailed past little beaches, some of them dotted with nude bathers defying the autumn cool and the ban on their preference, and anchored for a late lunch near Watsons Bay. I turned off the radio and listened to the slap of water and the call of prospecting gulls. They lulled me to sleep in the deck chair I'd set up on the roof of the small cabin.

Who needed to die to be in heaven?

***

Wesley Crowe lived in a splendid, fortified apartment block overlooking the water at Darling Point. As I approached the speaker grille with its row of bright chrome buttons and numbers set in the high stone wall, I checked the time. Eight o'clock suited my purpose nicely.

A throttled version of Wesley's voice answered my third ring.

'Ed Sharock,' I barked.

'I've been calling you,' he said after a long pause. 'I suppose you want to come up.'

'Not if you'd prefer to have a business discussion over this intercom.'

The buzzer snarled and the metal gate swung open. I followed the softly-lit tiled path through a heavily foliaged garden to the foyer of the building, where a second buzzer admitted me to the elevators. Appropriately, the Crowes lived in a high nest. I got out at the fifteenth floor where Wesley, done up in a bone cashmere polo and taupe pants, was waiting to meet me.

The sight of my sun-reddened face and wild hair made him hesitate for just a moment before shaking hands. 'Come on in Ed,' he said, groping for light-heartedness. 'We just sat down for dinner. Perhaps you'd like to join us.'

'No thanks Wesley, I had a couple of pies at the yacht club.'

I followed him into a spacious lounge room with a broad balcony beyond, and a dazzling view of harbour lights. Enid Crowe was sitting at their marble table in the peach-coloured dining room with two other people. I waved, then threw myself into one of the cream damask lounge chairs. Wesley winced and remained standing.

'Did my lawyer call you today?' I asked.

'Not that I know of,' Wesley replied cautiously.

'That's because I didn't tell him to,' I said, grinning. 'Wesley, I've come here to tell you something.' I stared out of the window to let the muffled dinner music fill the room. 'You know how I refused last night to come back to work?'

'Yes.'

'I was only joking.' I laughed, the volume enhanced by yacht club beer, and raised myself from the chair's feathery embrace. 'I'll be home tomorrow for your call to arms. And we must talk about my farewell dinner. I think I'm going to enjoy it.'

***

It wasn't Wesley who telephoned the next morning but Felix. I was engrossed in front of my computer screen, still challenged by Florence Formby. I also wanted to make Clarice suffer a little longer before telling her that I was back in the winners' circle.

'Ed, old boy,' Felix chuckled. 'Wes gave me the good news. I suppose we deserved for you to give us a serve. You haven't been too tough on Clarice, I hope.'

'I haven't had a chance. She's out running at Mosman Park. I'll probably give her a surprise over coffee when she gets back. Now, where do we go from here?'

'Okay, we get an internet cable put into your house for the direct link with Salt Lake City. I've got our computer people delivering you a new power PC and twenty-one-inch monitor tomorrow, and a laser colour printer as well. Now, as we said, we'd like Andy to work at your place too. Can you fit him in?'

'He can use the rumpus room down below,' I said. 'The girls never use it during the week.'

'Okay then, you'll get two of everything delivered plus a scanner for Andy, along with his usual artist supplies and computer programs. We'll add a rental component to your monthly salary. I'll fax over the whole package in a minute. Okay?'

Because I had now abandoned my career as a romance writer, the perverse Channel deluged me with ideas. I was compelled back to work on Florence Formby. I could hardly type fast enough. Florence had finished her morning shift on the dredge and was unzipping her rough navy boiler suit in the change room when she heard Boris the brutal boss calling her name. He barged in as she was stepping out of her knickers. Extra big knickers. Boris stood staring, immobilised. He'd only ever seen her in the boiler suit. He'd never dreamed how beautiful she was. My God, I realised, I'd made Florence plump.

The thought of her got me a hard-on but she couldn't be a Mills & Boon character ... although maybe I'd made an unfair assumption. Maybe romance readers craved a fat heroine. I stopped the story and began a query letter to the editors.

Trying to pitch a fat heroine proved to be harder than writing the story. I sat staring at the cursor blinking at the beginning of the first sentence as I listened to Clarice clattering about in the kitchen.

'Ed, come in here quickly,' she called shrilly.

Thinking she'd been confronted by a spider I left my chair and hurried to the kitchen. Clarice was standing by the fax machine holding a piece of paper.

'Ed, have you seen this?' Her voice was hoarse.

'How could I? It's just come out of the bloody fax.'

'You devil!' she laughed, and ran across to hug me. 'You didn't tell me. My God Ed, this is a deal and a half. You've played Felix and Wesley like a champion angler.'

She towed me after her to the bedroom where she urgently pulled off her clothes as well as mine. Her body was still glistening from the run she'd just finished. We fell on to the unmade bed. Where the hell was my fat girl? I wasn't getting hard. Suddenly I became Boris, fucking fat Florence on a heap of sweaty towels he'd flung on the change room floor of the Derwent River Dredge Company. Our eight-limbed machine came to life.

***

Andy appeared the next day. After we had given each other a high five and toasted our restored status with a mug of coffee, he helped me unpack the new computers and set them up. When I compared my little old PC to the new monster that appeared from the boxes I had to retire mine to the garage shelf to join the other stuff under the rug.

We set up my office first so that we could work out the best place for the cable before Telstra arrived. Then I took Andy down to the rumpus room to show him where he'd be working.

'This is so fucking cool,' he breathed as he looked around at the polished timber floor and out through the sliding glass doors into the garden and the swimming pool beyond.

'We can throw a sheet over the table tennis table if you need to spread your work out,' I said. 'And you can take a walk in the garden when you want a break.'

'Where should I smoke?' he asked. 'I mean *smoke.* '

'We're a non-smoking house,' I said, ignoring the conveyed meaning. 'So outside, if you wouldn't mind.'

A grey melamine desk and boxes of paints, brushes, repeater pens and pencils arrived early in the afternoon and then a consignment of art paper in various sizes.

'I won't use much of this stuff,' Andy said. 'With a computer and the Paintbox program and a scanner, paper's fucked. I told Crowe but he wanted me to have it just in case.'

Once I'd set Andy up so that the light coming into the rumpus room didn't reflect off his monitor's screen, we left each other alone to install the programs that had come with the machines.

I tested the new cable by going to the Good Fortune Pet-food internet site. The same material that was in the brochures came up, plus a load of information about the Good Fortune Court Network Marketing System. It seemed you had to know somebody who was already a member of the court to be admitted yourself.

I tried to get online with the company's personnel but didn't know the password.

At five, I took Clarice and the girls down to meet Andy. Sibyl was humbled by him. Later she told me he was the image of Slack, the new rock star. And when I told her that the Downheaval poster he'd stuck on the wall behind his desk was his work, and that he'd actually met Downheaval, she elevated him to sainthood.

'Andy is not here to play or be disturbed,' I told the small gathering. 'He's at work. I want you to respect that. So the rumpus room is out of bounds except on weekends and, even then, you don't touch any of Andy's things.'

Sibyl's dark head was bowed in reverence but Taya scowled. Neither said anything.

'Now, another thing, and this is very important. The reason Andy and I are working here at home is to keep our work absolutely secret. None of us must mention to anybody, even our best friends or families, what's going on here, and especially the name of the pet-food.'

'*cafe*,' Taya whispered and giggled.

Ignoring her, I continued: 'For the time being we pretend that I am writing a romance novel and Andy is a friend we are helping out with some work space for a while. After October everything will change and we'll go back to North Sydney.'

***

I'd never worked full-time from home before. I found that without the company rails to run on, discipline became difficult. It was too easy to start work when I wanted, dress without thinking and snack at will. Andy seemed to take to it better than I did. Artists, he conveyed in Andy-speak, were never very aware of their surroundings anyway.

When we weren't working on *cafe*, Felix fed through fill-in work. I even got to make suggestions for Awayaway and Dempster, although officially the agency had allocated those accounts to other creative teams.

After the disruption of being fired and reinstated had slid into the past, and I had built myself a new work routine, I found that I still had periods of dark pessimism. Although it had shifted ground, I now dwelt upon what might happen when I returned to North Sydney, and whether there'd be enough work from *cafe* after the name change had been launched. Did Felix and Wesley have a future planned for me or was I only to be part of the current year's profit and loss account?

***

Chapter Eleven

Iseemed to be the only person in the world who looked forward to my farewell dinner. While Wesley and Felix needed to make my removal from Lead Balloon look authentic, they loathed spending the money or the time on it. Wesley reluctantly booked a small private dining room at the Clarion Hotel in North Sydney and invited about a dozen people, also reluctant, from Lead Balloon.

'We'll get the bloody thing finished early,' he told me on the phone. 'Straight from work to have drinks at half-past six and dinner about half-past seven. I was going to ham it up a bit but I couldn't think of anything clever to do.'

I suggested we make it black tie, and have a woodwind quartet to give some sense of occasion, but Wesley said no, it would do the way it was, and we could all go home early.

On a Tuesday night, exactly two weeks after I'd been 'retrenched' from Lead Balloon, we gathered in the conference room bar of the

Clarion. Even though there was plenty to drink and talk about, it soon became apparent that the guests at my farewell were determined not to enjoy themselves. They clearly wanted my dinner to be designated bummer event of the year.

As the remains of the main course were replaced by plates of ice cream, tinned peaches and barely-there wafers, Wesley rose and unnecessarily struck his wine glass with his dessert fork.

'Ladies and gentlemen,' he said with a clearing cough, 'we're not going to waste good drinking and eating time on official speeches but this is a special occasion. Lead Balloon is saying goodbye to one of its longest-serving and finest creative people, Ed Sharock. It would not be fitting to let this moment pass without expressing our gratitude to Ed and to wish him well in his future endeavours where the pastures are undoubtedly greener. But I'll let him tell you all about that. Ladies and gentlemen, would you please be upstanding and raise your glasses in a toast of good luck to Ed.'

Chairs were pushed back and people stood holding their glasses of beer or cheap wine. Two of the chairs, also cheap, fell over backwards.

'To Ed,' they murmured and sank back to the table.

Felix leaned close to my ear and whispered: 'Make it short.'

I rose to my feet.

'Thank you Wesley, for making my contribution to Lead Balloon sound so grand. It really wasn't. I've had good clients and the overwhelming talent of the people at this table on my side. That's something I'm going to miss.

'As some of you may already know, my new career will involve romance fiction writing. This is something I've always wanted to do, something for which I believe I have a natural talent. I am sure you would like to hear a small sample of my work.'

Without waiting for confirmation I pulled a sheet of paper from my pocket and began to read.

'Florence Formby had done with men. She craved love but hated the cruelty that always seemed to go with it. That is why she went to work on a fifty-foot dredge at the mouth of the Derwent River.'

I glanced over the top of the paper. Indulgent smiles had turned to uncontrollable smirks. Some hands were covering mouths. I read on.

'She had finished her morning shift on the dredge and was unzipping her rough navy boiler-suit in the locker room when she heard her brutal boss, Boris, calling her name. He barged in just as she was stepping out of her size-eighteen panties. Boris stood staring. He'd never realised how big or how beautiful she was. He'd always thought of fat as being ugly, but in a flash Florence changed his mind with her voluminous breasts and buttocks, and creamy dimpled thighs. His own boiler suit became taut with his desire as he advanced upon her.'

When the laughter had begun to subside I said: 'And here's something else I've always wanted to do.'

I leaned across to the red wine decanter and filled my glass beyond the point of good form as recommended by *Vogue*. Then I tipped half of the contents over Wesley and the other half over Felix.

In the absolute silence that followed, Wesley got slowly to his feet. His face looked as though a make-up artist had tried to render him a fractured skull but had used the wrong strength stage blood.

'You motherfucker,' he said, picking up a full jug of beer. He threw the contents into my face.

Felix stood up and for some reason poured his white wine into Doc Sherlock's top pocket. A meteor of ice cream flew across the room and hit Joan White on the chest. She scooped it up, added a handful of peach portions and smeared them over Simon Quigley's new YSL shirt.

The battle continued until there was no more food or drink left to throw. That which had missed its mark created a slowly evolving art piece on the walls and ceiling of the room.

Felix, out of breath, said: 'Fuck the coffee. I'll order up some towels and then I think we should go home.'

As I dried myself I mentally apologised to my fat girl and to Florence. How cheap and convenient it had been for me to lead the mob in jeering at the thing I secretly loved.

***

Chapter Twelve

The interior of the grand ballroom at the Salt Lake City Conference Centre had been blacked out. The only way to find a seat was to be guided by ushers with torches. These spidery girls wore black leotards and became virtually invisible so that once seated I might have been in deep space, viewing a galaxy of darting stars.

I'd tried to persuade Ellis Sommerville to invite Andy Hope to the conference to see the new name launched. But later I'd been relieved at the refusal when I'd found I would have been sharing a hotel room with Andy. I imagined the burnt-bushland smell as he lit up a joint in our room for his daily adjustment to life.

Ellis hadn't invited me just as a goodwill gesture. After the grand opening I was to be taken on an intensive tour of the company's operations and shown the new products it had in planning. They would all need clever names and seductive descriptions.

Sitting there in the total darkness waiting to see the launch of the name I'd created certainly excited me, but I could feel pessimism close by. Although I'd take back with me more agency work for *cafe*, it was nothing compared to the amount that the name change had already generated. Would I again be put through a dismissal, but with no nocturnal laughing visit from Wesley and Felix to reverse it?

A rushing, whistling sound overhead stopped the chatter of the invisible audience in the cavernous room. Shafts of laser light crisscrossed one another like clashing swords. They became one huge pointer which wrote, in bright red above us, 'Good Fortune'. The faithful cheered. The word acquired a third dimension, as though it had been hewn from red crystals. Then, as we watched, the word began to weather. Rust and cracks ate away at the letters until they lost shape and fell into a heap of red sand which blew away to reveal something underneath. My word, *cafe*, hung above us like a newborn star, winking and gleaming in Andy's two colours of red and blue, minus the hyphen. A God-like voice boomed:

'Welcome to a new age. Welcome to *cafe*.'

The lights came up like a quick sunrise. We were in a huge medieval court. I was seated among the common courtiers who were designated by their navy jackets. In front of us were Earls wearing green jackets, Barons in brown, Lords in burgundy, Princes in yellow and Kings, the most exalted, in purple. The Kings were lined up on the dais facing the rest of the court. In the middle of them, dressed in what looked like sackcloth robes, were the three partners: Ellis Sommerville, Sally Ness and Gerry Silver.

Ellis stood and raised his arms like a possessed preacher and the Kings sat down. Then he stepped forward to the podium which appeared as a giant can of *cafe*. With only his head and shoulders visible at the top he could well have been a piece of talking dog-food.

'The *cafe* court is now in session,' he called. That brought the jacketed ones to their feet for the shouted response: 'Court in session!'

'As you can see,' he told them after they had resumed their seats, 'this was the surprise we promised you: a change of name. We've all wanted it and now it is here. The company is set to tackle the twenty-first century with a twenty-first century name.

'Our new name, *cafe*, will go on a whole range of new products that we'll be releasing over coming months. Like our pet-food, they will be cutting edge, state of the art. We'll have collars, combs and brushes, breath fresheners, tooth-cleaning snacks, blankets, shampoos, flea treatments. One of the most exciting products is in final trials now. It is a non-surgical libido deactivator to combat unwanted pregnancies in domestic pets.

'When I think,' Ellis's voice softened, 'that it was only eight short years ago that we were selling our first little product from my daddy's farmyard gate, it is hard to believe that three thousand of you have gathered at court here today. I am humbled before you and before God for such gifts.'

Ellis laid his head down on the edge of the can and became shaken by heavy sobs. The two other sackcloth-clad figures helped him back to his seat at the centre of the Kings, where he bent forward, head bowed, dabbing his eyes with a flowing white handkerchief.

Sally took up the story at the podium. She talked about the company's strong financial position, its credit rating and the numbers of network distributors compared to the potential throughout the world. Her speech, too, appeared to be unfinished when emotion overcame her and she was replaced by Gerry Silver.

'We're taking this business global!' Gerry thundered. 'In one month we open in Australia and then we go to England. Any of you folks who know people who know people who know people who know people in any of the new countries where we plan to set up warehouses can start talking to them right now. That's what I said, right now! Just think of all those beloved pussies and puppies deprived all these years of their *cafe*. Liberation is close at hand, and so is the banishment from the earth of their excremental odour. These furry and hairy creatures, whom we love so much, didn't choose to cause a stink.' Gerry had to pause to take out his white handkerchief to blow his nose.

As he spoke I looked along the row of Kings. There must have been fifty of them. Some of them were women, and I wondered whether they had mounted an internal feminist campaign to be called Queens. Being a King meant that you had recruited at least twelve courtiers who themselves had become Earls or higher. Commission earnings rose steeply at each court level. Some Kings were rumoured to be making millions as their down-lines and their distributors and their users multiplied along with the numbers of dogs and cats gulping down *cafe*.

The company made no secret of the fact that *cafe* was addictive. Why shouldn't an animal crave that which was so good for it? A dog or cat deprived of its *cafe* became depressed and refused other food, although the company was working on a new product which would cure the animal's dependence upon *cafe*. The new product, of course, was going to be very expensive.

Nat Cohen stood out among the Kings, with his black shirt and tie under his bulky purple jacket. I wondered what career he had forsaken to become a *cafe* distributor, and then what motivational forces he had summoned to take him to the top of the earning ladder. How ignorant I had been that day when he had come into my office with Morton Whitbread. I had been in the presence of a *cafe* King who was probably earning ten times the salaries of anybody at Lead Balloon.

After several other speeches, one being a very polished delivery from Morton Whitbread about the numbers of dogs and cats in the major nations of the world, and how much reeking excrement they produced per day, the court was declared adjourned. The following days would be given over to prospecting and marketing seminars, mostly conducted by the Kings to show the lesser members of the court how to also become Kings.

As I was filing out of the court Nat Cohen suddenly confronted me and enveloped me in a purple and black hug.

'Ed,' he said as he unclamped me, 'I heard you were coming, but with the annual court, you never know whose gonna turn up. Listen, we've got to talk. How are you fixed tomorrow?'

'Fixed is the word,' I replied. 'My dance card is full. I've got inspections, visits and conferences for four days straight, and then they ship me home with another load of work to do.'

'What about nights?'

'Same,' I replied. 'I'm eating dinner separately with Ellis, Sally and Gerry. I get the feeling that they're still very nervous about security. Maybe they think a rival pet-food company is going to kidnap me.'

'Don't joke about it,' Nat said, without smiling. 'Look, I'd better say this now. You know we're going to open in Australia next month. I think I could get the march on the other boys with a little help. And I love your country. I might settle there one day. Ed, let me ask you a question.'

'Ask away Nat.'

'Ed, are you happy with your job? I mean, does it give you all the time you want and all the money you need to live the way you would like?'

'Pretty much,' I replied, feeling myself being sucked into the networkers' verbal vortex.

'I thought the same when I was a New York lawyer,' Nat continued with a wistful expression. 'I was earning plenty of bread but I didn't see much of Ruth or the kids. Now I never see Ruth at all, and I only get to see the kids Sundays. The law business cost me my family, Ed.'

'I'm sorry to hear it,' I said awkwardly.

'I wouldn't like it to happen to a nice guy like you,' he continued. 'Marriage feeds on time and money. I'm glad to know you've got both, Ed. Tell me one more thing. Do you love your job? Do you feel good every day you roll out of the sack and head for the office?'

'I'm not really sure,' I replied, only just stopping myself from confessing to my secret pessimism. 'Advertising is a bit up and down, especially at my age.'

'Do you know what I'm hearing here Ed?' Nat dropped his voice and moved close to me. 'I'll tell you what I'm hearing. I'm hearing a guy whose career is taking water. He wants to row ashore because he thinks it might be sinking but he's not exactly certain, so he stays on a little longer. And then one day it's too late. Down it goes, dragging him with it. He finds himself sitting right at the bottom. Is this you, Ed?'

'Not really, Nat. I suppose I've been around Lead Balloon too long, but I don't see any realistic alternatives. The *cafe* account has given me a kick along, so I don't have to worry about my career for the time being.'

'Does it make sense to live day to day on kicks along?' Nat asked. 'If I could show you a better way, would you take a look at it?'

'What have you got in mind?'

'Do you want me to tell you, Ed?'

'Okay, tell me.'

'Let's storm Australia together. With your contacts and my know-how we'd own the whole country. We'd end up feeding every dog and cat and cleaning up every sidewalk. And while we were doing that, we'd make more money than you ever dreamed of. What's your heart saying Ed? What do you hear?'

'Are you asking me to join your *cafe* court, and to get involved in network marketing, Nat?'

'Ed, is that what you'd like to do?'

'To give you a simple answer, Nat, no. I hate the idea of using friendships to sell stuff. I don't like approaching strangers and I can't handle rejection.'

'Do you see those as challenges you'd like to overcome?'

'No, I don't see them as challenges, Nat. That's just how I am. It's how a lot of people are. I was tricked into a Prodmasters meeting once and I decided then and there I hated network marketing.'

'*Cafe* is nothing like Prodmasters, Ed,' Nat sighed. 'But I can understand how you feel. I felt like that, but I found once I got going with *cafe* I grew a new personality. But hey, I'm not here to huck you. Can I ask you one final question? Would you give me a few names of people in Sydney with dogs and cats who might come to a meeting?'

Almost everybody I knew had a dog or a cat, and how many would Sid know? Probably thousands.

'Okay Nat,' I said clapping him on the arm, 'that much I'll do for you. I might even come to your first meeting to hear you do your stuff.'

'You're a pal,' Nat said hugging me again. 'I'll be in touch when I hit Sydney in about three weeks. Deal?'

'Deal.'

***

Nat was only the first of a dozen approaches I had from members of the court over the next four days offering to sponsor me into making a *cafe* fortune in Australia. Australians were rare creatures in America, it seemed. Some of the members expressed surprise to find that I was white and spoke a language similar to their own. Others mixed up Australia with Austria or imagined that we lived in towns made from discarded American corrugated iron and plywood.

Once they knew that the company had booked up all of my time in Salt Lake City, the distributors became inventive in their methods to contact me. Twice hotel room service personnel turned out to be disguised court members and once, when I went to a public toilet, I received an abridged presentation while I stood taking a piss at a urinal.

I quickly found the way to shut them up was to say that I'd already signed under a King. The best they could salvage was to give me a business card for use if ever I should be unhappy with my sponsor.

I felt depressed the following Tuesday morning as I landed in Sydney. Jet-lagged and weighed down by the new briefs I had been given, I didn't want to face having to move back to my office at Lead Balloon. In fact, I'd decided to suggest that Andy and I continue working from Mosman.

Clarice met me at the airport with hugs and happiness, but once we had gained the privacy of the Range Rover she said:

'You've got to do something about Andy. Sibyl has a crush on him.'

I stared out at the green Sydney landscape sliding past. I didn't want to engage any more problems. 'It seems more likely that we've got to do something about Sibyl,' was all I could think of saying. 'I take it Andy isn't exactly ripping her pants off.'

'No, not yet anyway, but I don't trust him. She can't stay away from him after school. I can hear her in the downstairs room talking her head off and he hardly seems to say anything.'

'That's probably what attracts her,' I said. 'It's such a contrast to the rest of her friends – and family for that matter. But I wouldn't worry too much. Andy and I are both supposed to be returning to the agency building now that the *cafe* name has been announced, although I was toying with the idea of delaying the move. I'll bet Wesley hasn't told the staff about our mock dismissal.'

'I don't have any idea about that, Ed. But I'd like Andy to move soon because I'm worried,' Clarice said.

'I can't really tackle him if he hasn't done anything.'

'How do we know he hasn't done anything? She wouldn't talk about it and I can't ask him. You'll have to.'

When we reached home all I could think of was bed but, as if advised by telepathy, Wesley Crowe phoned.

'Ed old boy, welcome back,' he said jovially. 'I hear you've brought plenty of work with you. Can you come in this afternoon? We're having a few drinks after work to make the announcement about *cafe* and welcome you and Andy Hope back to the fold. And no tipping drinks on the directors.'

'Wesley, I'm pretty tired from the flight,' I said. 'Could we possibly make it tomorrow?'

'Afraid not, Ed. The rest of the week's booked up. Why don't you have a sleep and come in around four.'

'Okay,' I sighed, hung up and made for the bedroom where Clarice already had the bed turned down.

***

I seemed to have slept for only five minutes when the alarm woke me at three. I showered, had a cup of coffee and drove slowly to the office. Any plans I might have had about extending my time working at home had to be cancelled in favour of controlling Sibyl's sexual development.

As I walked through the front doors of Lead Balloon I realised I hadn't been inside the place for nearly four months. There were different plants in the foyer and a couple of new graphics on the wall. A new receptionist too, who asked me to spell my name before telling Mr Crowe that his visitor had arrived.

'Please go up to Mr Crowe's office,' her bright red lips and carnivorous white teeth told me.

It should have felt like a homecoming but it didn't. Wesley wore his jolliest face as he confessed, unconvincingly, how they'd all missed me.

'I've organised a get-together of just the key people,' he said. 'I was tempted to produce you and Andy from behind a curtain but it's probably better to do it straight and just have you in the room when they arrive.'

'And after that I can move back to my old office?' I asked.

'Well, not immediately,' Wesley said carefully. 'We've had a few temporary moves in the last few weeks. Simon has been camping in your old space. We'll set you up at the back of accounts for the time being.'

'Just as a matter of interest, Wesley, does the office at the back of accounts have a window?'

'Of course, Ed. We wouldn't lock you in the dark.' He forced a laugh. 'There's a glass wall that looks over the accounts open plan desks and then out across the street. If you want privacy you just close the vertical Venetians.'

'And Andy?'

'He goes back to his old desk in the art room. And while we're talking organisation Ed, we're going to give you a decent creative team now that *cafe* is going to be out in the open. You've carried the load on your own for long enough.'

'I don't need a creative team,' I said. 'All I really need is my old office back and maybe an assistant to do some donkey work.'

'Let's not worry about that now, Ed. We'll sort it all out tomorrow when you start back in earnest. Now we should go to the boardroom and set up our surprise.'

It was no surprise. Everybody who came to the gathering knew I was returning to Lead Balloon and some of them knew I'd been working at home on the *cafe* account. Andy stood inertly holding his glass of beer and looking cold. He'd never been very sociable in the company and this gathering wasn't going to change anything.

'How do you feel about moving back?' I asked him as a lead-up to talking about his contact with Sibyl.

'Good,' he said in a monotone. 'In fact, fucking good. That daughter of yours, Sibyl, was coming on to me. So it's better to get away. You oughta talk to her, Ed.'

***

Chapter Thirteen

In my intense application to the task of working on the *cafe* account, I'd forgotten about Nat Cohen's visit to Sydney. First there was an e-mail from him, and before I could reply his Bronxy voice was on the phone.

'Hey, Ed, how you doin'?' he said. 'Sydney looks to me like a big juicy clam ready to open. And inside it's full of hungry cats and dogs.'

The image made me shudder involuntarily.

'I got a week to organise meetings,' he continued. 'Listen buddy, could I talk to you at home tonight?'

I remembered that I'd offered to help Nat with contacts. 'That will be fine Nat,' I said. 'Would you like to come for dinner?'

'Sure.'

'Anything you don't eat?'

'Well you might have guessed I pass on pork and prawns,' he replied.

'Okay, I'll call Clarice,' I spoke with more enthusiasm than I felt. 'Come around seven. We can have a drink and a talk before we eat.'

Nat arrived punctually and, after some hallway chat with me, he applied himself to Clarice. She thawed and melted like a tub of ice-cream. By half-way through dinner he'd mesmerised the girls with his tales of the streets of New York and his consuming personal interest in their lives. He saved me up for the treatment until we were sitting in the lounge room with coffee.

'You've got such a beautiful family,' he said. 'I might'a had something like this if things hadn't gone down the turnpike on me. I love families, Ed. That's what I'm working towards, you know. *cafe* is going to give me the means to get another family. Wife, babies, the whole set.'

'Sure, Nat. That's how it will be,' I said, hoping he wasn't going to start crying. 'Now, how can I help you with your business?'

'Maybe you could suggest a place to hold our business opportunity meetings. And then give me a few names and phone numbers of pet owners,' he said. 'That's all. I'll do the calling. I'll say my friend Ed Sharock recommends they should hear about a revolution in feeding their pets.'

'I don't want to appear that heavy,' I said. 'You can say that I gave you their names but leave out the idea that I'm pushing them into buying something. Remember Nat, I'm never going to become a distributor. It just isn't me.'

'Okay,' he said, holding up his hands in mock defence. 'I'll be real nice to the folks you recommend. You don't have to worry, I do it mostly with questions. It's a technique I teach my down-line to use in marketing *cafe*. Let's role-play so I can show you how it works. Okay?'

He looked at me as though he'd never seen me before and said:

'Sir, do you mind me asking you a question?'

'No.'

'Do you have a dog or a cat?'

'Yes, one of each.'

'Do you care about what goes in one end and comes out the other?'

'I suppose I do.'

'Yes, but do you care enough to change their brand of food and pay only marginally more than you pay now for supermarket pet-food?'

'I don't know. I hadn't thought about it.'

'If there was a pet-food that made your animals very much healthier and removed the smell entirely from their excreta, would you be interested?'

'I might be.'

'And if this food came in biodegradable containers that are wonderful for your garden, would that make a difference?'

'Yes, I suppose it would.'

'If I told you that there is a pet-food called *cafe* which came in a number of flavours so that your pet would never get bored with it and that you could pick up its excreta in your hand without olfactory offence, would you want to buy that food?'

'Yes, I probably would.'

'And finally, if I was to tell you that simply by sharing the benefits of *cafe* with other pet owners you could build yourself a recurring income that could exceed your present income, would you want to take a closer look at *cafe*?'

'Yes of course I would,' I said, momentarily swamped by the logic.

'Okay Ed, you can see how we work. No hard sell, just soft

questions. I don't ask all of those questions on the phone call, of course. I just want to get them to a meeting. Then I get a hit rate of about seventy per cent of dog and cat owners. I can't get those who have to feed their pets table kitchen scraps because they're too poor. *cafe* is for people with money, to begin with anyway. Then it works its way down. In America we've found that once pet owners see the results of *cafe* they'll often go without themselves to keep up the supply to their dog or cat. But of course the business potential is so good that being poor doesn't last long if they become distributors.'

Clarice appeared in the room on the pretext of refilling our coffee cups, but I think she wanted another dose of Nat's attention.

'Where are you staying?' she asked him.

'That's a good question,' Nat replied. 'I only got in this morning. I haven't decided. I was going to ask you good folks for a recommendation. I didn't like the last hotel I shared with Morton.'

'How long are you staying in Australia?' Clarice continued.

'I'd say probably a month,' Nat replied. 'Depends on how quickly the lines build.'

'Why don't you stay with us, for a start anyway,' Clarice offered.

'Clarice, I couldn't impose on you good people like that. Ed, tell Clarice she's outa line.'

'Of course she's not out of line,' I said feebly. 'If you'd like to stay with us, we'd love to have you.'

'Exactly,' Clarice pealed. 'In any case, you can't leave here tonight without a room to go to. If you want to organise yourself a hotel tomorrow that's up to you, but tonight you spend with us.'

'That's so good of you,' Nat said, standing up to hug Clarice. He should have hugged me. I was the one he needed to convince.

***

Nat stayed more than one night. By the end of the first week I had the feeling that I was staying in his house. Clarice and the girls seemed to pay far more attention to him than they did to me.

Clarice went out and bought a menorah and two yarmulkes for Friday night. We stood around the candle-lit table while Nat read prayers from his Shabat book. We drank kosher wine from egg cups and ate pieces of bread from a loaf which he drew, like a magician, from beneath an embroidered cloth in front of him.

'You oughta be doing all this,' he told me, 'because you're the head of the house. But since you don't know the prayers I'm doing it for you. When you learn to read a little Hebrew you can run the show.'

I toyed with the idea of instituting grace before meals on the other six nights to win back a bit of religious territory, but thought better of it. After all, he'd only be around for a week or two.

While he was cutting the bread and sprinkling it with salt I managed to read what was tattooed on the back of his right hand. It said: 'prospect or perish'.

***

My yacht club readily agreed to hire out the dining room to Nat the following Tuesday for his first *cafe* meeting. As an office bearer of the club and a friend of Nat's and the creative director of the *cafe* account at Lead Balloon, I felt obliged to attend the meeting. But Clarice wouldn't come with me. Her dislike of network marketing was far greater than her liking for Nat. I called Sid to ask him if he wanted to come to the meeting for a laugh. If it became boring, I promised him, we could withdraw to the race committee room and drink rum like two old seafarers.

An unexpectedly large crowd arrived at the meeting. Nat must have put in many hours on the telephone to attract what must have been fifty or sixty people. He had set up a whiteboard at the end of the room, and a table of *cafe* containers showing all the flavours for dogs and cats. He'd also hung up giant photographs of the Utah headquarters and pictures of Ellis, Sally and Gerry.

At exactly eight o'clock Nat walked from the back of the room to the front at bridal speed, head tilted back as if in a religious trance. He wore his trademark black shirt, black trousers and black tie and, of course, his purple jacket. Nobody except me knew we were in the presence of a King.

He turned, stretched out his biggest smile and called: 'Hi everybody!'

There was silence.

'I said hi!' he bellowed.

'A few people muttered 'hi'.

'That's not much of a welcome for a lonely Yank,' he said. 'What about a big welcome from all of us, to all of us? Hi!'

This time they chorused a reasonably loud response.

'Okay,' he said clapping his hands together, 'We're here to take a look at something for two types of creatures, pets and people.' He picked up a purple marker pen from the table and went to the whiteboard.

'People first,' he said, drawing a stick figure. 'Now dogs and cats.'

He began to draw a dog but its back half looked like a cat. That got people laughing.

'Would you believe I went to New York art school?' he said. 'I'm sure you could all do better. Anyway, just pretend this is your pet.' He drew an arrow pointing at its mouth. 'Food in here,' he said. Then another arrow pointing out of its arse. 'What'll we call the stuff that comes outa here? Anybody want to tell me what you call it in Australian?' There was more laughter, but nobody spoke. 'Okay, let's call it X. Food in, X out. Food smells okay, X stinks. Anybody want to dispute that?'

Nat had them. I looked at Sid. He too was riveted by the presentation.

When Nat had spent about twenty minutes talking about the product he switched to the newly named *cafe* Corporation, telling the story of how it all began and how it grew and where it was going. That led into the payment plan for those who wanted to do more than make pets healthy and pavements pure. I'd heard the earlier stuff before – in fact I'd written some of it – but I'd never taken much notice of the money arrangements. The way Nat told it, nobody could fail as long as they earnestly prospected for distributors for at least an hour a day.

'I'm going to say something you won't believe,' Nat suddenly dropped his voice to a whisper. 'I'm telling you that *cafe* does not have to be sold. I've never sold a can of it. I hate selling. I'm not a salesman. I never will be. No, *cafe* is not sold, it is bought! Distributors make money from prospecting and signing other distributors who all buy *cafe*. They call up the company, give their credit card number, the company delivers *cafe* to their door and the distributor who introduced them gets a commission – paid automatically by the company's computer every month.'

He rubbed out his dog/cat and replaced it with a lot of people stick figures joined by lines and holding percentage signs in their hands. Then he calculated average household spending on pet-food multiplied by the number of distributors in a typical series of rectangular networks. The results were amazing. Kings like Nat averaged over half a million dollars a year. Even an unmotivated Lord, designated by the permission to wear a burgundy jacket, could make as much as I did at Lead Balloon, and do it in his own time from his own home.

'The compensation plan is hard to follow at first,' Nat explained. 'There's a whole lot more to it. We teach it all at distributor training. We have a system based on a medieval court to sort out levels of distributors.

'Everybody here will fall into three categories,' he said at the end. 'First, you might walk away saying that you have no interest in the product or the money – and that's okay. Or you may want to try some of the product on your dog or cat and I can arrange for the company to supply you. Or you may want to make *cafe* a business so that it replaces and exceeds the income you're earning now. It's your choice. I'll stay behind for anybody who wants to make either of the last two choices. Thank you for coming to our first meeting. God bless and good night.'

***

Chapter Fourteen

Nearly all the people at the meeting seemed to want one of the last two choices. Nat suddenly became a celebrity fielding questions at a press conference. Although he calmly opened a box of registration forms, he was clearly overwhelmed by the response. His plump hands were shaking as he tried to decide where to put the stack on the table. Sid said to me:

'Listen, we'd better help the poor bastard. I hate to see business go begging.'

Sid went across and spoke briefly to Nat who handed him a wad of forms and waved to me. Sid and I joined Nat at the table and lines of people immediately queued in front of us. I looked down at the forms.

'What do I write in the space where it asks for the sponsors and up-line name?' I asked Nat.

'Put your own name as sponsor,' he replied. 'And you can write me as your up-line.'

'But I don't want to become a *cafe* sponsor or a distributor,' I protested.

'Doesn't matter,' Nat hissed. 'We can sort it out later. Right now we need signatures on forms.'

I stopped arguing and got down to it. When my queue was finally exhausted I had seventeen people signed under me. Did that make me a Baron or an Earl, I asked Nat?

'No, it makes you a common Courtier in a navy jacket,' he said. 'But if you sign twenty, or any of your down-line Courtiers sign other people into the business you could become an Earl or a qualifying Baron. Or you and Sid could become partners and that would make you an Earl straight away.'

'How can two people be one Earl?' Sid asked.

'Yeah, seems funny but that's the system,' Nat replied. 'Some partnerships take three or four people to make one court level.'

'So what are we going to do about all this?' Sid asked, staring at me.

'How do you mean, "do about"?' I replied. 'I'm not interested in becoming a *cafe* distributor, Sid. Don't tell me you are'

'No, of course not. I'd only give it a go if you did. You know, a partnership or something. Just part-time. Have a bit of fun together. I mean, we've got a flying start already.' He waved his wad of forms like winning raffle tickets.

Maybe Sid was fascinated by the way Nat did his presentations and thought he could even improve on them. But apart from his skill in public speaking, the fact that Sid was a vet would have high credibility with any audience of pet lovers. If Sid wanted to do all the uncomfortable stuff like starting up conversations with hostile strangers, I could probably handle the detail work, I reasoned. After all, I did know the company and the products better than anybody in Australia.

I called an urgent meeting in my subconscious. A multitude of my brain cells that had previously voted against network marketing crossed the floor. Incredulously, I heard my voice say:

'Okay, let's give the fucking thing a try.'

***

Chapter Fifteen

I soon realised that my first major obstacle in becoming a *cafe* distributor had nothing to do with products or networking. It was telling Clarice. I asked Nat not to mention it to her when we returned home that night; I would choose the right moment when Clarice and I were alone. I suspected Sid would have the same problem. His wife Stacey had once lost a lot of money, and even more self confidence, on Magic Face cosmetics, and had since become a bitter-voiced opponent of crooked pyramid schemes, as she branded all network marketing.

The moment I chose to tell Clarice was not the right one, as it turned out. There was probably no right moment, actually. I waited until the next morning, and blurted out my decision around the bathroom door as Clarice was cleaning her teeth. She immediately spat white froth into the basin.

'You did what?' she shouted, the toothpaste around her mouth looking like advancing symptoms of a fit.

'Not just me on my own,' I replied with spirit. 'Sid and I are partners in a *cafe* distributorship. It's just a part-time thing. For a laugh.'

'I don't think it's a laugh at all Ed,' she said, holding up her toothbrush and pointing it like a ray gun. 'You know how I feel about those schemes, or should I say scams? I'm telling you, tear up the papers and get your sanity back.'

I'd always been prepared to discuss opposition to my ideas or decisions, but I'd never been able to tolerate being ordered about. Clarice should have known better than to deal with my *cafe* decision in the way she did. I could feel my face grow hot.

'You don't tell me to do anything,' I said. 'If I want to flog pet-food I'll fucking-well flog pet-food. When it starts to affect your precious standard of living I'll do something about it, but until then, back off!'

I dressed in silence and left the house without breakfast or saying goodbye to the girls or to Nat – who was no doubt busy calling the US, reverse charges, as he did every morning.

Clarice might have easily talked me out of becoming a Courtier – or to be more precise a half-Earl with Sid – if she'd taken it gently. The idea of buttonholing people to talk them about their animals' shit and then inducing them to become *cafe* distributors was no more appealing the morning after Nat's meeting than it had been the morning before. But now I had a point to prove. Clarice was not going to have me jump to her orders.

Sid called me at home the next evening with a similar tale. Stacey had thrown her coffee mug on the floor when he'd delivered his news after dinner. If he wanted something extra in his life, why didn't he take up photography, or play more golf, or sail more?

'Do you think we should forget it?' he asked.

'No, bugger them,' I said from the security of my study. 'It's not like we're going to give up our jobs to do *cafe*. It's just a part-time thing.'

'I'm glad you said that,' Sid said. 'They'll get over it. And what if we just happen to be very successful and the money starts to roll in? I'll bet they won't mind spending it.'

Before Nat Cohen would let us begin looking for prospects to join the *cafe* network, he performed a short ceremony of welcome, at the end of which he presented us each with an elaborately-wrapped gift. When we took the paper off we were each holding in our hands a leather-bound book of ruled, but otherwise empty, pages. The inside back cover had a pouch that held a blank sheet which, when unfolded, was a metre square.

'This is the most valuable book you will ever own,' Nat said, his voice quavering with emotion. 'This is your book of life for networking. In it you gotta enter the name, numbers and address of every prospect you ever contact. The sheet in the back is your network map. In the middle you write your name and draw a rectangle around it. Then you draw rectangles around the names of each new down-line and join it to your rectangle with a line. When they get their own down-lines you add to their rectangles. And write in pencil. Son of a bitch down-lines can drop out and you need to juggle the rest of the rectangles.

'Now I gotta tell you something serious, boys. If ever I catch you not filling in this book I will stop helping you and do everything I can to take you out. Okay?'

And so began my companionship with an empty book. At first I filled it in because I feared Nat's revenge, but soon it really did become my most valued possession. If the house was burning down and I had the choice of saving one item, it would have been my prospecting record book.

The protective presence of Nat delayed the hard reality of network marketing hitting Earl Sharock-Willis. Nat stayed in Australia for another six weeks after Clarice ordered him out of our house for turning me into 'one of those', as she put it. Nat responded by taking a spacious serviced apartment in Elizabeth Bay overlooking the harbour, and inviting us to use it as our *cafe* meeting place. The hostility of our wives meant that neither Sid nor I could do the at-home meetings that the court training specified. Instead, we worked through what the *cafe* training manual called our 'warm circle', at Nat's place. We invited prospects to meet us there for coffee, during which we'd try to get them to one of Nat's meetings. For those first six weeks in the business we had Nat always willing to work his magic on a difficult prospect, and we sat like disciples at his meetings, which were soon filling the yacht club room twice a week.

Every newcomer to network marketing begins prospecting with his warm circle, Nat explained. They are friends, work colleagues, or relatives who, because they are not strangers, remove the first discomfort, that of self-introduction. Some of our warm circle remained warm after our network marketing pitch but many, believing our association had been sullied by uninvited commerce, turned into our frozen circle.

Sid and I divided up the yacht club and the golf club members between us. Through my work on the race committee I had the names and telephone numbers of the whole Mosman Yacht Club membership. Sid sweet-talked the golf club secretary for a list of members. We managed to make a few calls during the work day, but most of them were made from home. I would close my study door and compete with my daughters for use of the telephone in the early evening, but I usually didn't mind losing because it let me off having to make prospecting calls. Every time I'd lift the telephone to dial, a knot of fear would form in my stomach and I'd have to push myself to continue. Sometimes I hung up when the line was answered. Sid said he felt the same way. But when we met at Nat's to make calls together it was not so difficult. If we got abused we could talk about it and laugh it off.

When I'd call a member of the yacht club, he would at first be flattered. Fancy hearing from race committee-man Ed Sharock. How's that old yacht of yours going Ed? What's new at the club? What's new in advertising? How are the wife and kids? Yes, I've got a dog, poor old bugger, needs a good bath. Of course it eats. I don't know which pet-food; my wife buys that. Where does it shit? I don't know. I don't follow it around. Of course it stinks. All shit stinks. What do you mean it doesn't have to? Listen Ed, what's this call about anyway? How do you mean, making money as well? What, me sell pet-food? No, I've got nothing against pet-food or money or my dog's improved nutrition but it's not something I want get into. What kind of meeting? Who is this Nathan Cohen again? At the yacht club, you say. Well, I'll try to make it Ed, but I can't promise.'

Of course sometimes I'd hit the bullseye and they'd come to a meeting, but I couldn't work it the way Nat did. Somehow he got a string of questions going and never let up until he had uncovered the prospect's pain. He'd begin with some friendly chit-chat and then ask them whether they were fulfilled in money, in leisure time and in career satisfaction. Then he'd suddenly switch to the health of their dog or cat. They'd wonder why he'd left the most important elements of their life hanging in the air. But, through his questions, he'd press on with the benefits of *cafe* to their animals. You could almost hear the prospect yelling 'what about me?' Then he'd present the solution. In one neat *cafe* package he would conjure money, time, career, healthy animals, well-mulched gardens and foul-free pavements.

I found it difficult to reconcile Nat's mastery and profound belief in network marketing *cafe* and Clarice's total opposition to it. After that first outburst of resistance in the bathroom, Clarice settled down to a steady, subversive campaign by pretending *cafe* did not exist. In spite of my offering to supply and feed *cafe* to our dog and cat, she would not have the wretched stuff in the house, she declared. I could see no point in trying to get to our dog and cat first in a daily feeding race. Clarice would always win and, in any case, the house was her domain. But it meant that I had to lie to people when I told them how my pets were thriving on *cafe*.

Apart from a becalmed pocket that *cafe* had created in our marriage, the rest of it seemed to sail along steadily enough in a quiet breeze. That was until we hit a squall the day my first *cafe* commission cheque arrived. I couldn't mistake the *cafe* embossed envelope, addressed to Earl Sharock-Willis, lying among the household bills on my desk at home. Clarice stood akimbo at my study door to watch me open it. I prayed that all the promises our customers and our down-line had made to purchase *cafe* had been kept. I nonchalantly removed the network printout and gold-edged cheque from the envelope.

'Ah,' I said, 'this only covers our early weeks in the business.'

'How much is it for Ed?'

'The amount won't tell you anything, Clarice.'

'How much is it for Ed?'

'Clarice, it is not important enough for you to know.'

'How much is it for Ed?'

'Sixteen dollars and eight cents,' I said quietly.

'And what will you spend all that on?' she said with a triumphant laugh.

'Half of it goes to Sid,' I replied acidly, 'so you and I can go out and celebrate with eight dollars and four cents, which has to cover the tip, don't forget. Does that make you happy?'

***

Chapter Sixteen

All too soon it was time for Nat Cohen to return to the US. Sid and I felt like little kids surrounded by bullies without our big brother. We'd built a reasonable down-line of people using *cafe* but if we were to lift our income we'd need to help them build teams of their own. Otherwise we'd be a low-earning Earl for ever. We also had to face up to continuing the twice-weekly business meetings at the yacht club without the comforting presence of Nat. Sid, with his Toastmasters training, didn't mind making a public presentation but I was terrified when I had to do it. Nat said that we should take half the meeting each and gave us a Powerpoint presentation as prompts.

Sid and I drove Nat to the airport the Saturday he left. He'd paid for three more days at the Elizabeth Bay unit, which he said we could use and then return the key. We went back there after we'd seen him off. Sitting in the two lounge chairs facing the sunny harbour we envied the people in their carefree boats.

'We're in the deep end now,' Sid said reflectively. 'We've got a meeting to do next Tuesday. Could be sixty people if our down-lines bring the guests they've promised. How do you feel about it?'

'Scared out of my wits,' I said. 'It's all right for you. You thrive on it.'

'Not true,' he said. 'I'm just as scared as you, probably more so. I've just learned a few techniques to ward off stage-fright. But there's a big difference between Toastmasters and presenting at a *cafe* meeting. Toastmasters is pretend speeches. The audience are all frightened fellow travellers. But a *cafe* meeting is full of doubting and suspicious bastards who would rather be at home guzzling beer and watching television. They're dwelling on us fucking up so they can walk away.'

'Maybe we'd better practise,' I said.

For the rest of the afternoon we took turns to stand at one end of the room and address invisible audiences of *cafe* prospects. We hurled abusive questions at one another, made diversionary noises like mobile telephones ringing, farting, and fits of coughing. By the time the sky had given up its sunlight and the harbour had turned into a black drape with bright, moving pinholes, we were braver men. But, as with drilled soldiers, training was poor preparation for battle.

***

Earl Sharock-Willis ran out of warm circle prospects one blustery October Sunday afternoon. Instead of playing golf, Sid and I had retreated to my study to make calls after Clarice had gone to visit her mother. We each had our precious prospect record books in which we'd written the names and telephone numbers of everybody we'd ever contacted. We'd worked our way through the yacht club members, the golf club members, our relatives, our workmates, our friends, our dentists, doctors and lawyers. Every time we got a rejection we'd ask for referrals, and if the referrals weren't interested in buying *cafe* pet-food or building a network marketing business we'd go on asking for referrals until the trail went cold.

My last call was on Carl Zimmer, a member of the golf club, who curtly told me he was opposed to the idea of suburban domestic animals, and to improve their health or make their excreta more acceptable would only encourage more people to acquire them.

'Finito,' I announced to Sid as I replaced the receiver. He'd made his last call three before mine. 'So what have we got?'

'We're down to one meeting a week at the yacht club,' he said, looking at notes he'd been making. 'We've got about two hundred people using *cafe*, and we've got about forty people who are trying to duplicate what we're doing by building networks. If five of them can each recruit five new Courtiers we'd become a Baron.'

'And our last cheque as an Earl was for three hundred and ninety-four dollars,' I added. 'We're working this business for less than twenty cents an hour.'

'That's what Nat said would happen early,' Sid replied. 'Remember he told us we'd work like dogs for a year and be paid peanuts. I remember it word for word because I thought we should get peanuts if we were working like monkeys, not dogs. Anyway, then he switched metaphors and said once we got the steam train moving nothing would stop it flying.'

'Well, the steam train seems to be stopped in a siding,' I said. 'We don't know anybody else to call.'

'Don't forget that our down-lines are still working through their warm circles,' Sid said. 'That'll make the business grow without us having to do anything. And if some of them see the big picture and work the business properly we'll become a Baron and get a higher commission.'

'But Sid,' I said, 'we still need more Courtiers on our front line, and the only way to get front lines is to prospect them ourselves. It's decision time.'

'What do you mean?'

'I mean that we're at a fork in the road. One signpost says stay as we are, which means our business will slow down until its stops. The other one says we cold-call.'

'You mean just march up to people we don't know and start talking about shit?'

'Maybe not march up, but certainly ring up. There's a whole phone book full of prospects. Just think how many cats and dogs there are waiting in the white pages. I'll bet every second name owns a dog or a cat and everybody would know someone who does.'

I couldn't help pitching a campaign in my head. There was a high fence with gates in the middle made from the two sections of the telephone directory. The caption read: 'Through here to dogs, cats and piles of money'.

***

Chapter Seventeen

'Would you be game to pick a name out the phone book and just call?' Sid broke my diversion.

'No,' I replied, 'I wouldn't. Getting up and presenting at the yacht club meetings is more than I can handle already. Thank God we've trained a few of our Courtiers to do presentations. Every time I have to do it I spend the day in a nervous sweat.'

'So what you're saying is that we're quitting? If we stop prospecting, we die. Nat said that. He said it was like Alice in Wonderland. You have to run as fast as you can to stay in the same place. He still prospects every day – and he's a King. You've seen that tattoo on the back of his hand.'

'I'm not saying we're quitting,' I said. 'I'm just uncovering the issues.'

'Uncovering the pain,' Sid replied quickly. 'Our pain is that we're not game to uncover somebody else's pain.'

'So what do you suggest we do, get ourselves tattooed?'

'We grow balls,' Sid said, 'real balls. We cold-call. And we start now.'

He reached across my desk and lifted the phone book. 'This is how we'll do it. I pick and you call, then you pick and I call. And the picking has to be done blind.'

He closed his eyes, opened the book, and laid a long index finger on the page.

'Ching,' he said, after looking down. 'L.P. Ching, 9924 0102.'

I could detect humour in his eyes, but his mouth was set in an unflinching line. I dialled.

While I waited I asked: 'What about no-answers? Do they qualify as a cold-call?'

'Of course not,' he snapped. 'You've got to talk to somebody. We'll count a wrong number as a call as long as somebody answers and you speak to them, but a no-answer is not a cold-call.'

'*Whey,*' a woman's voice politely answered.

'Is that Mrs Ching?' I gulped.

'Yes, Mrs Ching speaking here. What you want?'

'I want to ask you a question.'

'Why you want to ask?'

'Because I want to know if you own a dog or a cat.'

'Why you want to know these things?'

'I'm conducting a survey.'

'What is survey?'

'Questions, Mrs Ching.'

'Stupid questions,' she said, and hung up.

'I take it you didn't get an appointment,' Sid said.

'I got fuck all,' I replied sourly. 'She got going on the questions before I did. It's like an arm wrestle. Once your opponent gets you past a certain angle you're beaten. It's the same with questions. Now let's see how you go.'

I opened the phone book and pretended to close my eyes but I cheated. I said: 'Funicello's Delicatessen,' and gave the number.

'They have to be private numbers, not businesses,' Sid protested.

'Who said?' I replied. 'You made the first lot of rules. Now I'm making one. I pick, you call.'

Sid gazed at me, hoping for a sign that I was kidding but I remained impassive.

'I can't believe you picked this one blind,' he muttered as he dialled.

'Mr Funicello?' Sid began confidently, 'My name is Sidney Willis. Do you own a dog or a cat? No, I haven't found yours. Did it stray? I'm glad to hear it didn't. Now tell me, what food does it eat? *What food?* Yes, I know you own a deli but don't you think there is better food for your dog than leftovers from the shop? You're probably giving it too much fat and spice. I should know, I'm a vet. Yes, I understand the leftovers are free. Can I ask you a personal question, Mr Funicello? Do you have a problem with your dog's droppings. *Droppings.* You know, what comes out of the end of the animal's body: the opening that is furthest from the head. Yes, poopoo. You don't care? Well, are you interested in making more money or having more leisure time? *Leisure.* By becoming a distributor for *cafe* pet-food. Yes, I know you have a delicatessen and not a café. Look, for chrissake forget it.' Sid hung up.

'I take it you didn't get an appointment,' I said.

'We've just got to hone the technique,' Sid said wiping his glistening bald head with his handkerchief. 'Everything has to be a question until we uncover the pain, and then we give them the answer: *cafe*! Do you remember the way Nat Cohen did it? Nobody could break down his wall of questions. If they asked him why, he'd ask them "why why?"'

Sid gave me another name and number. This time an older sounding man answered. I got on top of him right from the start. Question followed question. I released questions like the start of a pigeon race. He lived in a flat with his wife, and they kept a Jack Russell in contravention of the lease. They were forever monitoring its bowel movements – as he liked to put it – and picking up the output before anybody could complain. There were others in the block who also had secret pets, including several cats operating in a very limited garden area. There was an acknowledged problem of the cats re-digging recent holes. Yes, Mr Peters would come to the meeting at the yacht club next Tuesday. Yes he'd buy *cafe*. And he'd like to find out how to become a Courtier. His superannuation was not as good as he'd thought, and he could do with some extra money.

I hung up and gave Sid a high five for my first successful cold-call.

'I'll tell you what we're going to do,' I said, riding the wave. 'We're going to pledge a solemn oath that we will each make five cold-calls a day. We'll number them in our record books. That's thirty-five cold-calls a week each, which equals seventy cold-calls by Earl Sharock-Willis. It would bring spectacular results. What do you say?'

'Five every day is more than you think,' Sid said cautiously. 'There'll be some days when you can't do any. Then the next day you'll have ten to do.'

'Yes, but on a good day you might do an extra five in advance and buy yourself a holiday,' I said. 'Swings and roundabouts.'

Mr Peters had inspired me far beyond my capability but, at that moment, I was alight and I ignited Sid.

'Okay, we'll give it a go,' he said. 'Let's try it for a month, and then we'll review it. A solemn oath?'

We shook hands.

***

My elation at cold-calling was short-lived. The next day, Sunday, I suffered cold callers' block. I slept in – on purpose I suspect – and then I had to hurry to get up and take Clarice and the girls for brunch at our friends the Parkers. That lasted into mid-afternoon, by which time I had a headache from drinking white wine in the sun. I arrived home in a non-cold-calling mood but I forced myself to go to my study and open the phone book. Then I remembered some unpaid household bills, and attended to those. After that, I gazed through the window and discovered that the lawn needed mowing. A dose of late afternoon air seemed exactly what I needed to freshen me up to make my calls. I returned the mower to the shed just before dark, showered, watched the football summary on television and then it was time for an early dinner because the girls had homework to finish.

'Do you want to watch a movie tonight?' Clarice asked. 'There's a Woody Allen that I don't think we've seen.'

'I've got a couple of jobs to do at my desk,' I said. 'They'll only take a few minutes. Then I'll join you.'

I went to my study and sat down. The phone book lay open where I'd left it. I stared at it like an opponent in a boxing ring. Maybe I'd specialise in Smiths, I thought, as I flipped it open at S. But what if Sid had thought of the same thing? We hadn't talked about allocating names to avoid duplications. I abandoned Smith in the belief that foreign names were better to call anyway. You could stuff up and recover while the prospect grappled with the language. What about Chinese, or Koreans? They were polite and they worked hard and they needed money. I should concentrate on them. But I remembered my wipe-out with Mrs Ching.

I closed my eyes and slid my index finger down the page. When I opened them I was pointing at Dr Lo. What if he thought I was a patient? Would an Asian doctor have a dog or a cat? Did Asians regard domestic pets differently to Australians? I remembered that in some parts of China they ate dogs. I did a couple of breathing exercises and dialled.

There was a recorded announcement giving Dr Lo's surgery hours and an emergency number. In my call book I wrote opposite Dr Lo: 'Interested, call back.'

My next random selection was the Ling household. Without Sid next to me I trembled with fear, but I vowed to only ask questions.

'Mr Ling?' I enquired of the cultured English voice that answered.

'Yes, this is Raymond Ling.'

'Have you ever heard of pet-food called *cafe*?'

'Who is this speaking?'

'Is that important?'

'Yes, if I am to have a conversation.'

'Would it satisfy you to know that my name is Edward Sharock?'

'Is it?'

'Do you accept that it is?'

'How do I know?'

'I'd hardly make up a name like that, would I?'

'How do I know you wouldn't?'

'Do you own a dog or a cat?'

'Why do you want to know?'

'Is your ownership of such an animal a secret?'

'This conversation is going nowhere, Mr Sharock. Please come to the point.'

I drew a deep breath. 'Do you want to better nourish your cat and dog, remove the smell from their excrement, aerate your garden, assist the environment, make more money and have more leisure time?'

'I do not want anything from your list, thank you,' he said, and hung up

As I recorded Mr Ling as the second solo call in my prospecting book I decided I would be in better shape tomorrow to do nine calls rather than disturbing myself and other people on Sunday evening. I joined Clarice and Woody Allen in the lounge room.

***

Cold-call failure gripped me like an infection. The next day at work brought a bad attack of pessimism. Felix dropped into my office, the temporary one that was becoming permanent, with its sterile outlook across the accounts cubicles. He apologised for the delay in selecting the new *cafe* creative team. While I would head it up, he said, one of the young writers who had come off a breakfast food account would progressively take over the writing role.

'You've got to think management now,' Felix said. 'Did you know that money-market traders are burned out by the time they're twenty-five?'

'Meaning what?'

'That creative advertising writers burn out too.'

'What are you trying to tell me, Felix?'

'Look Ed, I'm not suggesting you're burned out, far from it. Nobody but you could have come up with the *cafe* concept. It was one of the most brilliant pieces of creative work I've seen. But you have to be ready for the day when, suddenly, the flame just flickers out. It's better to have scooted off into management before that happens.

'I'm calling a meeting of the *cafe* team first thing in the morning to formalise it. Then you can run it.' He handed me a sheet with five names and titles opposite them. I was at the top as account director. 'You'd better get all the *cafe* material together and lay out a program. Work them hard Ed, and don't bust your own gut. That's good management.'

After he'd shut the door I pushed my chair back and stared out across bodies hunched over desks or marching, papers in hand, around the accounts room. I envied their permanence. Accounting was a mechanical process. You did. Creative writing was nebulous. You felt. Writers were in the dark, feeling about for other minds. If you felt none, you were executed. That was what I faced. The title of 'account director' at the top of the page in front of me was the last stop before execution. Felix wouldn't need to tell the members of the team that the weakest position was at the top.

I owed the cold-call bank nine calls. I was in danger there too. But at least if I was a failure I could measure it. I had a choice of whether to live or die. If I failed to make the calls it was suicide, not execution. Suddenly I saw the cold-call list as my strongest defence against career execution. With unnecessary force I pulled a telephone book from the bottom draw of my black vinyl-covered desk, threw it in the air and let it fall open. I closed my eyes and pointed. Without allowing myself time to procrastinate I dialled.

'Is this Mrs Macgregor?'

'Yes, who is calling please.'

'Do you own a dog or a cat?'

'We have a dog. Who is this calling?'

'What do you give it to eat?'

Perspiration was quickly forming on my face. I replaced the receiver with Mrs Macgregor still asking who I was. I called Sid.

'How is your cold-calling going?' I asked.

'Hard,' he replied. 'I'm two behind. But I'll make them up after work. I've got a couple of appointments though. How are you going?'

'Finding time to call is the problem,' I lied, 'but I'll catch up. Listen, can we have a lay day once a week if we need it? I mean, I don't need it right now, but I'd like to have it up my sleeve.'

'Ed, you're the one who thought up this cold-call schedule. You got me going. I'm committed. You're not wavering are you?'

'Of course not, Sid. I was thinking about you. I know how busy things can get in the surgery.'

'Good, and speaking of that, I'm busy right now with a wormy dog. I'll call you later.'

I selected another name from the phone book still open in front of me. I dialled a number and when a woman answered I hung up. Stupidly, I began to cry. I couldn't help it. How could I have led myself into this trap? I was being catapulted from hell into oblivion. I couldn't tell Sid and I couldn't tell Clarice. I turned over the pages of the phone book, my tears leaving forensic evidence of my complaint, as I searched the Gs for Greenstrum.

***

Chapter Eighteen

'I didn't know whether you'd still be in practice,' I said as I sank into the soft low chair opposite Dr Greenstrum's elaborate timber desk. I looked up at him from the same position in which I'd poured out my secrets about fat girls.

'Why did you think I might not still be in practice?' he asked.

'Well, it must be nearly ten years. I thought maybe you would not be working at this any more.'

'A lot of patients say that when they come back for revision,' he said. 'Perhaps it's a subconscious plea to be let off the hook.'

As he pulled out his notebook and turned on his tape recorder I thought how kind the intervening years had been to him. He had less hair, and what was left had turned grey, but the skin on his long face had not yet been badly affected by gravity. And his luxuriant eyebrows still worked like trained ferrets as they scuttled back and forth between his glasses and the top of his head.

'I'm not here about fat girls,' I began. 'Or girls at all, in fact. I'm having a career crisis, I suppose you'd call it.'

'What matters is what you call it,' he murmured as he started to write.

'It sucks,' I added.

'What do you mean by "it"?' he said, looking up suddenly.

'I mean where the hell my life is supposed to be going. I think I'm on the way out at work but they won't tell me, and I don't want to ask because that might set them thinking something they wouldn't have thought if I hadn't asked.'

The ferrets rushed down into a frown, but he didn't say anything. He let silence squeeze me. I quickly succumbed. 'Then I put my faith – I think I did anyway – in a network marketing business that means I have to cold-call prospects. You see, I can't do it.'

'Lets talk about network marketing,' he said, leaning back and half-closing his eyes.

I began with our Prodmasters' experience, and how Clarice felt about it, and how *cafe* came into my life, first through Lead Balloon and then as a business opportunity in its own right.

'You mean to say,' Greenstrum said, sitting up and opening his eyes, 'that if my dogs eat this *cafe* stuff their shit won't stink?'

'Yes, the product is outstanding,' I said.

'Can I get some?' he asked, leaning towards me across the desk.

'Of course,' I replied. 'You could even build a business in it if you wanted to. I want to, but I can't cold-call.'

'And the nutritional value is higher than any other dog food?'

'Much higher. But that doesn't do me any good because I've lost my confidence in talking about it.'

'Tell me again about the biodegradable can.'

I quickly ran through the benefit of burying the cans in the garden.

'My God,' he said, laying down his pen, 'you're on a bloody winner. Here, get me a mixed dozen to try out. We've got two dogs, both big fellas.' He opened a drawer and pulled out a cheque book.

When I'd given him the price and he'd handed me his cheque, he settled back and said, 'Now, you were telling me ...'

'I can't cold-call,' I said irritably.

'Ah yes. What do you think stops you?'

'Fear of rejection.'

'So how do you see me being able to help?'

'By getting me over the fear of rejection.' I felt trapped in a loop.

'Okay, you have three options.' He spoke as though this was a solution he often recited. 'One, you can give up the business. Two, you can try some sales courses that might help through role-playing. Or three, we could try a few sessions of hypnotherapy. I've had some success lately with people who have to speak in public. They suffer a form of rejection fear too.'

'I'll take option three,' I said, 'but it'll have to be quick because I'm already seventeen calls behind.'

'Behind what?'

'The schedule that Sid and I set for ourselves.'

'Ah, already there is an anxiety back-up we need to address,' he said, writing in his notebook. 'Okay, I'll fit you in Friday. Come at six. And be sure to bring me my cans of *cafe*. I can't wait to try it out.'

'And don't let me forget to tell you about the third stool rule,' I said as I strained to rise from the enfolding depths of the chair.

***

I didn't know what to expect from hypnotherapy. When I emerged from each of Dr Greenstrum's treatments I remembered only fragments of what had gone on. But afterwards, ideas about cold-calling kept popping, bubble-like, through the surface of my mind. In the midst of doing something unrelated to network marketing I'd suddenly think: the worst that can happen is that they'll say no, and nobody's ever died from that or, I can't be injured over the telephone or, I can't lose what I didn't have.

Not unexpectedly, Greenstrum liked Nat Cohen's technique of using a stream of questions to uncover the pain, observing that it had been stolen from psychiatry and modified to become a selling tool. He told me he'd concentrated on building Nat's questioning technique into the 'response implants' he'd fed me under hypnosis.

Even though my cold-call deficit built alarmingly, Greenstrum forbade me from prospecting on the telephone until he thought I was ready. Then, like a flying instructor announcing to his student it was time to go solo, Greenstrum pushed his telephone across his desk one Friday afternoon and read out a number.

'Smith,' he announced. 'Call 'em up.' His stern voice reminded me of Nat's at our first team calling.

I dialled the number.

'Yep?'

'This is Ed. Am I talking to Mr Smith?'

'Yep, Ed.'

'You've got a dog, right?'

'Yep, two. What's up?'

'Mr Smith, can I ask you a question?'

'What?'

'If I could supply you with a dog food that would save you money and would feed your dogs better, you'd be interested, right?'

'Dunno. Might be.'

'And if this dog food – let's call it *cafe* – was not only great for your dogs, but meant that their droppings were odourless and turned into harmless powder, you'd want to at least try it, right?'

'I s'pose.'

'And if I was to say that not only was this the best food ever produced for dogs but that you could develop a home-based business in marketing it, would that be worth coming to a meeting in Mosman to find out about it?'

'Na, I couldn't be bothered with all that.'

'With all what, Mr Smith?'

'Meetings and all that stuff.'

'You don't like meetings?'

'Look, I don't mind some meetings, but to come to Mosman to listen to stuff about dog food? I don't think so.'

'Mr Smith, may I ask you a question?'

'Yep.'

'If there was a way that you could get the information on *cafe* dog food and the business that didn't involve coming all the way to Mosman, would that make sense to you?'

'Yep, s'pose it would.'

'If I was willing to come to your home to give you this information, would you invite five of your friends who own dogs to share the benefits with you?'

'You'd come to my place? S'pose I could.'

'How are you fixed for next Wednesday night at eight o'clock, for no more than forty minutes?'

'Yeah, okay, you're on. Here's my address.'

When I'd written it down I hung up and pushed the phone back across the desk.

'My God,' I said to Greenstrum, 'was that me talking? Did I really do that?'

'You certainly did, Ed. Not only did you apply the questioning technique, you salvaged what could have been a lost cause. You switched from the Mosman meeting to an in-home, as you call it, without missing a beat.'

I left Greenstrum's office feeling as though I'd participated in a miracle. The holy ghost of cold-calling had descended upon me. How long my state of grace would last I didn't know, but for one cold-call, at least, I had felt The Power.

Clarice looked at me curiously during dinner that night. Afterwards, when Sibyl had gone to visit her friend next door and Taya was attempting cookies for a stall at the school fete, Clarice followed me to my study.

'Are you okay, dear?' she inquired as I sat down at my desk and reached for the phone book.

'Why, do I look un-okay?'

'No, you just seem different. Has anything happened at work?'

'No,' I replied. 'That's not to say it couldn't at any time.'

'That's good,' she said. 'You seemed preoccupied, that's all, like you were holding back some news.'

'The only news I'd hold back would be about network marketing *cafe*,' I said truthfully.

'Well, I'm glad you've remembered that I don't want to hear anything on that subject. I'm looking forward to the day when you tell me that you and Sid have had enough. You put such effort into it and it doesn't pay off. As I've said before, Ed, those things never do. And you and Sid never stop to think what effect it has on the people you approach. For the few that come to a meeting there's all the others who feel leaned-on or betrayed.'

The smell of burning butter interrupted any further wisdom Clarice had to dispense on the subject of network marketing. She hurried away, calling to Taya to turn off the gas. I opened the phone book. I had to know whether I still owned The Power or whether it had been one of those epiphanies that only happen in psychiatrists' rooms.

As I dialled I felt none of the usual fears. It was as though there was a glass wall between me and the person I was about to call. I was exercising a technique, not exposing myself to personal rejection.

The call followed the same pattern as the one to Mr Smith. This person, a Mr E. Patrick, had no pets but gave me the names and telephone numbers of three other people who did, and even said I could use his name.

I spent two hours making cold-calls that night, and nearly paid back the debt I owed to the cold-call bank. I got rejections, of course, but they didn't penetrate the wall. They were unfortunate people who hadn't seen the big picture, that was all. I didn't even dislike them for it. I simply placed them in a different category to those who said they would come to a Mosman meeting or would meet me for a cup of coffee and a half-hour chat about their dog or cat.

There was a price for owning The Power. It also owned me. The cold-call quickly became an obsession. Where previously I had seen the telephone as sucking me into a land of fear, now I rode into it like a conquering king. I cold-called every time I had an idle moment at work. I cold-called after dinner at home. I cold-called on my hands-free mobile as I drove my car. I cold-called so much that my peerless technique, coupled with the sheer weight of numbers, brought me abundant success.

Another truth emerged. If my years in advertising had taught me anything, it was this: when the marketing pendulum swings from under-demand to over-demand, the supplier becomes choosey. I became choosey. I refused to travel too far to meet people. As our network grew I passed on far-flung cold-call leads to our down-lines rather then sign them up myself. I patronised a coffee shop in Mosman and told prospects they would have to meet me there at times of my choosing if they wanted to know about *cafe*. Either that, or come to our Mosman meetings. People responded surprisingly well to this take-it-or-leave-it attitude. They saw it as a sign of strength, and wanted to have a part of what I appeared to have.

Sid asked me what medication I was taking. Although he had done his cold-calls with displeasure but steady determination, and had met with moderate success, I had streaked away from him. When our next commission cheque was over a thousand dollars he resisted taking half of it, saying that I'd been responsible for nearly all of it.

My blossoming questioning technique spilled over into my work at Lead Balloon. The *cafe* account meetings became opportunities for me to try out different types of questioning. I could manoeuvre my creative team into silence by asking increasingly more awkward questions. I did it for fun sometimes when there was no argument to win or product to sell. The Power positioned itself in my mind as a vaccination against pessimism.

I suppose I was in unconscious training for the day when Felix or Wesley would launch their next attack on my fragile future in advertising. Now I was prepared. They'd have a cold-call black belt grand master to deal with.

When I was a kid at school I used to imagine what it would be like to be involved in a serious fist fight. I wanted to prepare for it so that I could win, but I didn't have the courage to pick a fight just to try myself out. And rather than get into a ring with somebody at the gym, I bought a book on boxing and put it into practice in front of the wardrobe mirror. My reflection became my opponent, a fellow of exactly my height whose every move I could anticipate. He stood correctly on the balls of his feet, side-on, left guard raised, right hand cocked and ready to deliver the knockout blow. But apart from a few schoolyard scuffles a real conflict never arose, and I felt oddly cheated. What I didn't know was that fate had been saving me for an enemy engagement later in life.

***

Chapter Nineteen

When Wesley invited me to his office for a drink late one Friday afternoon I could hear the distant blood-calls of the boxing crowd as I ascended in the elevator. And when I discovered that Wesley and Felix were my only company, I knew I was about to become involved in serious, real-world combat; they armed with the crushing weapon of dismissal and I with my little slingshot of questions.

Uncharacteristically, they dithered. They could have gone for the kill immediately with one sentence but instead they sparred, with talk about holidays and the state of the advertising industry and football and even sailing – which neither of them had ever liked. It seemed as though they were amused by toying with me, but their attitude only built my anger as I chatted along, asking no questions.

Eventually it became apparent that they had chosen the popular 'our company is re-structuring' method of dismissal.

'You know, Ed,' Wesley finally launched the first salvo, 'advertising agencies are no different to the clients they serve. They're all driven by change. Not only change in their products but change in the way they run their businesses.'

'To put that graphically,' Felix cut in, 'if you run squares joined by lines for a few years it's not a bad idea to change to ovals, held in place by a big border around the outside.'

'Anyway Ed,' Wesley went on in his softly rasping voice that always reminded me of a carrot being grated, 'we're going for a different company shape. We're going to departmentalise by skill rather than by client. There'll still be account executives, but beyond that we'll have pools of writers, pools of artists, and pools of media planners, all working on all the accounts. It will be a company of specialist pools; young pools. There won't be room for combination people in their, how should I put it, ripening years.'

It was time for me to load my slingshot.

'Can you give me an example of a combination person of ripening years?' I asked.

'Well Ed, you for one,' Felix said with the oily smile of a man who is about to win.

'Apart from ripening years, when did you decide I was a combination person?'

'A long time ago,' Wesley said. 'I mean, you secured the *cafe* account, conceived the name, took the brief in America and wrote the copy. Now you head up the creative team. That's combination.'

'Aren't you and Felix combination people of ripening years?'

'No, we're management.'

'What do you see as the role of management?'

Felix and Wesley looked at each other, neither wanting to answer. Eventually Wesley coughed and said: 'Well, to take overall care of the business and the people in it. But Ed, we're not here to discuss the theory of management.'

'So you take care of people, right?' I said.

'Yes, that's right.'

'And does that cover the time when they leave the company?'

'Yes Ed.'

'Would you say you're caring people?'

'Of course we are, Ed.'

'Is caring a quality you admire in yourselves?'

'Yes Ed, it is.'

'Are you caring for me?'

'Yes Ed, of course we are.'

'Can you explain to me how you are doing that?''

Wesley crossed the room to his desk and picked up a sheet of paper.

'Ed, it's time for you to move on. We want to make it a positive experience for you. Now, for a start, your superannuation goes with you. Then we owe you about two months' holiday pay and the long-service leave you haven't taken adds up to four months. On top of that, we'll give you three months' severance pay.'

I let silence congeal the room. 'And you think that's caring?' I said at last.

'It certainly is,' Felix replied.

'Would you like to be cared for like that?' I asked him.

'It's not me we're considering here.'

'Who are you considering, Felix?'

'You Ed, you.'

'For chrissake,' Wesley muttered. 'All these fucking games.'

'Is that the kind of offer you make to a person you care about?'

'Listen, if you're not happy with the offer,' Wesley said, 'tell us what the fuck you want.'

'How would you feel about everything you've just offered me plus a year's full pay?'

Wesley Crowe's dusty rose facial colour upgraded to puce. 'I'd feel like you were robbing us,' he snarled, trying to keep his voice under control. 'And let me tell you one thing, we won't be robbed. You're not holding a gun to our heads when, in fact, you haven't even got a fucking gun.'

'Do I need a gun to get a fair deal from management after twenty-three years' service?'

'No, but fair's fair,' Felix said. 'Tell you what. We'll stretch the three months' severance pay to six months. There you go.'

'Where do I go?'

'For shit's sake,' Wesley spat.

'Don't you think that would make a good slogan for the next *cafe* campaign?' I asked with a smile.

'What are you talking about?'

'How would this sound: "*cafe* … for shit's sake"?'

'We're getting nowhere here,' Wesley said, hooking a finger under his collar to relieve some invisible pressure.

'Isn't it important that the staff members of Lead Balloon think that they are in the hands of caring managers?' I continued.

'Yes, of course, but what's that got to do with you, Ed?'

'How would you feel if my skill as a copywriter, poor though you think it is, was to be turned to producing an internal newsletter called, let's say, The Lead Bugle? And how would it be if the first issue comprised an insightful piece about the caring policy of management when an employee leaves after twenty-three years of service?'

'You wouldn't dare do that,' Felix said. 'We'd sue you for …

for inciting disharmony in a lawfully-constituted company. Or something along those lines.'

'Would you like me to e-mail you the first issue tonight?'

'As Wesley said, we'd sue you.'

'And don't you think the same information would then come out in court?'

After some eye play between Wesley and Felix, Wesley said, in a low voice, 'All right, a year's fucking full pay.'

'Dated three months from now because that's how much notice you want to give me?'

'Okay, okay, 'Wesley said. 'I'll get it formalised Monday morning. But I want you to piss off straight away.'

As I turned to go, I said, 'Are you going to give me another farewell dinner?'

'You can get fucked,' Wesley rasped, looking out the window.

I sang like a released prisoner on my way home. Between songs I delivered a short passionate speech as I handed the Nobel Prize for Applied Psychiatry to Dr Greenstrum in recognition of his work in cold-call therapy. I gave another to Nat Cohen for his contribution to the 'pain exposure through questioning' technique. By the time I reached my garage I was going through the guest list for a party I was going to throw, but I sobered at the thought of dealing with Clarice. Although I'd come home a winner, she mightn't see it like that.

Over dinner The Channel came to my rescue. I said that as a result of a meeting I'd had with Wesley and Felix, I'd be again working from home for a while. The Channel had saved me from lying, but I delivered the news with such enthusiasm that Clarice became suspicious.

'You'll be working at home on the *cafe* account?' she asked.

151

'Of course I'll be working on *cafe*,' I replied, wanting the topic closed.

'And how about Andy?'

'No, he won't be involved here. Just me.'

'I'm relieved about that, anyway. When do you plan to start all this?'

'Monday,' I said as I rose and began to collect plates.

Something's going on, Ed,' Clarice said. 'I can't remember when you last gathered up the dishes, humming to yourself.'

'I just wanted to get moving,' I said. 'I have to get to my study to do some work.'

That was true too. I needed to call Sid. I hurried to my study, closed the door and dialled his number.

When I told him I'd been permanently dumped from Lead Balloon and now I could work full-time on *cafe*, he said: 'You'd better take the lion's share of the *cafe* commissions.'

'Absolutely not,' I replied. 'This is my choice. You're still the star performer at the business opportunity meetings. We're partners, don't forget. I'll now have time to take over all the administration, and chase up appointments, and contact our down-lines – all of that stuff. I don't mind taking out business expenses before we divide the loot.'

'Listen Ed, this is a huge move for you,' Sid said, as the realisation of the change filtered through to him. 'Suddenly you're really out of Lead Balloon on your ear. Aren't you in shock? Won't you miss advertising?'

'Not a bit,' I said confidently. 'This is the second time my job at Lead Balloon has died, remember. I did all the mourning the first time. And the other thing is that I love the *cafe* business. Now that I'm on top of cold-calling, the fear of failure has gone. All I need now is to see that Clarice doesn't find out about me being fired. I'll tell her the full story when the *cafe* commission cheques become consistently big enough. Maybe by then you'll be full-time in *cafe* too.'

'I doubt it,' Sid said. 'There's only Stacey to fire me from our veterinary practice and she'd see to it that I left with nothing.'

***

Chapter Twenty

My study at home became the cockpit from which I drove our *cafe* juggernaut. Behind the closed door Clarice didn't know I was prospecting and contacting my down-lines rather than writing copy for Lead Balloon. I explained my frequent meetings in the Mosman coffee shop as company conferences – which, in fact, they were. By defining my words literally, I satisfied myself I was telling Clarice the truth.

In spite of the numbers of drop-outs that our team suffered, something that Nat had warned us about, Sid and I were still gaining more new distributors at the prospecting end than we were losing at the quitting end. Not only had I mastered the cold-call, but I even grew to enjoy addressing our weekly meetings at the yacht club, although I'd never be as good as Sid. He had improved his technique to the point where I compared his presentations favourably with Nat's.

With all this extra activity our monthly *cafe* commission cheques grew to around three thousand dollars. I banked my share in the secret account where I had deposited my Lead Balloon settlement and from which I was now paying a monthly cheque into my regular account. The amount was equivalent to my old monthly salary, so that Clarice, who had access to it, was not aware of any change.

Although my income was better than it had been at any time in my life, it was likely to be temporary. I had less than eighteen months before my Lead Balloon severance money ran out. After that, either *cafe* would have to provide enough to replace it or I would be out looking for another job. And who would employ a clapped-out copywriter of fifty-three?

I often thanked Greenstrum under my breath as I made my cold-calls. I would have been in a terrifying predicament if his treatment hadn't worked. He'd delivered me from the abyss of idleness into which I'd seen plenty of my unemployed contemporaries fall. Their crises weren't usually over money. Being unemployable quickly crushed the confidence backbone of rich and poor alike.

About two months after I'd been fired from Lead Balloon I received a telephone call from Nat Cohen.

'Ed, buddy! You and Sid are doing just great in Australia. I've been in touch with head office in Utah and they tell me you're a virtual Baron. You can trash your old green jackets and order brown ones. But listen, that's not the reason I'm calling. I've had the word that we're opening in London real soon. Now don't get me wrong, Australia is a great market, but population and distance make it such a schlep, right?'

'Right Nat, you know what it's like. So what are you telling me?'

'Now listen Ed, I don't want to take you away from your turf, but next month England will be firing up. You know how many people and how many dogs and cats, and how little room there is in London? And you know how they'll die for their dogs. They love big dogs, and big dogs make big turds. This is going to be *cafe* city Ed. Do you hear what I'm saying?'

'I hear what you're saying Nat. You think we should go to London. But for how long?'

'Look, you gotta work that out. If you want to tap into the serious money you're talking six months. Better a year. It takes follow up. People drop out, you know that. You gotta keep feeding the lines until they're concrete. You know what I mean?'

'We keep feeding the lines here and we're making concrete but the stuff won't set,' I said. 'How do you stop down-line courtiers from dropping out?'

'It's a numbers game, Ed. You gotta keep feeding 'em through, feeding 'em through. Give me a dumb prospector ready to wear out his telephone any time. Hey Ed, I'm not telling you anything you don't know. See, in London you got the whole population of Australia in a few neighbourhoods. The multiplier works much quicker. You're backing up your lines all the time.'

'I can't make a decision right now, Nat,' I said. 'Obviously I couldn't transplant the family, and I don't know whether I could leave them for that long. But at least I've got no work commitments apart from networking *cafe*. You knew I was fired from Lead Balloon?'

'That's not the story they got in Utah,' he said. 'They were told you walked out because you didn't get a big enough raise. You say you got fired? That's a plus. Nothing like a bit of rage to give you a lift. Your *cafe* results are showing it. So now you got time to spare.'

'I might, but I don't know about Sid. And Clarice still thinks I'm working for Lead Balloon – from home. I'd have to come clean on that.'

'Okay Ed, I see you've got some challenges and some re-scheduling ahead of you. But I'm going to move to London, and here's the real good news: I'm renting a big house in Barnes and letting rooms to my down-line. There'll be a maid on site to do the cleaning and a bit of cooking. The deal is eighty pounds a week per room. Let me know fast if you and Sid are interested. I haven't offered the deal around yet.'

***

Chapter Twenty-One

I'd so looked forward to the day when I could tell Clarice that I'd become a champion network marketer. I'd planned to do it when the Sharock-Willis commission cheque had exceeded thirty thousand dollars a month for three consecutive months. My half-share from that would have been more than my old salary at Lead Balloon. Whatever discomfort Clarice may have felt about network marketing would have been swept aside by my monetary triumph. Forgiveness and admiration would surely follow.

The problem was that our commission cheques were still struggling to pay me half my old salary at Lead Balloon. We needed more time prospecting and network building in Australia but, if we did, the opportunity of opening England would be lost. I called Sid for a strategy conference.

'I've always wanted to spend time in London,' he said after I'd told him about Nat's proposition. 'I wouldn't go on my own, but if you go, I'll come with you.'

'What about Stacey and your vet practice?' I asked.

'That's one of the reasons I'd like to go,' he replied. 'She can prove what a genius manager she is. She's always telling me how bad I am. Let her have a go for a few months.'

'It might be for a year.'

'All the better.'

'The hardest thing for both of us will be breaking the news to our families,' I said.

'Then we'll need to make a time pact,' Sid said. 'The time now is four o'clock on Wednesday afternoon. We've both got twenty-four hours to spill the beans. Agree?'

Of course I agreed. God had set Sid and me upon the earth to challenge one other whenever possible.

Trying to find an opening at dinner that night reminded me of the time, almost a year before, when I'd tried to tell Clarice and the girls that I'd been fired from Lead Balloon the first time around. Only on this occasion, Clarice was not part of a beneficial conspiracy. It suddenly occurred to me that I should call upon my network marketing skills. I waited until dessert before shifting gear into the questioning technique.

'Is anybody interested in my career?' I began in a fainter voice than I had intended.

After a silence, Sibyl said, 'You mean about pet-food?'

'How would you feel about me having to go to London for a while – on business?'

Clarice abandoned packing the dishwasher and came back to sit at the table. 'When, who with?' she asked.

'And would it surprise you to know that I left Lead Balloon five months ago and that I've been doing full-time network marketing for *cafe* and that I'm earning almost enough for us to live on already?'

'No, there is no surprise in you telling me that you got the sack from Lead Balloon,' Clarice said icily. 'I knew the day after it happened. Wesley called to see if I was all right. And there is no surprise in you telling me you've got sucked right into that pyramid selling scheme either. What do you think happened when your gullible cronies called while you were up the street in the coffee shop? I've been wondering how long it would take you to come clean, Ed. As for going to London, I think it would be good for you to get it out of your system – if that's what it takes. I don't want to have to live in the middle of endless meetings and grovelling to people and scheming to sell things out of our garage. This is our home, not a flea market.'

'Jessica's got fleas again,' Taya remarked distantly.

I abandoned my network marketing training.

'Okay, so I got fired. What did you expect me to do, go down to the Centrelink office and line up for work on a dredge?' Florence Formby had found her way into the argument.

'No, but you could have started looking for a job in advertising,' Clarice said.

'What, at fifty-three, after having been chucked out of a leading agency because I was burnt out? And then having to admit that my last three accounts were pet-food, a country bus line and a funeral parlour? Get real, Clarice. I had to make a change of career.'

'You didn't tell us why you're going to London, Dad,' Sibyl said.

'Because *cafe* is opening there and I can get in on the ground floor,' I replied. 'Believe it or not, Sid Willis and I are good at network marketing. Very good, in fact, in spite of what your mother might think. It takes time to get people to join and build networks but in the end it all runs itself.'

'How long will you be away?' Taya asked with a sniff.

'Oh, only a few weeks. Just to get the thing started. Then I'll be home and you can all help me count the money.'

'Don't we have enough money?' Taya continued.

'We do right now,' I replied. 'When I left Lead Balloon I made them give me enough to last eighteen months. We have to be ready when that runs out. That's why I'm trying to get the *cafe* network marketing business going.'

'Why doesn't Mum get a job?' Sybil asked.

There was an awkward silence which I didn't want to break because I was enjoying seeing the blowtorch switched on to Clarice.

'She could keep fit by running around the streets putting leaflets in letterboxes,' Sybil pressed on with calculated innocence.

'If I have to go to work, I will,' Clarice said, returning to the urgent demands of the dishwasher, 'but right now I'm full-time looking after the rest of you. Sure, I can look for a job – I don't know what – but you'd all have to get used to doing your own washing and ironing and cooking and cleaning.'

'Are you going to take all our money to London with you?' Taya asked.

The Channel leaped in. 'No,' I said. 'I'll leave it all here for you to use while I'm away. The only money I'll have is what I earn from *cafe*. If it's not enough I'll starve to death in the London snow. Then Mum will have to go out to work.'

Taya began to cry while Clarice laughed. 'Don't worry darling,' she said, 'your father isn't the starving-in-the-snow type.'

I left the table and called Sid from my study.

'I've dropped the load on them,' I said, 'with half a day to spare. But I think I've done something stupid.'

'You agreed to live overseas only on the money we earn from

cafe,' Sid said.

'How the hell did you know that?'

'Because I've just done the same stupid thing.'

***

Chapter Twenty-Two

London welcomed us with an icy morning drizzle. Cowering and shivering in our thin Sydney clothes, we took a black cab from Heathrow to Barnes, our four suitcases stacked in front of us. They hid the fare meter, protecting us from knowing what a misshapen dwarf our Australian dollar had become in comparison to the English pound.

'I feel like I'm on some sort of macabre honeymoon,' Sid remarked as he stared out at the moving history book of London.

'I'll do my best to make you a good wife,' I replied, 'and I'll have a black slave to help me.'

'How do you know she's black?'

'Nat Cohen told me. Black and doesn't say much. Her name is Winsome.'

'Maybe she wants to talk,' Sid mused, 'but Nat uses up all the available broadcast time.'

Eventually we drove down past a row of sinewy black trees and found the sign 'Padlock Mews' set into a stone fence. Down a soggy gravel driveway we came to a two-storey house that might have been a grand residence once, but now needed paint and extensive restoration of its masonry. A more careful inspection revealed it was actually a three-storey house, the first being a basement with worn stone steps going down to a little door.

'Did you say we had a choice of rooms?' Sid asked, following my gaze. 'I hope the upstairs ones are not all occupied. I don't want to live like a rabbit.'

After the cab driver had taken most of our cash and had departed in a fine haze of water and mud, we heaved our cases up the loose-tooth marble steps and pressed the button beside the door.

Trying to stamp the cold out through our feet, we waited for the reassuring sight of Nat Cohen to welcome us into warmth and comfort. I imagined a farmer's breakfast waiting for us, with eggs from calm British hens. Instead, the door was opened by a lanky black girl in jeans and a pulled-about orange mohair sweater. She stood in the cavernous, draughty hallway and said nothing.

'You must be Winsome,' I broke the silence.

'Who's arskin'?'

'I'm Ed Sharock and this is my friend Sid Willis. We've just arrived from Australia to stay here with Nat Cohen.'

'Yes, he told me you might be along. Well, he ain't' here is he. Gone back to America 'cause 'is mum's sick.'

'We're jolly sorry to hear it,' Sid said, faking an Oxford accent, 'but that won't stop us moving in as arranged, will it?'

''Fraid it will,' Winsome said. 'Mr Cohen put me in charge of renting the rums 'cause he didn't know when he'd be back.'

'And when might that be?' Sid continued his role of superior gentleman.

'I'd say least a week,' she said, lifting her round chin defiantly.

'That's fine,' Sid continued, a little louder. 'We'll stand here for least a week until everybody has gone and then we can move in.'

'You can't hang around,' she said equalling his volume. 'Come back in a week and I'll see what I can do.'

Sid was irritable from not having slept during the flight. 'Bullshit,' he said, picking up his two suitcases and advancing into the hallway. 'We're coming in.'

'Absolom!' she turned and called loudly.

A black man detached himself from the gloom and appeared next to Winsome. He was as tall as Sid and twice as wide. He politely picked up Sid's cases and placed them back outside, then returned to stand, arms folded, behind Winsome.

'Can I call Nat from here?' I asked. 'I think I can sort this out.'

'We don't have no international dialling,' Winsome said, 'and, as well, I'm freezin'. You'll have to split. Like I said, you can have your rums in a week. I got to give other people notice.'

We held our ground in the hallway.

'Absolom,' she called softly.

Like a well-rehearsed dance duo Sid and I moved back in unison, after which the door was shut quietly in our faces.

'Let's go back to the airport,' Sid said. 'We'd be home in time for tomorrow's dinner.'

'Are you serious?' I asked.

'No, just a bit disheartened, that's all,' he replied. 'What now?'

'We'd better find a pub,' I said. 'I can only remember the Ritz and Claridge's. But if we stay at either of those we'll be bankrupt after one night.'

We picked up our cases and trudged back along Padlock Mews

and on to the high street. It wasn't long before another black cab came along and we resorted to the cunning of international travellers in trouble: we asked the cabbie for advice. He took us to the Grosvenor Court Hotel, whose ornate stone foyer and generous lobby belied the size and style of its bedrooms. There seemed to be a conspiracy between the cab driver and the management to manoeuvre weary travellers into registering before inspecting the rooms.

***

Chapter Twenty-Three

After sleeping until late afternoon, we showered, dressed and seated ourselves in the lobby lounge on worn velvet armchairs separated by a low oval table. The place was quite busy, its breathy warmth seeming to suck people in from the cold storage square outside.

'The trouble is,' Sid said after he taken his first sip of warm brown ale, 'we didn't come here with enough contacts to make a start without Nat's help.'

'Yes, but look at all these prospects wandering around the lobby,' I said with more cheer than I felt. 'We could just get up and start talking to them.'

'You can get up if you like,' Sid said. 'I'd rather wait for the list of prospects that Nat promised us.'

'You know we haven't been able to raise Nat at his New York number,' I replied. 'Until he gets back here we're on our own. We don't want to be struck down by galloping inertia. We ought to start prospecting now.'

'What, here? In this lousy hotel?'

I remembered something that Greenstrum had told me. He rated cold-calling much harder in your own town. He called it 'reputation consequence'. He said that you would take a far greater risk of making a fool of yourself in a foreign country because you were not known and you had the option of disappearing.

'Wouldn't it be better to open the phone book and start calling the way we do at home?' Sid said defensively. 'I mean, we know the routine.'

'We could, and no doubt we will,' I replied as my mind returned from Greenstrum's room, 'but if we want to make dialling seem easy, we should cut our teeth on something harder.'

'Like?'

'Like getting up out of these museum chairs and buttonholing the Brits on their own ground – in this case their own worn carpet.'

I found it hard to believe I was saying this. If I'd been sitting there on my own I would have drunk my beer in silence, unable to move.

'So who will go first and how do we pick our prospects?' Sid asked.

'Remember the day we first cold-called from the telephone book?' I said. 'We took turns of picking and doing. I'll toss you to decide first picker.'

I pulled out a fat one pound coin and flipped it. Sid won.

'Okay,' he said rubbing his hands and looking around. 'Who will it be?'

'Before you decide,' I quickly interjected, 'remember the old saying: "what goes around comes around". If you give me a bummer I'll do the same to you.'

'You'll do that anyway,' Sid replied dryly. 'Now, let's see.' He stood up and swung his gaze around like a periscope. Choosing a prospect for me should not be taken lightly, I quickly pointed out to Sid. Approaching somebody sitting down would be an invasion of their campsite and they would be put off before I began to speak. The prospect had to be standing – and not in a group or in a rush. I formalised a rule to that effect.

'If we're setting rules,' Sid said, 'here's another one. The pickee is not permitted to look around the room to influence the pickor. The pickee must look at the floor until told by the pickor who the prospect is. Only then may the pickee look up.'

'Okay,' I muttered, bowing my head in readiness for bad news. This had nothing in common with cold-calling on the telephone. Greenstrum's cure had not gone as far as the physical cold-call, or the 'walk and talk', as Nat has put it. I thought about my appearance. I could not be taken as threatening, surely, conservatively dressed in a navy jacket, open-neck business shirt and grey trousers. But my ponytail might put people off. I could make a joke of it. I could tell people that I wore a pony tail because I had a face like a horse's arse. No, that would be definitely off-putting to a prospect. I had to appear friendly but not pushy, business-like but not greedy, well-mannered but not superior. Sid tapped me on the arm.

'Over there near that plastic palm tree.'

'Where? There's nobody there except a Salvation Army collector.'

'Right,' he said briskly, 'a good one to warm up on. God will be watching over the deal.'

'Fair go. Give me somebody normal. I can't just go over to her and strike up a conversation about shit.'

'You can and you will,' Sid said sternly. 'And here's another rule. If the pickee refuses an assignment, he is fined the next three assignments in succession.'

I got to my feet and took a long, slow detour to reach her. She wore the traditional burgundy and black outfit: high buttoned dress and little pill-box hat. I pulled out the pound coin that had led me into this situation and dropped it through the slot in her out-held tin.

'God bless you,' she said smiling.

'Thank you,' I replied, 'I need it, particularly now.'

'Oh?' she said, 'are you troubled?'

'Yes I am,' I said, 'by a great need to know if you own a dog or a cat.'

'Yes, we have a dog,' she said, 'Pete, a poodle.'

The Channel immediately chipped in. I couldn't stop it.

'A peck of pickled pepper Pete the poodle pooped,' my caption suddenly found voice. 'I'm sorry, I didn't mean to say that,' I added quickly, red-faced.

'Whatever are you talking about?' she asked, her smile of charity now weighed down at the corners.

'Just a private joke,' I stumbled along. 'The point is, if there was a dog-food for Pete that was highly nutritious and, as a result of his eating it, his excrement didn't smell, and the can was good for the garden, would you be interested in taking a closer look at it?'

'A closer look at what?' she asked, frowning.

'At *cafe*. It's pet-food.'

'Oh,' she said, and hurried away quickly towards the door.

I watched her go, annoyed at Sid for picking her, and disappointed with my own blundering. What had happened to my impenetrable walls of questions? I shambled back to Sid.

'So when are you going to address the parish colonels?' he asked brightly.

'I fucked up,' I said sourly. 'She thought I was crazy. And it cost me a pound as well.'

'How about we break for dinner?' Sid suggested.

'Good try. You have to do one before we even think of eating. Get your head down while I survey the scene.'

My sweep around the room came to rest on a man who reminded me of Felix Crouch – in shape anyway. He was reading a paper from which he looked up every few moments.

'Over near the elevator,' I said to Sid. 'Tweed jacket and baggy green corduroy pants.'

'Not that roly-poly,' Sid said. 'He wouldn't have a dog. He couldn't keep up with it. Give me somebody bright and likely.'

'Like a Salvation Army collector? Listen, I've been very good to you. Now, get on with it before I claim a forfeit and you have to take the next three – according to your own rule.'

Sid pulled himself out of the deep chair and sauntered over to the fat man. After a few moments they shook hands. I'd made it too easy. Next time he'd get the hardest prospect in the room. I watched as they talked at some length. Then Sid was leading him back to our table.

'This is Henry Throgmorton,' Sid said.

I stood up and we shook hands.

'Henry tells me he has several dogs at his country cottage at High Wycombe.'

'True, true,' Henry said, nodding, 'Let me see. There is Alfred the Rottweiler, big brute he is, and Cynthia the Chihuahua and Henry, a King George spaniel.'

'That's strange to call a dog after yourself,' I observed. 'I mean, if somebody calls "Henry!" who comes?'

'Usually both of us,' he said, straight-faced. 'My wife Emily named the dog Henry because she said it looked like me.'

I took a more careful look at Henry. I could see his wife's logic.

'I might be able to help you with introductions to a couple of clubs we belong to,' Henry said. 'You can't have a rottie without taking it to obedience school, you know. We've made a lot of friends through the school.'

'I asked Henry to join us for a drink,' Sid said. 'We'll keep a lookout for his guest.'

'I don't think he'll show up now,' Henry said, as he sat down heavily. 'It's always a bit of a gamble meeting somebody to talk about network marketing.'

'Network marketing?' I almost shouted.

'That's right,' Henry replied. 'As I told Sidney, I'm in Prodmasters. I understand you're in some kind of pet-food direct selling. I think Prodmasters has pet-food too.'

'Not like our pet-food,' I affirmed.

'Really,' Henry said, settling back in his chair and summoning a waiter. 'Tell me about it.'

Sid and I were like two kids recounting our first day at school. Henry fuelled us with questions. After the rejection at the hands of Winsome and the Salvation Army collector, he was like a comfortable bed. Eye contact with Sid confirmed that we had to persuade Henry to join *cafe*. He had it all: dog owner, dog club member, and proven networker. His obesity and his hiccupping laugh immediately became dear to us.

After a couple more rounds of drinks, and in the middle of telling us about the rottie club's rules, Henry took a flourishing look at his watch.

'I've got to make a phone call,' he said. 'Must tell Emily what time to expect me for dinner.'

'Please dine with us,' Sid offered, just beating me to it.

'Well, if that's not putting you to too much trouble,' Henry said, 'I'd like that very much.' He summoned the effort to launch himself out of the chair and wombat-walked across the room to the telephones.

'My God,' I said to Sid, 'we've run into luck here. 'He'll lead us just where we want to go.'

When Henry returned he remained standing in front of us. 'I'll buy you a round and then we might eat,' he suggested.

'You'll have to pick somewhere,' I said, as Henry paid the waiter. 'We don't know London.'

'Well now, let me see,' Henry said, curling a long lonely strand of hair around an index finger. 'We don't want to go too far, do we. Not a cab ride, I mean, otherwise I'd take you to my club. We'll do that another time. There's a nice little place I sometimes eat at a few doors down. You won't even need a coat to walk there.'

Protected as he was by tweeds and girth, Henry certainly didn't need a coat, but Sid and I were both shivering as we idled along at Henry's laboured gait. We passed a couple of presentable little eating places but with a dismissive parry of his umbrella Henry led us on. Eventually we arrived at Piatella, an Italian restaurant with soft lighting, an exotically-tiled floor and too many waiters. We seated ourselves in an intimate alcove where Henry immediately ordered a large bottle of Italian red encased in a basket.

'Better value if we're going to down a bit of plonk,' he said cheerily. 'This is on me,' he added as he tasted the wine and nodded to the waiter.

'I wonder if you'd like me to order,' he asked almost immediately. 'I know what they do well here.' We both nodded and he waved away the offered menus.

Henry turned to the stooping waiter and spoke rapidly and confidentially, punctuating his instructions with fingers pinching imaginary dumplings and mixing invisible sauces. The exercise made him salivate, and he dabbed his moist mouth and grey moustache with his napkin.

'That should get us started,' he said with a chuckle, as he eased back in his chair. 'Now, you must tell me about life in Australia. I have a queer uncle living there, in Sydney I believe he is.'

Henry knew his questioning skills well. We were into coffee before we succeeded in turning the conversation around to our mission in London. Henry, now flushed and guffawing at almost everything we said, had difficulty in focusing on dogs, cats and shit.

'My dear friends,' he announced, laying his hands palms down on the table, 'please forgive me but I must go, otherwise I shall miss the last train to High Wycombe. I hope we can get together for another talk soon. It has been so interesting. I'll fix the bill on my way out.' He began grappling with gravity to get up.

'Just a minute, Henry,' Sid said with a restraining hand, 'is there any possibility that you might stay the night at our hotel.'

Before Henry could reply I added: 'as our guest, of course.'

'I'd be happy to continue our conversation,' Henry said, 'in fact, I'd probably be more coherent over breakfast, but I couldn't possibly accept. I came out without very much cash. The fellow I was supposed to meet was going to pay me quite a bit of money for Prodmaster stock. So this meal sort of cleans me out.'

'We never intended you would pay for this meal,' I said firmly. 'You were always our guest.'

Henry twirled his hair strand. 'Goodness,' he said, looking into the middle distance, 'you are very kind. I'll have to make another call to Emily and visit the loo.'

He rose to his feet and went off in search of a telephone. In the meantime we called for the bill. I suppose because Sid was the tallest, they handed it to him. His gaze froze at the bottom of the page.

'Two hundred and eight quid,' he croaked.

'I think we have to look at him as an important investment,' was the only positive thing I could think of saying. 'I'll hit on him to become a *cafe* distributor the minute he comes back.'

Sid placed his credit card on top of the hill like a lonely flower on a coffin, and crossed himself. By the time the waiter had returned with the receipt, Henry had rejoined us. As we left Piatella, I loaded up my question magazine and began firing before Henry could set an agenda.

'Do you like the sound of the *cafe* products?' I asked, walking close to Henry and directing my voice to his hairy ear.

'I certainly do,' Henry replied.

'Would you feed them to your own dogs? You know, Alfred and Cynthia and Henry the dog.'

'Oh, our dogs,' he said with a belch. 'You'll have to forgive me. A little too much of the good Italian red. Yes, yes, I would feed them calf.'

'*cafe*,' I corrected, and then pressed on, 'and that being the case, would it make sense to introduce it to your dog-loving friends, and build a substantial income at the same time?'

'Indeed it would.'

'Then you'd like to become a distributor?'

'Subject to a review when I'm sober, yes.'

'We'll need to sign you up as a first step,' Sid said. 'Then we'll work with you to prospect all the dog clubs and all the owners you know.'

'Sounds fine to me,' Henry said. 'I might even be tempted to put Prodmasters aside for a time and see how good your calf is. But I have one request. May I sign up over breakfast? As you can see, I'm a bit three sheets to the wind.'

In the close warmth of the hotel foyer, I made a booking for Mr Henry Throgmorton on our account and was given his key. When I had transferred it to his short-fingered hand, Henry yawned like a cat, and said: 'Let's meet for breakfast, say around eight-thirty? I'll go to my room now and call Emily to fax my master Prodmaster list to me here. If we add that to my dog owners we'll have plenty to work with.'

'Excellent,' I said. 'I'm sure you know that one of the first things a new distributor has to do is make a big prospect list.'

Henry shook hands with us and toiled across to the elevators.

***

Chapter Twenty-Four

Sid and I sat down at our breakfast table just after eight the next morning to arrange the papers for Henry to sign, and to set out his prospecting program. Even if Henry was not an industrious prospector we could do it for him. This would keep us busy until Nat returned. Dog owners knew other dog owners. Referrals were so much better than cold-calls.

When eight-thirty came and there was no sign of Henry, I went to the reception desk to call his room.

'Throgmorton,' the clerk mumbled as he punched the name into the computer. 'Yes, here is the name, or was. Room eight one four. He's checked out.'

'Did he leave a note or anything?'

'No sir, only the account to be settled by Willis-Sharock Marketing.'

'What, no forwarding address, no phone number, no list of dog owners?'

'No sir.'

I returned to our table. 'The old prick's shot through,' I announced.

Sid sighed deeply. 'I had a nasty feeling last night. I thought Henry was too good to be true – and he was.'

I'd felt the same way, but I still preferred to be conned by Henry to being excommunicated by the Salvation Army collector.

'I'll bet he never was a Prodmasters' distributor or even a fucking dog owner,' Sid went on. 'We should have done telephone prospecting. No more of this walk and talk crap.'

'I don't agree,' I replied. 'At least we can see who we're talking to. At home, we know something about the prospect on the phone from the way he talks and where he lives. Here, we'd never know. I think we ought to try some more buttonholing. We've learned not to buy drinks or dinners or bedrooms. They can't hurt us if we don't spend our money on them.'

'I'm losing confidence,' Sid said dejectedly. 'I don't think I can prospect anybody live right now.'

'You don't have to, not straight away anyway. It's your turn to pick the prospect for me. Tell you what. If you can make me chicken out of presenting, I'll agree to withdraw to the telephone, okay?'

'And if you do go through with it?'

'Well, then you have to do the next live prospect that I pick for you. Same as before. Look, we were just unlucky. We could have picked two winners. We've got to keep trying.'

'Let me have some eggs and bacon while I think about it,' Sid said, but I knew he couldn't turn down the challenge. I also knew that he'd try to force me back telephoning by finding an impossible live prospect for me.

***

Chapter Twenty-Five

Neither of us wanted to finish breakfast. We strung it out until half past nine. Although I'd made the deal, I wasn't looking forward to leaving the dining room. Telephone calling looked far more agreeable than scouring the hotel for prospects. And what if Sid took it into his head to look outside? He might pick a policeman or a Grenadier Guard. I braced myself as we walked along the carpeted corridor leading to the street. As we passed an open doorway Sid suddenly grabbed my arm and pulled me back.

'There you are,' he said. 'The rule is you have to speak for four minutes before you can leave.'

'What are you talking about?' I said as I peeked into the room. A conference was about to start. About fifty delegates were seated facing an empty podium, whiteboard and overhead projection system at the ready. It appeared that the speaker had not yet arrived.

'I can't,' I said. 'They're waiting for the speaker. He'll walk in.'

'Not if you stop farting around. I'll stand here and detain him while you do your four minutes. Just think. How many chances do you have to talk to all those people at once? Or do you want to chicken out and we'll go back to the telephone?'

I walked numbly into the room, then mounted the low platform and looked at the rows of men and women who had suddenly stopped talking to give me their attention. Fortunately they were casually dressed, so my open-neck shirt and jacket didn't look out of place.

'Good morning,' I said loudly, which drew some faint responses. 'Firstly, may I ask you to rise for one minute's silence as a mark of respect for the great visionaries who have gone before us, the men and women who started it all.'

They clearly had not anticipated such a beginning to their day, but they rose and hung their heads while I looked at my watch and tried to work out how I would fill the next three minutes with a pitch about *cafe*.

'Thank you,' I said at the end of a minute and a half. 'Now, before you resume your seats, let's do some simple exercises to get the blood circulating. Follow me.'

I began bending forward and back from the waist and swinging my arms. After half a minute I called a halt and they sat down to a shuffle of chairs and repositioning of papers and notebooks.

'What I am going to say may not immediately appear to be related to today's program, but please bear with me. Would you raise your left hand if you own a cat and your right hand if you own a dog.'

Many hands went up.

'You may well wonder what is the relevance to this conference of dog and cat ownership. I'll tell you what the relevance is. England is among the world's leading sufferers from an excess of animal excrement, its smell, its spread of disease, its accumulation in pleasant parks and waterways. How can we deal with the subject before us today without first considering our environment?'

I could feel a stir at the door and hear some intense, controlled-volume talking. I didn't look around, although I noticed that my audience was showing more interest in the doorway than in me.

'But there is a solution,' I continued with conviction. 'In a word, *cafe*. Now, that may sound like a place to eat, but let me assure you, in this context, it isn't. Just the opposite, in fact. It is a pet-food company, Utah based, with a remarkable product that feeds your animal and helps get air into your garden soil.'

The noise outside the door was now considerably louder. I could hear Sid's voice trying to talk above the rest.

'And you can make recurring income by moving these products through network marketing,' I continued.

Two security guards were advancing on me. It was obvious they had not entered the room to listen to my address. 'And their shit doesn't stink,' I sang out as four arms reached out and half-carried me from the room.

Outside, Sid was talking with two men in navy suits. When he saw me he said: 'Edward, you silly old fellow, you've been speaking at the wrong meeting. The Domestic Animal Interface Society meeting is in a different meeting room.'

'Oh no it is not,' one of the men said. 'I am the manager of the conference centre so I am in a position to know that this is the only meeting here this morning. This man is either a nutter or some kind of impostor sent here by the Royal Pennant Group to bring our conference centre into disrepute.'

He turned savagely around to me. 'Go on, admit it, you're working for the Royal Pennant, aren't you?'

Before I could answer, he grabbed me by the lapels. Sid fastened on to the back of his coat collar to try to pull him away and the two security guards attempted to intervene but instead became part of the affray.

The boxing stance I'd learned in front of the mirror came back to me. I didn't know who I was matched against. It didn't matter. With the exception of Sid, they were all opponents.

I'd only got a couple of jabs into the shoulder pad of one of the security men when Sid grabbed my sleeve and pulled me down the corridor, calling over his shoulder: 'Sorry about this. Must have been another hotel altogether.'

I tried to look back to see if the legitimate speaker had arrived but Sid shoved me into the elevator, the door closed, and we rose like departing spirits.

'I picked a tough one for you there,' he said. 'Sorry, I didn't think it would finish up in a blue.'

'Don't worry,' I said as I examined my jacket for damage. 'My turn is coming.'

'What do you mean?'

'I pick next for you.'

'Look here,' Sid said in his best conciliatory tone, 'isn't it time we stopped playing this silly game. I mean, we'll finish up in the Tower of London at this rate.'

'I agree,' I said evenly. 'We'll stop, but after I give you the one I owe you. Then we'll get back to less risky prospecting.'

'What have you got in mind?'

'If I told you it would spoil a nice surprise.'

***

184

Chapter Twenty-Six

I made sure we arrived early enough at St Stevens Anglican Church in Richmond to secure a seat in the front pew although, as it turned out, nobody else wanted to sit there anyway. The faithful were in short supply that morning. The congregation looked to be no more than about fifty people.

While the asthmatic organ being played from some unseen woody cave put us into a soul cleansing mood, I looked around at the worn splendour of the church with its stained-glass windows in dire need of the removal of pigeon shit. I wondered briefly whether there would ever be *cafe* for birds.

My musings evaporated as the six-strong choir filed in, followed by the elaborately-robed vicar. I was tempted to let Sid off. What I was about to make him to do was surely against the law – although which law I didn't know. But then I remembered the inflexible dedication with which Sid had thrust me into the meeting at the hotel the previous Friday.

During the singing of the first hymn I leaned across and delivered an unambiguous message into Sid's ear. He pretended not to hear, but when I repeated it he shook his head.

'For God's sake Ed,' he pleaded.

'Precisely,' I said impassively. 'And like me, you only have to go four minutes.'

I could feel Sid twitching as the service progressed. We both knew he would have to go through with it but after it was over I was ready to call a truce on speaker crashing.

When the vicar retreated to the rear of the nave I nudged Sid. 'You're on,' I said.

To Sid's credit, he didn't hesitate. I thought he might climb into the high pulpit, but fearing being trapped up there he stepped on to the low platform at the edge of the altar.

He faced the congregation with his eyeballs rolled back in his head and eyelids fluttering.

'The spirit of the Lord is upon me,' he boomed. 'I bring a message.'

The vicar stopped what he was doing and peered at Sid over the top of his glasses. By the look on the vicar's pinched face I don't think he had ever had one of his services interrupted before.

Sid continued: 'And that message is to do with the creatures of the earth, especially those which share our lives, day by day. Yea, I say unto you, they should suffer not, our dogs and cats.'

The vicar began to advance on Sid but then changed his mind, and instead scurried out through a side door. I looked at my watch. Sid had only used up a minute. I reasoned that if the vicar had gone for help Sid could last through his remaining three minutes and we could escape – as long as nobody in the congregation decided to challenge us.

Sid then resorted to speaking in tongues. The words reminded me of the films we had watched as kids, when the agitated black men with spears would address each other in the jungle clearing.

'*cafe cafe cafe!*' Sid concluded.

'Hallelujah!' I shouted, and drew a few mumbled responses from the congregation.

Sid opened his eyes. 'I will translate for us,' he said. 'The Lord's message is that the dogs and cats of our lives shall eat the food of heaven, and that food shall be known as *cafe*, and they shall wax healthy upon it and their excrement shall not have an unpleasant smell but shall dry and thereafter be blown away upon the four winds.'

Sid saw the doors at the far end of the church open before I did.

'And now the Lord commandeth me to go forth from here,' he said as he beckoned to me. I leaped up from the pew and we both hurried past the altar to where the vicar had made his exit. There was a low door beneath the choir stalls. We opened it and found ourselves in a small vestibule. From there, another door, thankfully unlocked, led outside and down a hedged path.

We walked quickly around to the front of the church. The double front doors were standing open. A police car stood in the driveway. Walking as fast as we could – without running – we headed for the railway station and stood in the lee of the wall at the far end of the platform until our train lurched through the tunnel and stopped.

As we sat down in the train bound for Leicester Square, Sid looked me in the face and said solemnly, 'You are a fucking turd.'

'At least I didn't get you into a punch-up,' I said. 'Anyway, that's the end of unauthorised public speeches.'

***

Chapter Twenty-Seven

When Sid and I made our next attempt to move into Padlock Mews we found there had been changes in our favour. Gone were the surly Winsome and her companions. In her place was Mrs Warboys, live-in housekeeper. She had been recommended by somebody in Nat Cohen's vast *cafe* down-line. Nat had not yet returned to London but left a message for us to keep the faith, along with an invitation to move in immediately. He gave us a month's rent free to make up for some of our hotel expenses.

Mrs Warboys was a short woman, as shapeless as a sack of wheat in her grey tracksuit, but compensating for a lack of bodily angles with a sharp nose. As she walked, her fake fur slippers gave the impression of two rodents trying to escape from her. She never looked up when she spoke, but always appeared to be talking to somebody lying on the floor. There her apparent reticence finished, however. She came equipped with a penetrating voice and an impressive range of expletives.

Inside, the house was like a once-grand, but now condemned, picture theatre foyer. The folds in the burgundy velvet curtains were edged in fade marks, and the springs in the floral brocade furniture were permanently bowed from the weight of the people who had sat in them.

Mrs Warboys was a passable cook in the British tradition of chewy meat and multiple, imploded vegetables. We soon learned to be on time for meals or to give her plenty of notice if we would not be home. Even though our board included an evening meal, Mrs Warboys would not tolerate tardiness.

Apart from the basement flat which had become Mrs Warboys' burrow, and the master front room upstairs reserved for Nat Cohen, we had a choice of several large bedrooms. I chose a ground floor one at the back which led out through draughty French doors into the overgrown garden. Sid went upstairs into a side room with a view over that British curiosity, the private allotment. With winter just finished, the allotment holders were busy digging and planting vegetables and flowers which would make the place worthy of a David Attenborough wildlife documentary. I could hear his voice praising the creatures for their industry after the long, barren winter.

'There's one bloke,' Sid told me soon after we'd moved in, 'who reminds me of somebody; his walk or something. He's too far away in the corner plot to see his face, but I have noticed him meet a woman there and take her into his shed.'

***

Chapter Twenty-Eight

Familiarising ourselves with the house and the huddle of shops that formed the village gave us an excuse to become tourists at the expense of our *cafe* prospecting. But our respite finished when Nat Cohen suddenly arrived. One lead-coloured afternoon, after we'd gone walking along the river tow path in the forlorn hope of running into somebody with a dog, we returned home to find our King in residence.

Nat must have heard us arrive. Wearing his habitual black outfit he hurried down the stairs and embraced us like family.

'Goddamn, it's good to see you guys,' he boomed as he half-carried us, a fatherly hand hooked under each of our forearms, into the parlour. 'I've been waiting for you to come back. We're gonna have us a little celebration.'

Mrs Warboys had set up a substantial high tea, with smoked Scottish salmon, caviar on crackers, various patés and champagne in an ice bucket. Nat poured us a flute each and raised his towards the peeling rosettes in the ceiling.

'Here's to owning the British Isles,' he said, and emptied the contents of his glass down his throat in one pass. 'Now tell me, how have you been doin'? I haven't seen the printout for England in weeks. Why, you ask? I've been away at the King's retreat in Hawaii, and my God, I gotta tell you, the company's going through the roof. Already we've got two per cent of the dog food market in America, and about one per cent of the cat. We expect England to be an even better market. I'll bet you guys have been having a ball.'

I took a deep breath. 'No,' I said, 'we haven't. We keep drawing blanks.'

'Are you filling in your prospecting books?' Nat asked sharply as he refilled his glass.

'Yes,' we said in school unison.

'Are you working with beacons?'

'No,' Sid replied. 'We'd kind of forgotten about beacons. We've been a bit haphazard in our prospecting, I suppose. We've tried con-men and Salvation Army collectors and rooms full of bankers and church congregations, but we haven't done any good.'

'All that work,' Nat said with eyebrows raised, 'and you got nothing. Tell me how that can happen.'

Sid and I recounted our unsuccessful campaign, sounding like two children explaining their misbehaviour to a stern parent. When we'd finished Nat let out a yelp of laughter and hit the side of his chair, sending up a fine cloud of dust.

'Oi, you got balls,' he roared. 'You got up to prospect in a church? You could have been jailed. Listen, with that much chutzpah you're gonna make millions and zillions. But seriously, you need beacons. You want to do a beacon session right now?'

'Might as well,' I said. 'It's got to be better than stalking along the river tow path like a couple of Jack the Rippers.'

Nat went to his room and returned carrying a small whiteboard with telescopic legs. He erected it next to the fireplace where the coals placed there by Mrs Warboys glowed quietly in the cracked grate.

'Okay,' he said, taking out a marker pen, 'let's do some beacons. By the way, as Mort might have told you, don't mix up beacons with goals. Goals are finishing points. Beacons are continuous. Their flashing light brings you in and then shows you the path to the next beacon.'

Nat was good at drawing beacons – no doubt from plenty of practice. He drew six, side by side at the bottom of the page.

'Let's give them prospect category names,' he said. 'Okay gimme one.'

'Dog and cat clubs,' I said.

'Good,' Nat replied, labelling the first one. 'So let's say you get to the dog club president. What's the connecting beacon?'

'Addressing one of their meetings to tell them about *cafe*,' Sid suggested.

'Right,' Nat said, and drew a beacon above the first. 'And then where?'

'Referrals from owners to other owners. Then a whole lot of people using the products.'

'Good, good,' Nat enthused. 'Now you're getting the idea. Let's have some more beacon names.'

'Dog ownership,' I said with the help of The Channel. 'If we had a dog we could engage other people with dogs in conversation and prospect them. Even if the prospect didn't have a dog, our dog would be a conversation starter.'

'Right,' Nat said, and drew two more beacons above the one he'd marked 'dog ownership'.

Sid next suggested council dog and cat pounds where he thought there was a chance to sell *cafe* to help defeat the assumed squalor and smell of the kennels. Then I came up with famous people who are associated with pets.

'Gimme an example,' Nat asked me as he was drawing a second beacon above the base one.

'Well, this is a stupid example, but you could say somebody like the Queen of England and her corgis.'

'That's very good,' Nat said, 'and then where?'

'The rest of the royal family,' Sid laughed, 'and then a royal decree that all dogs and cats living on royal property had to eat *cafe*.'

'And then referrals,' Nat continued. 'How many pet owners would the Queen know? Yeah, and then, how many could she influence?'

'If a loyal subject fails to feed his dog *cafe*, off with his head!' I said, cutting the air with the edge of my hand.

'Hey guys,' Nat protested. 'Don't spoof it. The Queen's got dogs, the dogs shit, the Queen doesn't like shit around the palace. Know what I mean?'

'I don't think it would affect her personally,' Sid said. 'She's got people to clean it up.'

'They can't clean it up before it comes out of the dog's arse,' Nat replied. 'If the Queen spends any time in the company of her dogs she's gonna see them shit, right?'

'Okay, that might be the case,' I said, 'but getting to prospect her would present a bit of a problem, don't you think?'

'Not at all,' Sid said, with a smirk playing around his mouth. 'Just call her up and ask her for ten minutes of her time. Or how about knocking on the front door of Buckingham Palace with a couple of cans of *cafe* under your arm for her to try out? And don't forget to warn her about the third stool rule.'

'Hey, guys,' Nat said, holding up a hand, 'you're still spoofing it. I know you won't prospect the goddamn Queen, but I will. In America we're not scared of big shots. I'm taking over this beacon, and when she becomes a distributor I'll put her in your down-line. Now, let's do some more beacons you can get serious about.'

An hour later we came out of the parlour born-again networkers, fizzing with enthusiasm for our *cafe* business. Sid went away to make notes of cat and dog organisations from the telephone directory so that we could begin prospecting them the next day. Nat was going to go through his down-line to see who knew somebody who knew somebody who knew the Queen well enough to give him a referral.

The beacon I got was to buy the Padlock Mews household a dog, but first I had to clear it with Mrs Warboys because she would be looking after it when it wasn't on prospecting duty.

While Sid and I were on the telephone the next day calling dog and cat clubs, Adolph moved in with us. I had hoped for something small, taught and intelligent. Adolph was none of these, and I immediately understood Mrs Warboys' sister's enthusiasm in getting rid of him. Adolph was not old, he just acted that way. Rather than a bark, he emitted a loud croak when he wanted to publicly express an opinion – and that was seldom.

Nat, however, quickly saw Adolph as an outstanding opportunity to bear witness to *cafe*.

'Just imagine,' Nat said the next evening as Adolph, imitating a flokati rug with a nose, lay down near the fire in the parlour. 'You take him down to the village, or even into the centre of London for that matter, he shits on the sidewalk, and you pick the turds up in your hand. What a sensation! You'd stop the traffic. Folks would want to know you. You could do a quick presentation right there.'

'And get arrested right there,' Sid added.

'Yeah, well maybe you'd have to pick the right situation,' Nat conceded, 'but you got so much potential with this dog. Now tell me, how are your other beacons going?'

'Promising,' Sid replied. 'We've got three appointments next week with dog clubs and one with the cat breeders association. How are you getting along with Her Majesty?'

'Still working on it,' Nat said. 'So far, I know somebody who knows somebody who knows somebody who knows her horse trainer. But I gotta do better than that. Maybe I'll go around to the palace and talk to some of those guards outside in the high fur hats. Might be quicker.'

'I'm taking Adolph on the first walk and talk tomorrow,' I said. 'Thought I'd try the village and then take a stroll through Worsley Common.'

'And I'm going to the council depot to see the dog pound warden,' Sid added.

'Okay, that's just fine,' Nat said. 'Now it's time we organised a meeting place where we can invite people to hear the good news – like we had at Mosman in Sydney. Ed, if you're going into the village, how about you ask around? We want a club room or a school house or something. You know the style of thing. I'll get calling too. The local synagogue might have a hall. As soon as we get prospects we'll need to hold business opportunity meetings.'

***

Chapter Twenty-Nine

A dolph was in no mood to go walking the next morning. He didn't want to leave the parlour fireplace, even though the fire had gone out some hours earlier. I lifted him to his feet and took him by the collar into the scullery where his enthusiasm suddenly came to life when I opened a can of *cafe*. That seemed to change his attitude to becoming active, a fact I stored as a *cafe* selling point.

We set off in the clearing mist of the morning looking like a photograph from *English Country Life*: a woolly dog with a floppy gait leading a man in a thick coat of a similar colour to the dog, and also imitating the dog by wearing a tweed hat with ear warmers hanging down. I strode out, my antenna tuned to other people walking their dogs.

We had been walking along the main street for about twenty minutes when I saw a woman approaching followed by her dog, a prancing red setter.

'Okay Adoph,' I said, 'you tackle the dog and I'll prospect the lady.'

As the distance between us closed Adolph went into action rather too well. After quickly examining the other dog he decided to start a fight with it. This was not the introduction to the owner I wanted.

'Adolph, calm down,' I cried out, pulling him away. And then to the woman, 'So sorry about my dog's behaviour towards your dog.' She peered at me from the oval frame of the plaid scarf she wore around her spectacled face.

'What dog?' she asked, looking down. When she saw the object of Adolph's belligerence she said, 'That's not my dog. I don't have a dog.' She clutched her bag closer to her and hurried on, leaving me to restrain Adolph as the setter bounded away.

A few minutes later we arrived at the village. I had no enthusiasm for Nat's idea of a public exhibition of the benefits of *cafe* – even if Adolph had been able to perform on demand. I wandered past the quaint shops, most of which had been around for at least a century longer than I had. On my side of the road there was a small wine shop, two Indian restaurants, a book shop, a travel agent and finally, near the corner, a bread shop called Go-to Bakery. I stopped outside, seduced by the smell of fresh bread and thinking I should buy Mrs Warboys a conciliatory bun. For a weekday morning, the shop was quite busy. I tethered Adolph to the bus shelter post, and opened the door of the shop.

The shock of seeing the woman behind the counter took my attention away from the low step and I stumbled heavily into several people waiting to be served. But my eyes never left her as she busied herself counting flour-dusted rolls from a rack and placing them in a tall brown-paper bag. As I took in her roundness straining beneath her white uniform I began to tremble. My stomach wanted to float off its mountings. I had never given her a name in my fantasies but knew her better than any other person on earth.

My stare must have caught her attention because she suddenly looked up with her deep green eyes and smiled. My lips quivering, I grinned back, and for some reason I took my hat off. When my turn came to be served she had moved to one of the ovens at the back of the shop, and I was attended to by a quick-moving older woman.

'Your other assistant was about to serve me,' I said, pointing towards the back of the shop.

'I don't think so,' the woman said. 'Hilda is in training from Germany. She won't start serving customers here until next month.'

'Oh,' I said, 'no matter anyway. I just want a couple of Bath buns.'

As they were being wrapped I watched Hilda bend over to pick up a box and bring it to the front of the shop. I was grateful that my overcoat concealed the lump that was growing in my trousers. All too soon the buns were being handed to me and I had paid for them. Other customers pressed into my space and I had to leave the shop.

I'd forgotten that I was in charge of a dog as I stepped, blinking, into the street. I had walked away from the bus shelter when Adolph's loud croak reminded me of our project. I went back and absent-mindedly untied him, and we set off for Worsley Common.

We walked the length of the Common and on into the gardens with its expansive pond. There were not only ducks on the pond but a large number of geese which, when they saw me with a paper bag, left the water like an amphibious army and surrounded me. Adolph approached one and received a peck on the nose for his interest. In contravention of the notice not to feed the living creatures of the gardens I took out Mrs Warboys' Bath buns, broke them into pieces and made a hero of myself.

As I accompanied Adolph back along the Worsley Common path I felt well pleased. With his help, I had managed to engage five people in conversation as they walked their dogs on the common. The questioning technique paid off with their names and addresses and an interest in coming to a meeting.

I became light-headed as I strolled back through the village, but not from my prospecting success. The glow in my groin felt like a warm towel stuffed into my underpants. The bread shop became a beacon which threw a light to Hilda's beacon. From there, a line of beacons, semaphoring unspeakable pleasures, stretched away.

Perhaps I had subconsciously fed Mrs Warboys' Bath buns to the geese so that I could return to buy more at the Go-to Bakery. As I approached it again, the smell of fresh bread immediately evoked Hilda. This time there was only one customer in the shop and two assistants behind the counter. Hilda was arranging loaves of bread in one of the glass display cases, enabling me to gaze apparently at the bread, but view her instead. I half-hoped I would discover I had made a mistake, that she was not my fantasy girl. I looked for her shortcomings, gaps in the delivery of my expectations. There were none. The woman I had created in my mind had also been created in the flesh: the short dark hair, the small, well-structured nose, the clear, milky-tea skin. And then the body, so grandly shaped.

Perhaps she was not my creation. Perhaps some cosmic reflector had beamed a real person into my mind after Greenstrum had set me up for it. Eventually she felt my eyes on her and looked up.

'You were here before,' she said. '*Zwei* Bath bun, *ja?*'

'That's right.' I wanted to shout in jubilation, but restricted myself to adding: 'and now I need two more.'

'You have the healthy appetite for Bath bun,' she said, and opened her full, soft mouth in a brief laugh. How many times had those lips been around the end of my cock? Often, yet never. I was hardening up again and knew I'd have to siphon the python that night or put up with an attack of lovers' balls.

'Actually I didn't eat them,' I explained, 'the geese did. They ambushed me in the gardens and went through my pockets like customs inspectors. Fortunately they don't eat money.' As I drew the wallet out I was pleased to see that Hilda was laughing. I dropped my voice to a whisper. 'Can you sell me another two?'

'Not until next month,' she replied. 'I must finish the baking course first. Then yes, on to business side and serving the customers.'

'I can't stand here that long,' I said. 'Incidentally, do you have a dog or a cat?'

'Yes, back in Hamburg. Why do you ask this question?'

Did I want to prospect Hilda for *cafe*? This would be mixing unlikely business with just as unlikely pleasure. Before I could decide, the other woman took over the sale, and again I was returned to the street with two Bath buns and a boner.

The winter afternoon light was seeping from a pewter sky as I walked home with Adolph. Passing the allotment next to our house I almost collided with a round, tweedy figure busy locking the iron gate that kept vegetable and flower pilferers out. I judged Adolph's interest in sniffing the man's shoes to be a prospecting signal. I eased off the lead and readied myself to apologise and deliver my familiar lines about dog shit. The man jumped when he felt Adolph's twitching nose on his shoe and turned to face me.

'My goodness, now here's a surprise,' Henry Throgmorton said with a lopsided grin. 'Well, nice to see you again. I must be getting on home. Yes I really must.'

'Where to, High Wycombe?' I blocked his path as Adolph sat down on his shoe.

'High where? Oh no. We don't live there now.'

'Well let me tell you where Sid and I live, Henry. Right next door. And we have been observing you carrying on in that shed. We've taken pictures with a long lens. We didn't like being conned, Henry.'

'I had no such intention,' Henry replied, trying to look hurt. 'Emily called me in the night. She was ill. I had to leave early.'

'Give me your wallet,' I said, 'otherwise I'll command my guard dog to tear your throat out.'

Henry fumbled in his coat and handed me a worn brown leather wallet. 'Are you robbing me?' he asked.

I ignored him as I opened the wallet and took out a business card and checked it against his driving licence. His name was Henry Thorpe with a stated occupation of 'chartered occupier'.

'What the hell is a chartered occupier?' I snapped.

'We look after houses for people when they're away.'

'And how about your rottie and your Chihuahua and Henry the King George spaniel and your wife called Emily?'

Henry looked down at Adolph who was now lying on his shoe. 'I certainly have a wife called Emily but the dogs, well, I must admit I made them up on the spur of the moment. Actually, I don't like dogs.'

'All that bullshit for a free meal and a room?'

'We were between occupations,' Henry whined. 'Emily was staying with her sister in Essex and I had nowhere to go, except there, and I really can't stand her wretched sister. Look here, I'm sorry. If there's anything I can do for you, you know, to sort of make up, you only have to ask. Now do be a good chap; give me my wallet back.'

'So you can walk away a free man for a second time? No, Henry. I'm going to turn you into a *cafe* networker whether you like it or not. Actually, you'll like it once you see the money rolling in. Do you agree?'

'Of course, old chap. Just tell me where to be and I'll be there. Now, my wallet?'

'No. I'm going to hold it as a deposit.'

'So you really are robbing me. You're just a scoundrel and a common thief.'

I didn't like the feel of Henry's wallet in my hand. 'I'll trade,' I said. 'Your wallet for the key to the allotment gate. And you get the key back when your first cheque arrives from *cafe*. Deal?'

'That's preposterous,' Henry huffed. 'You can't have the key. It's registered and I can't get another one. This allotment is part of the house we're looking after. I'm supposed to look after this garden too.'

'Then you'd better hurry along to our meetings and win the key back,' I said, holding the wallet in one hand and opening the palm of the other.

Henry poked a middle finger into the fob pocket of his vest and hooked out a long black key.

'Let me see it open the gate,' I said.

'You have no trust,' Henry muttered as he opened and closed the lock. He handed me the key and I passed across his wallet, along with my business card.

'Call me tomorrow,' I said, 'and I'll tell you where your first meeting is.'

* * *

Chapter Thirty

Even after three months in London, Sid and I still hadn't decided how long we should stay. As I expected, the *cafe* cheques from Australia were diminishing because we had left the business free-wheeling in Sydney. A shortage of money might therefore set a time limit on how long we could stay in England. But what would happen if we became tied to London because of our success, or if the fantasy of Hilda turned into an uncontrollable reality? Already Clarice was growing impatient for me to come to my senses.

I entered the Padlock Mews house through the back door and delivered Adolph into the care of Mrs Warboys. Her usual scowl struggled into a half smile when I gave her the Bath buns.

'From Go-to Bakery,' I said, desperate to talk about the place where I had seen Hilda.

'They're 'spensive,' Mrs Warboys said, 'but look here, thanks Ed.'

That was the first time she had called me by my given name – or any name, for that matter.

I left the kitchen and went inside to see if Sid had returned. I couldn't wait to tell him about our born-again recruit, and show him the key to the allotment gate. But in the hallway I was confronted by the second woman that day to cause me a nervous reaction. Winsome stood by the staircase, wearing the same orange mohair sweater and jeans in which she had soured our arrival in London. I looked instinctively to see if Absolom was in the shadows but instead found Nat.

'Ed, you've met Winsome before,' he said breezily. 'She's gonna move in. Actually she moved in today already.'

'Pity I couldn't have answered the door to her,' I said darkly.

'Everything's cool,' she said, slipping her hand under his arm. 'I've taken the bedroom upstairs next to Nat's.'

The front door opened with a rush of cold air as Sid let himself in.

'Do we have to go back to our least favourite hotel?' he asked as he caught sight of Winsome.

'Sid, you're such a funny guy,' Nat laughed. 'I was just telling Ed that Winsome moved back in here.'

'To do *cafe*, obviously,' Sid said dryly.

'Well, maybe, maybe,' Nat replied. 'She'll help me for a start, doing clerical work and then, well, yeah, she might do a little prospecting. You know we need a meeting place. Winsome's on the case right now.'

Sid shrugged his shoulders and said to me: 'In spite of the fright I've just had here, I've had a good day. I need to talk to you about it.'

'The parlour fire is on and I put some drinks in there for you boys,' Nat said, pointing. 'I might join you later but right now I've got a little work to do with Winsome.'

When Sid and I had settled down in the old chairs and had poured ourselves drinks from the line-up of new bottles that stood on the cabinet, Sid said: 'First, the Barnes pound warden wants to do a deal. He thinks *cafe* is sensational. The pound places lots of dogs and cats with new owners. He's prepared to include a pack of six cans as part of the fee they charge for each animal, and they will give me the names of all new owners so we can prospect them. In return he wants to buy *cafe* at wholesale price.'

'In other words, we make nothing out of it,' I said.

'Right,' Sid replied, 'but in exchange for the names of all those new owners, who will be *cafe* users by the time we talk to them. Looks like a good deal for us, right?'

'A top deal,' I said enthusiastically.

'That's not all,' Sid continued. 'The Barnes warden will write to all the other council pound wardens in Greater London and tell them about us and about *cafe*.'

'What a coup,' I said.

'And to cap it all off,' Sid went on, 'I've met a prospect out of the blue. If I tell you too much it will spoil a surprise. You'll have to meet him. How about tomorrow?'

'Okay,' I replied, 'I'll move a few appointments. Now, let me tell you about my red-hot prospect. You already know him. His name's Henry ...'

***

Chapter Thirty-One

Sid was evasive about his plans next morning. All he would tell me was to bring plenty of small change. I asked him if we should take Adolph with us but he said no, we would be doing some bus travelling. He kept consulting his watch during breakfast, explaining that it was imperative we be at the Barnes village bus stop by no later than five past nine.

We left the house at a quarter to nine and strode through drifting, misty rain towards the village. I suddenly remembered, with rising excitement, that the bus stop was right outside Go-to Bakery. Well before we reached it, the smell of fresh bread wafted up under my umbrella and powerfully evoked Hilda. For the rest of my life fresh bread would weaken me the way Kryptonite weakened Superman. While Sid peered through the drizzle trying to read the numbers on the approaching armada of red buses, I could not help but look behind us. The shop was busy, just as it had been the previous morning, so that the customers hid the employees behind the counter. Nevertheless, just knowing Hilda was in there doubled my heart rate. If it hadn't been for Sid pointing at the approaching number 443 bus, I would have been in the shop buying Bath buns.

The bus stopped, the door swung open with a hiss, and we clambered up, paying our fare as we passed the scowling driver. The elevated position in the bus gave me a sudden and unexpected view into the shop. And there was Hilda, her white cotton bonnet over her adorable bob of dark hair. She was carrying a wire basket full of rolls.

'Good,' I heard Sid say at my elbow, 'he's on the 443 just as he promised.' Sid was leading me to the back row of seats where a small man in a green coat and matching felt hat sat hunched in the corner. An old metal suitcase was stowed under his knees like an egg under a hen.

'This is Tommy Hackett,' Sid said. 'Tommy, meet my partner, Ed Sharock. Ed, you sit next to Tommy so you can hear what he has to say.'

Tommy's creased face put him into his seventies but he had unexpectedly clear blue eyes and a crooked grin made roguish by several vacant spaces between his teeth.

'Tell Ed what you told me yesterday,' Sid said to Tommy.

'Which part, then?' Tommy asked.

'Well, for a start, tell him where you live.'

''Er majesty looks after me,' Tommy replied seriously.

He works at Buckingham Palace, I thought. He's a footman to the Queen and he's in charge of her corgis.

'You know her then?' I said.

'Na, no more than you does,' he replied. 'What I mean is she provides me with somewhere to live.'

'And where is that?'

'Right here on the buses. Not only buses, either. There's all them trains and even a few ferries if I'm in the mood.'

'What's he talking about?' I turned and whispered to Sid.

'Tommy lives on the public transport system,' Sid explained. 'Do you remember that report on *60 Minutes* last year about people who live at airports, always pretending to be going somewhere, but they never leave the building? Well, Tommy does the opposite: he travels all the time. He only gets off for meals and to use public bathrooms.'

I looked at Tommy with new interest. 'It must cost you a fortune in fares,' I said to him. 'How do you manage to earn enough money to stay on the bus, if you never get off to go to work?'

Tommy rummaged in his breast pocket and produced a grubby plastic card with a royal crest above his photo, and the words 'Unlimited Public Travel Permit' printed across the bottom.

'How did you get this?' I asked.

'Falklands War,' he replied. 'Part of me navy pension, isn't it?'

'And they can't put you off the bus; is that how it works?'

'That's it. I had a bit of trouble at first but now they all knows me. Fact is, I'm a kinda celebrity. They like me ridin'.'

I turned to Sid. 'A great story,' I said, 'but how do you see Tommy as a prospect? The navy might be grateful to him, but it would draw the line at him travelling with a couple of cats or dogs.'

'Tommy's had a change of fortune – or the need for a change anyway,' Sid explained. 'He's fallen in love. He met a woman trying to do the same thing as him, but with only a disabled travel permit; and she keeps getting put off the bus.'

I looked again at Tommy. 'Why don't you quit travelling and live a stationary life together?'

'Don't 'ave the money,' Tommy said. 'Never thought I'd need it.

And let me tell ya, 'avin' a bit on a bus or a train ain't easy. Ya gotta pick ya time and we take longer, us bein' a bit older and all. And there's the danger of 'er bein' put off before we get through wiv it.'

'Coitus interruptus transportia,' I translated.

'Tommy is on friendly speaking terms with more people than you and I will meet in our lifetimes,' Sid said. 'With a bit of training and a few sample cans he could become a King.'

'King of the road,' I suggested. 'Possibly, but first, does he like the idea of network marketing *cafe*, and second, would anybody give him a hearing?'

'Yes on both counts,' Sid said. 'I watched Tommy yesterday. He's a celebrity. People love sitting next to him. He has their attention. And he thinks *cafe* network marketing is the ideal way for him to earn a living.'

'Tommy, you know you'll need to do a bit of training,' I said to him. 'You'll need to know all about the products and about the pay plan.'

'Course,' he said. 'Like I says to Sid, now I got goals.'

'We'll change those into beacons,' I said quietly, 'or Nat will. He's our up-line. He's a King.'

Tommy looked through the bus window, then down at his watch and stood up, lifting his case from its nest under his legs.

'Gotta get off here to connect to the 351,' he said. 'That'll get me on to the Northern line later so I can take a bath during the peak hour. If you gents wants to keep talking to me about business you'll 'ave to come along.'

For the rest of the day we travelled on buses and trains with Tommy. On some legs we would sit and watch him have animated conversations with people he knew – dozens of them – and between times we instructed him about the *cafe* products, and how to build networks. Sid had brought some brochures and a couple of sample cans. By mid-afternoon we let Tommy fly solo with a bunch of women he knew from the Hoxton Park Bowling Club. We sat in the seats behind him and listened. He really had absorbed a lot of what we'd told him.

We parted in central London when Tommy's schedule took him in the opposite direction to Barnes and to his bath somewhere on the way to Cornwall. By then he had trial orders for about fifty cans of *cafe*, along with the names and addresses of people who said they'd come to a meeting to find out how to become distributors themselves.

As we shook hands with Tommy at Kensington Station he said, 'I'll try to call you at a loo stop somewhere, but if you need to contact me, I'm always on the 443 Mondays, Wednesdays and Fridays, stopping at the Barnes bread shop at five past nine.'

He hurried away, a small springy figure in green on a tight travel schedule, carrying a case. His mention of the bread shop started me thinking about Hilda again. She was the direct opposite: a large, slow-moving figure in white, personifying a piece of moulded dough ready for the oven.

***

Chapter Thirty-Two

'Tommy is going to be good and so are the people who buy animals from council pounds and so are those people who have come to our meetings and so are your walk-and-talk prospects, and maybe even tubby old Henry.' Sid ran out of breath.

'Meanwhile,' I said, 'we're down to our last few quid and the rent is due, right?'

'Exactly. The question is, how is Nat going to react?'

'Well, he'll certainly be more sympathetic than our wives would be if we were to ask them for some carry-on cash,' I replied. 'But I'm not sure that Nat is getting it easy, either. He's building a good English business but he told me his American line has stopped growing without him there to push it. And his Australian business is suffering the way ours is.'

'On top of all that, Winsome is something of a drain on him,' Sid said.

'Poor bugger,' I said with an ironical sigh, imagining the joy of just one draining distraction with Hilda. I had restricted my contact with her to purchasing two Bath buns from the Go-to Bakery each day I took a walk up to the village to buy the newspaper.

'As I see it, these are the alternatives,' Sid said as he looked at the cheque still attached to the down-line sales printout that the company provided. 'We could go home to Sydney and never see through the potential of our *cafe* business in England, or look for supplementary work here – illegally I might add – while things get going. We could also move into a hostel somewhere and join the nouveau poor.'

I stared into the quietly hissing fire. Sid was right, but I hated all of the alternatives. Going home would be a terrible defeat. If we could find work in London it would only be manual labour and it would eat up our essential *cafe* prospecting time. Anyway, we were too old to be builders' labourers or railway fettlers. As to the third alternative, I couldn't face living in squalor any worse than that of the old house at Padlock Mews. Even Mrs Warboys had become tolerable since I had begun to supply her with regular Bath buns.

'What about we try to stay here but tighten the budget?' I said at last.

'How can we do that?'

'Well, we'd have to share a room, and also see if Nat would give us credit until we get on our feet.'

'Worth a try,' Sid said. 'Your room or mine?'

'Yours, I suppose. We'll be in a better bargaining position because Nat will get more for mine if he lets it out.'

Nat turned out to be a hard sell. We had to paint and re-paint an optimistic picture of our prospects before he slowly nodded and agreed to provide our accommodation on credit for a maximum of

three months. He insisted on sighting our monthly cheques from
cafe, and to take a bite out if he thought there was more than was
essential to keep us alive.

'And if you guys flame out you'll pay me back when you get to
Sydney, okay?' he concluded.

I moved upstairs into Sid's room. It easily took two beds along
with another cupboard which we positioned to roughly divide the
room in two.

The move brought an immediate improvement in our prospecting.
We thought we'd been busy before, but now we aggressively planned
each day to make every minute work. Because we had only one
telephone, we competed at being the slickest and the quickest in
telephone prospecting. Every cold-call became a hot opportunity.
We sticky-taped beacons all over the walls, and wrote motivational
messages on mirrors and on the backs of cupboard doors.

My only concession to pleasure was a regular morning trip to
the newsagent and a painfully exciting Bath bun purchase from
the bread shop. A cloud of depression would settle around me on
Hilda's days off but I was elated when she graduated from cook to
front-of-house. I quickly became her exclusive customer and would
hang back in the crowd so that I could be served by her.

Winsome secured us regular hire of the Goat Hair Weavers
Guild Hall, an ancient stone structure in Hertfordshire. There Nat
and Sid would take turns to tell the story of *cafe* and animal shit to
increasing numbers of interested listeners. Afterwards they would
deal with the usual barrage of accusations about pyramid schemes
and the fear of losing friends in their 'warm circle' of prospects. In
the process they usually sold enough sample cans of *cafe* to pay for
the rent on the hall.

Two months after being forced to share a room, Sid and I saw our commission cheque pull out of its dive. In spite of Australia suffering decline, England began to move forward. Tommy's sign-ups started to build down-lines of their own and so did others. I counted thirty-seven distributors who I had prospected with the help of Adolph, and Sid had a long list of people from the council pound contacts. We both spent nights addressing dog and cat clubs all over London, and from there we began to link into organisations in Scotland, Ireland and Wales. Nat told us that *cafe* would soon reach 'critical marketing mass', a state where, he explained with the help of his whiteboard and an infestation of beacons, a product became well enough known to generate demand on its own.

***

Chapter Thirty-Three

Although Nat's business was growing much faster than ours, he was disappointed with his failure at Buckingham Palace. His attempts at friendly conversation with Coldstream Guards had resulted in him being warned off the palace precincts upon threat of deportation.

'It isn't as if I'd demanded to talk to the goddamn Queen,' he said over dinner the night of his banishment. 'I only wanted to help with her goddamn dogs. I'll bet she's got cats too. Those guards are rude bastards. You go up to talk to them and they act like you're not there. Then four cops came over and read me the goddamn riot act.'

'So you're going to give up on that prospect?' Sid suggested mischievously.

'Hell no,' Nat retorted. 'I don't care how much money I make out of England, I won't be happy until those corgis are eating *cafe*. I'll just have to work from the inside, that's all. It's the golden rule of network marketing: everybody can be prospected. You just have to find the links. This whole business is a game of links.'

'What about beacons?' Sid asked.

'And beacons too,' Nat said, not realising he was being sent up.

'And rectangles?' Sid continued.

'Yeah, them too,' Nat said with growing excitement. 'Beacons in front, links at the side and all forming beautiful fucking rectangles.'

We were seated at the long table in the dilapidated dining room. The evening mealtime had become the report event of the day. It was as though we all earned our food by our success with *cafe* prospecting. In the case of Sid and I that was true, because we were still living at Padlock Mews on Nat's credit. Without a tale of endeavour or triumph to tell every night, our meagre lifestyle was in danger of collapse.

Mrs Warboys did not eat with us. That left seven for dinner each night when we were all home. There was Sid, myself, Nat, Winsome, and three new *cafe* boarders from America: Anne O'Grady, a former nun from Ohio; Owen Lissa, a lawyer friend of Nat's; and Bobby Einstein, a young flautist from the Chicago Symphony Orchestra who'd lost his job for being stoned during a performance. The new influx of boarders filled all the bedrooms, including my old one, which meant that Sid and I were stuck with each other for the foreseeable future.

Our shared quarters became more awkward the night I took sick. When I got up from the dinner table I was gripped by a pain low in the stomach. I immediately thought Mrs Warboys had poisoned us, but since nobody else was affected I concluded it was my ailment alone. Sid told me that if I was a horse I would have colic, and if it was bad enough I would have to be put down. But he was not prepared to venture a human diagnosis.

Instead of going to a meeting of Citizens Revolt Against Poo (CRAP), I begged a hot water bottle from Mrs Warboys and went to bed. Sid woke me coming in after midnight, which prompted me to get up to refill the hot water bottle. The pain had intensified and I had trouble walking down to the kitchen. At that point all my bravery at coming to England to start a new business left me, and I quietly whimpered for the comfort of my Mosman bed and Clarice to look after me. By morning I was experiencing excruciating pain coming in spasms. If I was pregnant, Sid remarked kindly, I was having contractions and should be taken to the delivery room immediately. Eventually Sid decided that I was seriously ill and called a doctor.

At nine o'clock Mrs Warboys' rodent slippers darted into my room followed by their owner. She announced the arrival of Dr Singh who, she told my carpet, had driven up in a pale blue Rolls-Royce and did not look like a proper doctor. Dr Singh swept in behind her, bringing with him a clinging smell of tobacco smoke. Short and middle-aged, he was running to fat, with the white hairs on his head making a successful assault on the grey.

'Bit of tummy trouble, my friend,' he said with a quick smile that showed all his teeth at once. 'There is nothing worse than a severely aching guts, nothing. Of course, there could be many answers. Yes, many. Tell me, are your bowels operating to your satisfaction?'

'Yes, complete satisfaction.'

'Well, that's one thing out of the way. Now, I'd better take a look at you.'

Mrs Warboys quickly withdrew as Dr Singh pushed up my pyjama top and began to prod.

'No lumps and bumps evident,' he said, drawing his stethoscope from his sagging black bag. 'Let's listen to the engine room.'

In the middle of his examination my ailment decided to reveal itself by delivering a demonstration spasm which doubled me up and turned my face white.

'Oh my goodness,' Dr Singh said as I rolled around the bed moaning. 'My dear friend, you have plenty of pain going on there. Plenty. I need my other bag. I'll just pop out to my car.'

As he left the room, Mrs Warboys' head appeared around the edge of the doorway. 'The Rolls-Royce isn't the latest model,' she told the opposite wall, 'but still, it's too good for an Indian doctor to drive. You just watch his bill now, Ed.'

When Dr Singh returned and had given me a painkilling injection in the buttocks, he said: 'Almost certainly I would say you had a kidney stone, or maybe more than one. I will take a blood sample to run a few tests but I am a very good kidney stone detective. Maybe the best in London.'

'So what happens now?' I asked between clenched teeth.

'Well, one of two things. Either you will pass the stone or you won't. If you do, that could be the end of it – except that you must watch your diet very carefully indeed. You see, not too much calcium. If you don't pass the stone then you must go to hospital to draw it out through the penis. I therefore suggest it is much better to pass it.'

The injection began to work and I relaxed back into the pillow.

'Do I have to stay in bed?' I asked.

'Oh most certainly you do,' he said. 'Get yourself a big jug of water and go at it. I want to see you turn into Niagara Falls. For at least three days. Now I'll give you a script for painkillers for when you get your next attack.' He drew out a pad and began to write.

'Our housekeeper is worried that you drive a Rolls-Royce,' I said to fill the silence.

'I used to make my calls on a motorcycle,' he replied, 'but it worried my patients very much. They thought I must be no good if I could afford no more than a motorcycle. So I bought the Rolls-Royce from one of my patients who died. Now those who are still alive are convinced I am a good doctor but they worry I will overcharge. So you see, you can't win.'

Since I now faced the prospect of spending at least three days out of full prospecting action, I had to attempt some sort of compensation for our *cafe* business.

'Tell me,' I said as the doctor was packing up his bags, 'do you have a dog or a cat?'

'Yes,' he said, 'three cats. More my wife's than mine, I should say.'

I launched into my well-oiled presentation, but it was the first one I had delivered horizontally. Dr Singh was not overly attracted to the product, because his cats had the run of an adequate garden, but when I explained the money he could make by building a network he set his bags down.

'Many people I visit have dogs and cats,' he said with enthusiasm. 'I could carry some samples in my number one bag. Yes indeed, it could be a very good business Here is my address. If you like you can pay your bill in your *cafe* products. I well understand this system of doing business.'

After the doctor had left I went to the kitchen. I found a large glass jug and filled it so I could prime the headwaters of the Colorado River. I also talked Mrs Warboys into going to the village to get my medicine by giving her some extra money to buy two Bath buns and to tell Hilda I was too sick to buy them myself.

Then I settled into bed to drink myself back to health. Mrs Warboys arrived with my medicine just in time for it to deal with another pain spasm – although the two yellow tablets were not as effective as Dr Singh's injection.

The day passed between drinking, pissing and painkillers. When not occupied with these pursuits, I managed to make some gasping follow-up *cafe* phone calls from my bedside table. Mrs Warboys brought me dinner on a tray and afterwards I fell into an exhausted sleep.

The next day passed in the same manner, punctuated by a call from Dr Singh telling me that yes indeed I had kidney stones and to keep on drinking.

By around midday on day three I thought I heard a tiny metallic ping as I was in my familiar position above the toilet bowl. When I returned to bed the pain had subsided. I called Dr Singh on his mobile.

'Might be a flash in the pan,' he said without realising his pun. 'I think it is probably good news but just to be on the side of safety, stay on the water for the rest of the day and if there is no more pain you can resume your normal life tomorrow. Afterwards you must come to see me so we can plot your diet. And don't forget to bring me your pet-food. Already I have some interested patients.'

I refilled the glass jug and went back to bed, now feeling I didn't belong there, but resigned to giving my kidneys some after-sales service.

I became drowsy after lunch and let my mind drift down to the village and the Go-to Bakery. So intense was my reverie that I began to smell fresh bread, and when I lifted my eyelids just a fraction I imagined I could see Hilda. I opened them a little wider and Hilda became clearer. With a start I opened them all the way. Hilda stood there smiling and holding a paper bag that I knew contained two Bath buns. She wore her familiar bakery white uniform and bonnet. I imagined she must have engineered an errand from which she had robbed a little time to see me.

'I hear that you are ill and I thought that you would miss your buns that might make you feel not so ill,' she said. 'You know me? My name is Hilda. From the bread shop.'

'Of course I know you, Hilda. I don't think I ever told you my name. I'm Ed Sharock. I'm sorry I can't be a better host.'

'This is okay,' she said. 'I will not stay. I will be missed at work. Your lady downstairs would not let me come up but then she sees the bag and then she says I must see you.'

She advanced towards the bed and laid the bag on the bedside table. I wanted so much to implore her to lie down with me, but my voice acted otherwise.

'This is very kind of you,' I said. 'When I'm better, which should be very soon, I would like to invite you for a drink to say thank you.'

Hilda regarded me with her soft eyes. '*Ja*, this will be okay, but no talking together in the shop. I must call you.'

I leaned out to the bedside table and took a card from my wallet and handed it to her. 'I will look forward to it,' I said as her soft fingers closed around the card. In other circumstances I would have put on a dressing gown and escorted her downstairs but my cock was running the show. I desperately needed to piss and I had a massive hard-on as well.

'I must go,' she said. '*Auf wiedersehen*, Mr Eddy.' She left the room, a mobile sculpture of mountains and ravines that the universe had created for my most exquisite pleasure.

***

Chapter Thirty-Four

Should fantasies ever be allowed to become realities? I thought about this as I stood on the threshold of a change in my association with Hilda. My cock craved her, but reality rang a warning bell. If it had been left up to me I might have procrastinated until the trail had gone cold. She now had my card, so the next move was in her doughy hands.

She didn't call. She wrote me a letter instead, in skinny upright handwriting not at all in keeping with her appearance. It told me that she would be at the Purple Turnip pub at six o'clock the following Tuesday. That was the evening on which Sid and I had arranged to speak at the monthly meeting of the Pit Bull Terriers club in Shepherd's Bush. I could have told Sid a lie about having to follow a hot lead somewhere else that night, but when I found we were alone in the parlour after dinner I decided to tell the truth.

I poured us both a glass of Nat's port and said: 'About next

Tuesday with the Pit Bulls, can you handle that meeting without me?'

'Why, have you got a better offer – like a date with that roly-poly from the bread shop?'

'How did you know about that?' I said, round-eyed.

'I didn't know,' he replied. 'I just said that as a joke. Don't tell me it's true.'

'Yes, kind of,' I said. 'I wanted to thank her for bringing me some buns when I was sick. And I feel a bit sorry for her too, with all that weight to carry about.'

Sid was trying not to laugh. 'She probably tipples on the icing when nobody's looking,' he said. 'Ed, you do what you want, but hey, it's not a serious thing is it?'

'No,' I said, grinning unconvincingly, 'not at all. It's just that I can't change the night. Okay with you?'

'Sure,' Sid said. 'And while we're on the subject, I may have a favour to ask you in return.' Now it was his turn to look uncomfortable. 'Anne O'Grady has been passing some nasty remarks about me.'

'I don't believe it,' I said. 'She's one of the nicest people I've ever met. An ex-nun like Anne couldn't make nasty remarks.'

'The remarks are not all that nasty,' he said. 'She doesn't mean them to be, anyway. The other day, when you were out with Adolph, she said it was a pity that two such engaging men like us were gay.'

'Because we share a room?'

'I suppose that's the basis of it. I couldn't tell her the reason, that we were broke.'

'And?'

'She kept on about it. The more I denied being gay the more she pretended to disagree.'

'Pretended?'

'She challenged me to back up my claim. She didn't leave the convent just to do network marketing, she said.'

'So what are you going to do about it?'

'About as much as you're going to do about the dumpling in the bread shop.'

'Are you suggesting a pact?'

'I suppose I am. We have to be ready to cover for one another if anything develops.'

'I'll go along with that,' I said. We touched glasses. 'Here's to two old queens trying to go straight.'

The Purple Turnip looked as though it had been built on the banks of the Thames before building regulations had been invented. It was warren-like, with low ceilings, tiny fire places, little windows and time-rubbed furniture. The rear opened up into an obviously newer section where the dining room ran across the entire width of the building, providing an expansive view of the pale khaki water.

Hilda's short note had not said exactly where in the Purple Turnip we should meet. I went to the back room and sat at a table in a corner to give me the best view of who was coming and going.

I hardly recognised her when she entered the room. Instead of all in white she was all in black. And instead of a uniform she wore a loose top and defining pants, which showed off her grand arse. I stood up to take the hand she extended and we both sat down simultaneously.

'You got my letter,' she said. 'I was not surprised if you didn't come.'

'But of course I would come,' I replied. 'I wanted to thank you for your kindness in bringing me the buns. I didn't think you would have remembered me.'

'Of course I remember you. Every day. *Zwei* Bath bun. I am

always looking for you. And sometimes your dog comes too. This dog makes me laugh. I hope you are not angry that I laugh.'

'No Hilda, I laugh at him too. Adolph is not strictly my dog. He is a jointly-owned dog. I just take him for business walks.'

Before Hilda could ask me to explain further, the drink waiter came for our order. The smell of food wafted out at the same time. I asked Hilda if she would join me for dinner.

'*Ja*, this would be good. But not late. You see I am watch by Eva and her husband which own the bakery. He is my husband's brother.'

When the waiter left us Hilda looked me in the eyes. 'Your wife is also living in the house?' she asked.

'No,' I said, feeling tempted to tell her that I was single. But I quickly decided that it was better to deal in truth. 'She is in Australia.'

'You are separated then?'

'Only by distance. I came to London to start a network marketing business in pet-food.'

'Net? Like for trapping the butterfly?'

'No, network marketing is when you sell products through people you meet. It's about making contacts and they make contacts and soon you have many customers. But there are no shops involved.'

'We could sell bread this way?'

'I doubt it. Bread would go stale before it could get through the network. You can sell almost anything that isn't perishable. You've heard of Prodmasters?'

'*Ja*. My brother was crazy about it. Soap for the clothes and the dishes and many other things.'

'*cafe* is something like that, except we sell only pet-food and a few other things for dogs and cats.' I didn't want to put on my prospecting hat for Hilda. I changed the subject. 'Tell me about the bakery.'

'Well, I am coming from Hamburg to learn Go-to Bakery business. In Barnes shop my sister-in-law Eva she teaches me. Then I go back. Wolf and I will begin Go-to Bakery in Hamburg.'

'Wolf?' I imagined feeding this fierce creature *cafe*.

'My husband. He drives the bus but he is tired of always going here, going there and coming back. He says I should learn from Eva and he should learn from me.'

I'd never thought about my fantasy girl being married. I'd never needed more than her body. Fantasies were good like that. You could take just what you needed.

Drinks came, and then dinner came, bringing with it a tide of trivial conversation. The French red went to work on our tongues, and even more so on my groin. After dinner, when she pulled out a thin black cigar and lit it, the sight of her full lips around the end of it suddenly prodded my subconscious into uncensored talk. I could have been reclining in Greenstrum's low chair.

'Hilda,' I said, 'I have a story to tell you, and I am able tell it because I expect nothing from you, now that I know you're married, and you know I'm married, and you live with your watchful brother-in-law from the bread shop.' I drew a deep breath and readied myself to confess my fantasy. But her eyes, softened even more by the wine and heady haze of cigar smoke, were on mine.

'I must tell you something first,' she said, holding up a padded palm. 'A most strange thing. Ever since I was about sixteen years I had in my crazy head a man. Before I married to Wolf I thought about this man when I was alone – you know what I mean?'

I nodded.

'This man I thought about was not real man because he was make-up in my head. Anyway, when you came into the bread shop I had a shock. This man had come to life. I said *Gott*, this is spooky.'

'You mean to say I am your fantasy man?'

'*Ja*, Eddy,' she said, taking a powerful drag on her cigar.

There now seemed little point in my confession. I would have sounded like the other bookend. Instead, I reached across the table and took her hand. As I expected, it was like fresh bread. 'And what do you intend to do about this fantasy?' I asked, struggling with a suddenly dry throat.

'Such difficult,' she replied. 'My Wolf is a good man. I love him. Our marriage is happy. But in the darkness comes the other man, you know what I am saying.'

'Tell me,' I had to ask, 'when you are with Wolf, making love I mean, do you sometimes pretend it is … me?'

'Not only sometimes,' she replied quickly, 'always. But I am not bad girl. I would not be going with another man. You ask me what I will do now and I must tell you I do not know. But since you walked that first day into the shop I am going crazy.'

'I would suggest,' I said, trying to sound like Greenstrum, 'that you take the mystery out of the situation. You see, fantasies can never really be fulfilled. There are always shortcomings. In your case, our case actually, getting the physical mystery out of the way might release us from the fixation.'

'You are saying that we should go to bed?'

'Yes.'

'But even if this was the good idea, where would we go? And I cannot be late back also.'

I ran over the options. Even if Hilda had sufficient time, I didn't have sufficient money to take a hotel room, nor did I have the benefit of a car which might have offered a youthful struggle on the back seat. There was the bus. Tommy had the necessary skill for sex in transit but I didn't. The last square on the board was the room I

232

shared with Sid. I looked at my watch. If Sid had run a successful meeting of the Pit Bulls, he would be back late.

'We must go back to my room,' I said, standing up.

Before the bus ride was over I had explored Hilda's soft lips with my own, and by the time we had reached Padlock Mews we were well into foreplay behind the seats. We walked on the halls of our feet up the stone steps of the house and in through the front doorway like burglars on their first job. In the darkened hallway I could hear quiet voices in the parlour but none seemed to be Sid's. All I needed was half an hour – of which my cock would have settled for ten seconds. As I led Hilda to my bedroom door, I whispered:

'Wait here a moment. I'll make sure Sid is out.'

'Somebody else is in the room?' she asked apprehensively.

'Don't think so,' I replied as I opened the door and peered around the edge. Sid was sitting up in bed with his beanie and glasses on, reading.

'I hope you had a better night with the dumpling than I did with the Pit Bulls,' he remarked, looking at me over the top of his glasses. 'Only three turned up and they wanted to talk about breeding instead of feeding.'

'Sid,' I said, 'there have been some developments. I need the room for half an hour.'

'What, with me out of it, you mean?'

'Yes. Look, I'll explain later, but I'm pretty desperate.'

'I can see that by your flushed face. Okay, give me a moment to pull on a tracksuit and I'll sit in the parlour and read for a while.'

I shut the door and turned to Hilda. 'It is important that we deal with this now,' I said, trying to remain therapeutic.

'I am not so sure,' she replied. 'Already it is late for me to be home and your friend is having to leave his bed ...'

I stopped her talking with kisses, during which I felt the air move as the bedroom door was opened and closed.

I tiptoed into the darkened room, drawing Hilda after me. We felt our way on to the bed where we undressed ourselves and each other in a shaking matrix of fingers and buttons and buckles and fasteners. As we slid between the sheets I ran my hands over Hilda's warm volume, so familiar yet so unbelievable. I quickly rose over her and sank between her smooth thighs.

***

Chapter Thirty-Five

Two weeks later as Sid and I were about to leave the dinner table, Nat pulled a newspaper from his jacket. When he held it up we saw it was *Private Eye*, the London gossip paper.

'How do you like this for a headline?' he suddenly boomed. '"No Pong at the Palace".'

We knew immediately this was Nat's finest hour. He'd cracked royalty. He read on.

'"The Queen's Corgis are now stink free, according to sources inside Buckingham Palace. The royal keepers of the dogs have been feeding the Corgis a new American pet-food that makes dog turds odourless. Even the cans biodegrade into soil nutrients. Our source said that the Queen was seen in the garden actually picking up a corgi turd after being assured by a palace employee that it was safe to handle".'

'There's more, but you can read it later,' Nat said, looking around the table. 'Do you know what this means? Do you really know what this fucking means?'

'What does it mean, Nat?' Anne O'Grady asked dutifully.

'It means that we're off the launch pad. We're riding the fucking rocket to the stars. You watch the rest of the media take it up. *Private Eye* has started an avalanche.'

'Is *cafe* mentioned in the story?' Sid asked.

'No, and all the better,' Nat replied. 'Leaves something for the other boys. You watch. The company will be named and then every paper and television station will run the story. All the contacts we've made will ride with us. Pet owners will all want to be using the Queen's choice.'

I thought immediately of Tommy. I imagined him in a crowded train holding a whole carriage spellbound with his affirmations about *cafe*. He was doing very well without the media's help but with a boost like this he could become a King. And if he became a King, the *cafe* rectangular payment system would also abundantly reward Sharock-Willis. I could see Sid and me having to buy new jackets.

'What should we do about all this?' Bobby Einstein asked with a sudden new eagerness. He'd seemed ready to drop out of network marketing *cafe* and return to flute playing. He needed a break.

'Sit tight until the media storm hits,' Nat said, 'but in the meantime review your beacons and links and rectangles. Yeah, and turn up the prospecting gas. We're not the only group doing *cafe* in England, you know. There's dozens of 'em, all over the goddamn country. I oughta bill them for getting this publicity.'

Nat was right about the media. *Private Eye* acted like a nursery for a good story. The tabloids picked up on *cafe* with such headlines as 'Eavesdropping on Royal Droppings' and 'Leave your Pooper Scooper at Home'. Then the television channels took up the story.

They interviewed Ellis, Sally and Gerry in Utah, punctuated by normally unshowable footage of squatting dogs and vigorously digging cats. Finally *The Times on Sunday* succumbed to the excitement with an analysis of pet-food, culminating with *cafe*'s groundbreaking formula and a reminder that is was protected by worldwide patents.

While all this was happening Sid and I worked our down-lines and our prospecting like a gold rush. I stopped only to eat, sleep and see Hilda. We shared a permanently recurring hunger for which there seemed to be no satisfaction. Had it not been for her watching relatives and my absorbing excitement over *cafe*, we might have spent the rest of our lives in bed. I was surprised that I felt no guilt about Hilda. My weekly call to Clarice and the girls was no less loving because of Hilda. I suppose I had lived with her for so long in my head that, when I met her, she was already accounted for. One day I would tell Greenstrum the sequel to his fantasy treatment.

***

Chapter Thirty-Six

About six weeks after the media explosion over *cafe*, the first ripple of a money wave lapped into our mailbox. Sid, who handled the accounts for Sharock-Willis, took me into our bedroom and threw a thick computer printout down on the wobbly wicker table.

'That's now our down-line,' he said, 'and this is what they've earned for us.' He showed me a cheque for fifty-eight thousand pounds. 'If we kept this up, we'd be on an annual income of nearly two hundred and fifty grand. And remember these are pommy pounds. In Australian dollars that's even more serious money.'

***

I stared at the *cafe* cheque, remembering our first one for sixteen dollars and eight cents. 'That's as long as it keeps up,' I said. 'You know how distributors can drop out.'

'I spoke to Nat about that,' Sid replied. 'He reckons that with the momentum we've got going, and the fact that *cafe* is addictive to the animals that eat it, the network should just keep growing. But that's no excuse for taking it easy, he says. Going on with prospecting will stop the money going to our heads until we can subconsciously handle it. He's been through it all.'

'I certainly don't intend to stop,' I said. 'One good month doesn't create a recurring income. In any case, we owe Nat quite a bit of money. We'll have to pay him back before we can claim any of the income as our own.'

'There's one more thing,' Sid said, taking a letter from his pocket. 'The company congratulates us for going from an Earl to a Lord. We leapfrogged over being a Baron. Now we can wear the burgundy jacket, but Nat says to wait for a month because he thinks we'll graduate to a Prince.'

'That's only one below King,' I said. 'My God, how did this happen so quickly?'

'When you go over the network genealogy you'll see why,' Sid said. 'As soon as we get twelve Earls or higher on our front line we become a King. Right now, we've got seven and when we get to eight we can wear the yellow jacket of a Prince.'

'How is Tommy going?' I asked.

'He's flying,' Sid said. 'He's a Lord already and could be a King in two months. And Tommy's got a certain queen to thank for his accommodation on the public transport system and for her dogs eating *cafe*.'

***

Two months later, with the English summer turning on the occasional day worthy of the season, I came in from a twilight walk with Hilda and found an envelope on my pillow. It was an unwelcome contrast to what had just taken place in the gardens. As I opened it I feared it might be from Wolf, who had somehow found out about Hilda and me, and was challenging me to a duel. But the note gave away very little. It was typed, and invited me to dinner the next night at Claridge's. It implored me to tell nobody about the invitation, but if I was unable to attend, I was asked to call the restaurant and cancel my name from the list.

The list? Did that mean there were many people going? I guessed it would be a *cafe* celebration organised by Nat, with maybe Morton Whitbread or even Ellis or Sally or Gerry. I knew that we had the most successful group in England, and that we would be making plenty of money for the company. But it was rare for the directors to spend time congratulating distributors; the commission payouts did that by demonstration. If the invitation had something to do with *cafe*, then Sid would have been invited too. But the note clearly asked me not to discuss it with anybody.

At supper that night I tried to get some clues about the meeting by finding out the immediate plans of our *cafe* distributor group. Most said they had prospecting appointments the next night. Luckily I had nothing booked, but Sid said he would be going to Charing Cross to help run a big meeting for Tommy.

I spent a night of broken sleep, dreaming of finding money under bushes in the twilight and being shot by dry cats' turds from Wolf's gun.

I welcomed the dawn and the busy day ahead of me. A letterbox drop of a brochure on which I had lavished my pent-up advertising energy was bringing results. The responding suburban animal owners had to be followed up before they lost interest, and I had an appointment each hour for most of the day. Apart from the chance to sign up users and distributors, the campaign gave me a look inside hundreds of London homes, with their furnishing oddities and their feeling of impending financial ruin.

I arrived home about six o'clock, took a shower and dressed in my yellow jacket and dark grey slacks. If this was to be a *cafe* function I wanted to appear in my princely garb. Although our bank account was only just getting on its feet, I splurged on a taxi to Claridge's and arrived at the invited time of seven-thirty. I looked across the lavishly appointed tables for a familiar face or a group sitting in formation. A voice at my shoulder made me turn around. I was facing Sid.

'So you got this *cafe* invitation too,' I said, noting his yellow jacket. 'Do you know who the host is?'

'You're looking at him,' Sid said. 'Since we virtually sleep together I thought I'd like to take you out to dinner.'

'You raging old queen,' I said. 'Come on, what's the real reason?'

'Let's eat and all shall be revealed to you,' he said as he signalled to the waiter to seat us. I followed to a table next to the window, where the lights of London looked posed for a tourist brochure. A bottle of champagne sat in a bucket beside the table. After the waiter had poured each of us a flute Sid raised his to mine.

'Here's to us,' he said. 'I'm glad we defied gravity to do network marketing.'

'Okay,' I said as I put down my glass, 'you've got the toast out of the way; make the speech.'

'You and I are due to be separated,' he said.

'Has a room come up at Padlock Mews?'

'Not only that, but something else has as well.' He pulled a piece of paper from his pocket. It was a cheque, its familiar gold edge telling me it was from *cafe*. I took it from Sid and looked at it. The amount was ninety-eight thousand pounds.

'In the words of Andy Hope at Lead Balloon,' I said, 'this is fucking rad. As long as it keeps up.'

'Oh, it will,' Sid cut me short. 'I've done some calculations on the automatic delivery system that almost every customer has taken up. This is probably the smallest monthly cheque we will get from now on. Hence this dinner, the champagne and the separation suggestion. We can afford to move to virtually wherever we like. We could take a mansion with bedrooms to burn.'

'Well I'd like to get my own bedroom again,' I said, 'although I don't say that just because of Hilda. I don't know how much longer she will be staying in London.'

'How serious are you about her?' Sid asked.

'Physically I'm hooked,' I replied, 'but we don't have a lot going for us apart from that. I don't think we could live together. We don't share the same sense of the absurd, or the same taste in food or movies or opinions on a whole lot of things. We don't have to face our differences because our situation is occasional and temporary. Wolf, her husband, has been to visit her a couple of times, and I can see that he makes her happy – even though she can't wait to get back into the sack with me. We're each other's narcotic. Now, you tell me about Anne O'Grady.'

'It's out of steam,' Sid said. 'Well for me it is. Fucking a nun was exciting because it was kind of forbidden. But now she's become just an ordinary woman – and a good friend as well.'

***

Sid and I tried to ignore the money now flooding into our bank account. Apart from buying a car each, we kept our financial position out of sight. In particular, we did not share it with our wives, who were becoming more and more insistent that we return home and put our network marketing failure behind us.

Sid kept his old room and I got Anne O'Grady's downstairs when she moved in with Bobby Einstein – which immediately silenced his flute playing.

The business opportunity meetings we held at the Goat Hair Weavers Guild Hall became so popular that we decided to discourage the half-hearted by charging admission. Instead of stemming the flow, the numbers increased. Prospects believed that if a network marketing company had the gall to charge admission to its business presentations it must be good. We had to run meetings four nights a week to fit in everybody who wanted to hear the gospel according to *cafe*.

***

Chapter Thirty-Seven

With the money tap now turned full-on I became more and more of a slave to *cafe*, although money had little to do with it. Rather, it was a lesson learned from my years spent in advertising where I'd seen companies struggle to get a product right, win public acceptance for it and grow rich. But then a mysterious force always arose against them, as though a certain law of nature disallowed anything, good or bad, to dominate for too long.

Sid did not have the same feeling. He looked at the wealth we'd created, and imagined how he might use his share. He began to talk again about animals and their ailments, and how he could set up an animal hospital with a casualty department and operating theatres and an obstetrics ward for creatures with difficult pregnancies. He even suggested hospital counsellors for people whose animals had died.

I don't know how long we might have kept working the *cafe*

money machine at Padlock Mews. I suppose at some point we might have earned enough or prospected enough people or created a large enough network to stop feeding it. But the mysterious force was at work well ahead of any decision we might have made.

As autumn began decaying the leaves of London trees and sharpening the air, there came a short message from the company. Nat was asked to organise a meeting of English *cafe* Kings, Princes and Lords in London so that the company could make a face-to-face announcement. We wondered why it couldn't wait until the annual *cafe* court convention in Salt Lake City in three months' time. Sid and I had planned to visit Australia after the convention, clad in our purple jackets, and smite our wives with our success. Then we would decide on the best course for our families. But now the London meeting had put everything on hold.

Had the company invited all its English distributors, it would have needed Wembley stadium to hold them. Even as it was, there were almost two thousand Kings, Princes and Lords. Bobby Einstein convinced Nat to book the Royal Festival Hall, remembering the time he had played there as part of the Chicago Symphony Orchestra on tour.

Anybody who could get the Queen's dogs to change their diet could surely book the Royal Festival Hall at short notice for one night, Nat reasoned. He followed the network marketing principle of looking for a referral from the highest level. He called Buckingham Palace. Using the questioning technique he got as far as the assistant to the Queen's private secretary before he had to declare his hand. Like seconds at a boxing match we sat with him in the parlour while he made the call.

'Okay, so you don't have anything to do with booking the Royal Festival Hall,' he said close to the mouthpiece, 'I follow that. But goddamn, if the place is called royal, Her Majesty must have some say in it. Listen, I'm the guy who cleaned up the corgis; you know what I mean? All I want is a name I can use when I call the hall. Does that make sense to you?'

Nat gestured urgently for paper and pen.

'Colonel Potherington-Finch I got that Just spell it for me please, miss. Okay, got it. Now, he's head of what you might call royal events, right? Yeah, I'll call him to make sure I can use his name before I go call the hall. Thank you miss, you've been very helpful. Before I go, can I ask you a question? No, forget I said that.'

He hung up and turned to us. 'Once you've got prospecting in your balls you can't switch it off,' he muttered. 'Now for these precious jerks at the hall. Winny, get the number will you?'

Winsome, the telephone book on her tight-skirted lap, ran a red fingernail up the page, wrote down a number on a piece of paper and handed it to Nat. He dialled again. This time he questioned his way right up to the Royal Festival Hall director of marketing.

'You know Colonel Potherington-Finch, right? Did he tell you Nathan Cohen was going to call you? And did he mention that Her Majesty is very interested in the outcome? Does that all make sense? Did he tell you he wants you to find a night in the next three weeks for a court function? No, a different kind of court; nothing to do with the law or the Queen. But why is that important to you? If I was to say this is just a company meeting with no catering, would that answer the challenge that is worrying you?'

Three weeks later to the day we were on our way to the Royal Festival Hall. The Cohen line, as we were known, hired a small bus to take us from Padlock Mews, except for Nat, who was already at the hall supervising the setting up. He told Winsome that the company had asked him to order a tonne of autumn leaves as decoration for the meeting.

As the hall filled around us with people dressed in purple, yellow and burgundy it looked as though we'd arrived for a contest between three sporting teams.

The decoration of the hall was nothing like the convention I remembered in Salt Lake City. It did not imitate a medieval court, with the Kings lined up in front. Instead they were mixed in with the Princes and Lords, giving the effect of a giant marble cake. The autumn leaves that Nat had been asked to procure were piled up on the stage, as if awaiting burning off by a council. There were no laser lights, no mystic entry in the dark and no food-can podium as there had been in Salt Lake City. Instead, the top of a simple wooden lectern was just visible above a pile of leaves in the middle of the stage. Harp music filled the gaps in whispered conversation.

As the lights went down, a spot followed Morton Whitbread as he walked from backstage. With a few forehands and backhands he cleared a space behind the lectern. There was some applause for his efforts.

'For you good folks who haven't been reading the *cafe* newsletters,' he said pushing his smile beyond its natural boundaries, 'I'm Morton Whitbread, *cafe* vice-president for international marketing. I want to welcome you to a very special meeting and I want to thank you, one and all, for giving us the time from your busy lives to be here tonight.'

'Puke,' Sid commented quietly.

'As this meeting progresses, I want you to remember one thing,' Morton continued. 'We could have sent all our distributors letters to make this announcement. Nothing compelled us to travel here and arrange this meeting – except our love for you.' He paused to blow his nose and continued with more creamy talk. After a couple more references to love, accompanied by more nose-blowing, he introduced Gerry Silver, one of the three company partners.

Gerry began with a few amusing stories about dogs and cats that the company, he said, had collected for a book it planned to publish soon. Then he went on to elevate the attendees to angelic status, and repeated the fact that the company did not have to hold this meeting at all. We waited patiently for him to get down to the gristle.

'Well, why are we all here?' he asked finally. 'I'm here to tell you that *cafe* has not only rewritten the pet-food industry record book, it has also rewritten the network marketing record book. We've gone faster and further than any company in history in either pet-food or network marketing. Let's give ourselves a round of applause for that.' Spindly clapping washed around the seats.

'But that has taken its toll on everybody,' Gerry continued, with furrowed brows. 'Sally, Ellis and I haven't had a good night's sleep in three years. I guess that might go for many of you too. Network marketing is a fine way to sell product but it takes a power of work and organising.

'What I have to tell you is that our company has accepted an offer from Uncle Ben, America's biggest pet-food company. In four weeks' time *cafe* will cease to be sold through the network and will start to become available in supermarkets.

'We know that many of you have come to rely on your businesses in *cafe* but now, like us, you're going to get a rest from your labours and you're going to walk away with the money you deserve.

'If you read the terms and conditions of your distributor agreements you'll see that we have the absolute right to terminate the network at any time. We could just walk away with our sale money and say "too bad guys, it's over". But we are not going to do that. No sir-ree. We love you all, and we're going to share our good fortune with you. I'm going to ask Morton here to present the plan to you.'

Gerry scuffed away to one side through the leaves and Morton replaced him at the top of the pile.

'Pretty big news, huh?' he chortled throatily. 'Now here's what's in it for you. We're going to pay out all commissions owing on goods sold and on forward orders. And here's the good part. We will pay triple commission from tonight until all the deliveries have been made. And after that, you will have the lifetime right to purchase *cafe* at wholesale prices. How's that for a deal?'

At this point I think Morton and Gerry expected, or at least hoped for, applause. But the Royal Festival Hall was so quiet it could have been empty. Morton cranked up his smile again which set off a round of booing.

An angry King stood up and yelled 'Fucking robbers!'

'We'll take questions in a few moments,' Morton said holding up his hand. 'First we need to go over how to handle your down-lines. We have some suggestions as to how you should approach them.'

The angry King, still standing and embellishing his opinion of the company owners, was joined by twenty others, including some other Kings. They each had a different way of expressing their opinion. None was flattering.

'Folks, folks, please be calm,' Morton pleaded. 'We don't have to be here, you know.'

Now everybody was shouting. The Royal Festival Hall had seen many standing ovations, but this was probably the most enthusiastic standing denunciation. People began moving down the isles towards the stage. Morton stood in his pile of leaves pleading for calm until a muscly young Prince leaped up on to the stage. The Prince was grabbed by a couple of security guards but it was obvious that the small security team could not control the major uprising that was brewing. Morton and Gerry turned and dashed away backstage through a swirl of leaves.

What would an angry English mob do with its victims if it caught them? Morton and Gerry decided not to find out. Well before the crowd could intercept them outside at the stage door, they had been swept away in their waiting car. That didn't stop the Kings, Lords and Princes from charging out on to the pavement and scurrying about looking for them, like dogs after lost balls. And, as the distributors came to realise that this was the end of the meeting, and the end of *cafe* network marketing, they craved a vent for their anger. In hotter-blooded parts of the world the mob would have gone on a looting rampage, but the *cafe* distributors were not violent people, especially those who had won the right to wear leaders' jackets.

In the street I found myself close to the King who had been the first to stand up in the hall. His anger had passed the point where shouting abuse would relieve it. He had to take some action. He tore off his purple jacket and, twirling it high above his head, ran to the low wall that separated the forecourt from the river and flung it into the Thames.

This was the lead that the distributors wanted. As if on fire, everybody began tearing off their jackets, swinging them around in the air and throwing them into the dark water. I saw some camera flashes go off and wondered who was taking pictures.

'Are you going to chuck yours?' I asked Sid. He replied by taking his glasses and wallet from his purple jacket and, with a warlike shout, running to the wall and hurling it over. After quelling a brief pang of remorse for throwing away something that I had taken such effort in acquiring, I followed Sid's example. Below, in the water, a massive creature had been born. Its back was a patchwork of yellow, burgundy and purple, and it swam just below the surface, moving deeper as the river carried it away from the Royal Festival Hall. Above, on the pavement, the creature's parents were now beginning to feel the autumn cold and wanting to go home.

***

Chapter Thirty-Eight

The next day marked the beginning of a permanent holiday from prospecting that nobody wanted. We lingered over breakfast, knowing that afterwards we would have to spend the day telephoning our down-line of Barons, Earls and Courtiers to tell them that *cafe* network marketing was finished, and that their work would not give them the everlasting income that the company had promised.

I delayed starting the task by taking a walk up to the village to get the paper and a couple of buns for Mrs Warboys. I was curious to see if there was any press coverage of the Festival Hall meeting.

Considering I had just lost my primary source of income, I marched along inhaling the sharp morning air with unexpected exuberance. Perhaps it was because a difficult decision had been made for me by the company, and I could indulge myself in an indignation not deeply felt. As I cautiously greeted Hilda at the bread shop I realised that I would have more time for her now that *cafe* would not be occupying me. I relished the arrangement we had made to meet that evening.

I bought the *Mirror* from the newsagent and glanced at the front page as I prepared to fold it and walk home. There was a large, poignant photograph showing a *cafe* jacket caught in the fork of a stump that had been exposed when the Thames tide had run out. The heading read: 'Police Search for One Man and Find a Thousand'. The story told of a mystery flotilla of jackets that had caused alarm when the outgoing tide had left them strewn along the banks of the Thames. At first police believed that one person had been drowned. Then they thought there had been a mass suicide of sect members. Eventually they discovered that the jackets had been thrown into the river by disgruntled distributors of a network marketing company after a meeting at Festival Hall. The story spilled to page six where there was a picture of the angry King twirling his jacket and a small shot of Morton and Gerry running through autumn leaves.

I hurried home to tell my fellow *cafe* travellers but, by the time I arrived, Nat was chairing a meeting at the dining table.

'Sit down Ed,' he said as I walked in. 'I see you've got the paper so you know what's happening. What you don't know is that I organised the photographers last night. I found out what the *cafe* bastards were up to while I was setting up for them yesterday afternoon. Also, what nobody knows is that I've been in touch with all the television stations. I know where Mort and Gerry are staying, and so do the news editors by now. Boy, are they going to get some hot poker.'

'Well, that might be good for revenge,' Anne O'Grady sniffed, 'but it doesn't give us anything.'

'Don't bet on it,' Nat replied. 'I wouldn't have wasted my time just sticking it up them. See, they're about to launch *cafe* to the general public all over. This story is going to fuck their publicity unless they make a big about-face. They'll be asked to go on the news tonight and if they give a re-run of last night's spiel the news boys will start getting opinions from the distributors like us. What are we gonna say? Nice stuff about them? I don't think so.'

'Do we have a legal case against them?' Sid asked

'Legal schmegal, what can I tell you?' Nat replied with shrugged shoulders. 'You can always make a case but this would be a hard one to win, to say nothing of the cost, and international lawyers as well. I'd forget about it. Better to hit them on reputation. Let them have to take us to court to shut us up.'

'So do we still tell our down-lines the game is over?' Bobby Einstein asked.

'You might as well let them know straight away,' Nat said, 'but tell them the Kings have gone to war for them on the compensation deal.'

We left the dining room and began telephoning. The business presentation meetings that had been booked, the appointments that had been made, the samples that were being tried, the dreams of wealth; it all had to be disconnected. Winsome cancelled the Goat Hair Weavers Guild Hall and everybody who was booked to come to meetings there over the next couple of weeks had to be notified. We found we were just as busy stopping the network as starting it. Telling the same story over and over, and listening to the same anger and threats from the distributors soon became exhausting. My capacity for sympathy thinned towards the end of the day and it was only the thought of Hilda's cherry-topped mountains and deep, warm gullies that kept me from hanging up on people.

We gathered around the television set in the parlour for the evening news. First came the international disasters, the death of a famous soccer player and a political scandal, before we reached the local news. And then, across wind-whipped Thames waves, we zoomed into the river bank where seagulls strutted carefully among a muddy wash-up of purple, yellow and burgundy jackets. It could have been an orgy of dead embracing people, except that the bodies were missing.

'This is what distributors of a pet-food company thought of being given their marching orders last evening,' the voice-over said. 'After they got the news at a meeting at the Royal Festival Hall they threw their company colour-coded jackets into the Thames in protest.' The picture panned up the river bank to an old brick wall where Gerry and Morton stood gazing down at the jackets. Then it moved to their right where a young male interviewer stood, his sandy hair flying in his face as he tried to stop his concerned look being contorted by the wind. He put a microphone close to his mouth.

'Company directors Mr Gerry Silver and Mr Morton Whitbread addressed the meeting last night, but they say that they were only halfway through explaining their offer when infiltrators disrupted the proceedings. Mr Silver, tell us what happened.'

'Look, we'd called a meeting we didn't have to call,' Gerry replied, also through flying hair. 'Our company is making a switch from marketing through a multi-level network to conventional retailing. We wanted to be ethical and tell the distributors face to face.'

'Your company markets pet-food, is that correct?'

Gerry nodded at the camera.

'That's the *cafe* brand which produces odourless excreta, isn't it?'

'Yes, that's the one,' Gerry agreed enthusiastically. 'The Queen's corgis eat it.'

'But isn't it a fact that you have sold the company and left the distributors high and dry?' The camera panned down to the jackets.

'We've sold, yes, but our distributors are being well compensated.'

'What was the sale price, Mr Silver?'

'I can't give you an exact figure on that,' Gerry said, blinking his long lashes rapidly in discomfort.

'Would it be more than a billion dollars, Mr Silver?'

'A confidentiality agreement prevents me from confirming or denying.'

'If it were over a billion, wouldn't the distributors be entitled to some of that?'

'They would and they are,' Gerry replied. 'We're sending them letters to explain it all. They didn't let us finish last night. We believe a competitor set out to sabotage the meeting. We expect *cafe* to make life very difficult for all other pet-food companies.'

'*Mazel tov!*' Nat shouted, and clapped his meaty hands. 'They're on *shpilkers*.'

***

It took Sid and I four days to get messages to all our down-lines. We told them that even though *cafe* network marketing was over, they would be hearing directly from the company on a generous settlement, forced upon it by the heroic Kings.

Two days of rest followed, the first of which coincided with Hilda's day off. We drove down to Nottingham Forest and went walking in the woody mush of autumn. The symbolism of decaying leaves that Gerry and Morton had chosen fluttered into my life too. Here was the end of summer, the end of *cafe* and nearly the end of my stay in England. As soon as the settlement letter arrived and we had received whatever the company was going to give us, there was nothing to hold me in London. Except Hilda. But it was autumn with her too.

'I am now the good baker and Wolf is impatient,' she said, on the way home. 'Soon I must be coming to Hamburg.'

'When is soon?' I asked.

'Maybe in one week,' she replied. 'I wonder how we will get on, Eddy.'

'Same as before we met,' I said, 'except we'll have our real memories to back up the fantasies.'

'Only I have one fear,' she replied, 'that in the middle of making love to Wolf I would call him Eddy. Because he will be Eddy at that time, otherwise I have no coming.'

'I'll probably face the same problem,' I said. 'We'll just have to learn to shut up.'

We ate an early dinner at a little restaurant in one of the villages off the expressway. With all the sexy talk, and Hilda's body straining to escape from its tight pants and sweater, I wanted to get her into bed at Padlock Mews as soon as possible, and leave enough time for her to arrive home to Eva's at a respectable hour.

We slipped into the house at nine o'clock and made the safety of my room without anybody except Adolph seeing us.

Of all the times I'd been with Hilda, I found that night the most exciting – and also the most exhausting. I had planned to stay awake to drive her home but instead I fell into a deep sleep, dreaming about being in an aeroplane where Hilda was the pilot, and laughingly admitting she didn't know how to fly.

I woke suddenly just before dawn and was alarmed to find myself still pressed against warm mounds in my bed. What would Hilda say to her brother-in-law now? Could she have made an excuse for being out all night or was this the beginning of a scary situation?

I groped my way out to the toilet and when I came back I cuddled into her back in the dark, pushing against the curve of her inviting arse. I woke again to her wriggling back against me until I got hard. Then she rolled over on to her stomach. This is the last time, I thought, as I saluted the twin hills and sank into the deep valley between them.

Fittingly, we climaxed together, producing a curtain-closing duet: groans from me and a torrent of strangely familiar God-talk into the pillow from her.

She rolled on to her back, took my face in her hands and kissed me.

'You might remember me – from some time ago,' a fat Clarice said. 'I've come to claim my Ed back. I love you.'

Was this an extension of the dream? I had to sit up in bed and focus on the window, where light was seeping around the edge of the blinds, to convince myself I was awake. Clarice sat up too, looking carefully around the wearied room.

'Poor darling,' she sighed. 'Just look at this. You've worked so hard and gotten nowhere. I never had faith in your pyramid scheme from the beginning. I hope you've had enough and that I can take you home. The girls miss you so much – and so do I. And don't worry about money. I've got a job with a travel agent. They flew me here for nothing.'

I kissed her delightfully plump cheek. 'You'll have to forgive me darling, I'm a bit dumbfounded,' I replied, trying to keep my voice from slipping into falsetto. 'But to answer you, yes, I'm done with *cafe*. The company has sold out on network marketing anyway. There's just one matter to clear up and then we're out of here.'

I swung myself out of bed in a concealed state of shock, took a shower and dressed while Clarice stayed to sleep off her jet lag. I left the darkened room and found Sid sitting in the parlour reading the paper.

'I've just been through a paranormal experience,' I said shakily. 'I went to bed with Hilda and woke up with Clarice.'

'Thanks to some fancy footwork on my part,' Sid said, smiling over the top of his glasses. 'Clarice arrived from the airport after midnight and luckily I let her in. Then I had to make sure there was room for her in your bed. I thought three might have caused overcrowding. I pitched Clarice a story about looking for a duplicate key to your room because you might have been still out at a meeting. Luckily I found that Hilda had already departed for the bread shop.'

'I owe you one,' I told him.

'Several,' he replied. 'There's more. Hilda phoned. She wants you to call her about a bridge game – if that makes sense.'

'Yes, it does,' I said. 'May I use the phone in your room?'

Sid nodded. I went quickly upstairs and dialled the Go-to Bakery number.

'I am available for bridge again tonight,' Hilda said formally.

'But I can't,' I replied. 'My wife has turned up unexpectedly.'

'This I don't believe,' Hilda laughed. And then quietly, with her hand cupping the mouthpiece, 'Can you come to the bakery in one hour when Eva is on break? Only the new junior will be here at that time.'

'Okay,' I said, and hung up.

I went back to the parlour.

'If Clarice wakes up could you tell her I took the dog for a walk?' I asked Sid.

Adolph was both surprised and pleased at being roused from the kitchen floor to accompany me on the familiar stroll towards the village. Along the way he showed he still remembered our routine as he approached another small dog on a lead and looked around for me to begin a conversation with its owner. When I failed to play my part he sat on his haunches and stared at me. He had to shake off the habit of networking too. I wondered what might happen to him now that he was no longer needed for *cafe* assignments. I made a mental note to talk to Sid about an annuity for Adolph, with Mrs Warboys as the executor – as long as she could be trusted with the money. No, better we should place an ongoing food order for him. I couldn't see Mrs Warboys sitting down to a plate of Adolph's *cafe*.

I was too early for my appointment with Hilda so I took Adolph on a sentimental journey to Worsley Common, remembering the prospecting I had done there and a twilight crawl into the bushes with Hilda.

We returned via the bakery where I tethered Adolph to the bus stop post and went in.

'*Ja*,' Hilda said when she saw me, 'you have come to check the oven, yes?'

I raised my eyebrows and then nodded.

'Please you will come and I will show you,' she commanded. 'Sophie, watch the shop and call if you need that I should help.' She led me through the back of the shop where there were the preparation tables and three ovens. Although the day's baking was done, the ovens were still warm and the smell of fresh bread lingered overpoweringly.

Hilda took both my hands in hers and rested her soft eyes on mine.

'This is not the romantic place,' she said, 'but there is no time to find a better one. This morning Wolf calls and he is coming tomorrow. I think he stays for a few days and then takes me back. And your wife comes also, you tell me. This is again spooky, Eddy.'

'You'll never know how spooky,' I replied. 'So this might be our last meeting.'

'It is,' she said. 'I am sad, but not too much. It will be good to go home with Wolf.'

I closed my eyes and took her in my arms and gently kissed her mouth. When I opened my eyes she was thankfully still Hilda.

Sophie called for assistance. On our way back into the shop Hilda put two Bath buns into a bag and gave them to me. I left the shop without looking back as she began to show Sophie how to make a box from a flat-pack for a customer's birthday cake.

When I reached Padlock Mews Sid was waiting for me outside.

'I think Clarice is still asleep,' he said, 'but I didn't want to take a chance. The mail has just arrived with an agreement from *cafe* for us to sign.'

'What do we have to agree to?'

'Not to make any further financial demands on the company, and not to speak to the press, and to write a testimonial saying, to our knowledge, that the performance claims made for the products are absolutely genuine.'

'And what do we get in return?'

Sid coughed and giggled. 'As Kings, we get a settlement equal to double the amount of commission we earned in the last twelve months. Do you know how much that is?'

'Not exactly,' I replied, but it must be huge.'

'Enough to retire on,' Sid said.

'If we were the retiring types,' I said clapping him on the arm. 'Let's get inside and get the paper work done before Clarice wakes up and starts investigating.'

'You're not going to tell her?' Sid asked as we crunched along the gravel path leading to the back door.

'No. She's come all the way to London to bring me home under her wing. I love her for that. I'm not going to spoil it for her. Are you going to tell Stacey?'

262

'Not straight away. I'm going to enjoy her believing I was a bloody idiot. I'll pick my moment. It's nice to have an ace up the sleeve.'

'More like a whole pack,' I said as I went into the kitchen to give the paper bag I was carrying to Mrs Warboys.

We went upstairs and began work on our written assignments. I paused midway to ask Sid to dispose of my nice Jaguar before Clarice connected me with it, and to ask Nat not to reveal our financial position.

***

Chapter Thirty-Nine

Clarice brought me back to Sydney as a wounded soldier from a war. I fell easily into the role she set up for me. I wasn't smug about being secretly rich but I was cautious about revealing it. I needed to give myself time to reassess the dynamics of the family.

Clarice was revelling in being saviour and provider. Through her own efforts alone she had secured a job and an income. She had organised the girls to take more responsibility for themselves and had developed an appreciation for money that she would never have while I was earning it all. To show her my bulging bank balance would have risked destroying her self-esteem. I had to wait, and in the meantime allow myself to be nursed back to sanity.

I naturally fell into the role of house-husband. I learned to use home appliances efficiently and to shop sensibly at the supermarket and even to cook a few simple but unpopular meals.

I felt guilty about opening a secret bank account and the fact that just the interest from it could have enabled us to live very much better, but I was being led by some, yet to be revealed, divine purpose.

Clarice insisted I take a good break before looking for a job. What I couldn't tell her was that I didn't want a job – even if I could find one. Outwardly I appeared to be the husband she'd rescued from network marketing deep space and returned him to the Earth of normal, decent living. But like certain other doomed space travellers, I carried the alien inside me. The questioning technique was growing impatient to be used. I yearned to sell products you couldn't buy in a shop, nut out compensation plans, run business opportunity meetings, inspire up-lines and down-lines. Take all that away and what was I? A worn-out advertising writer.

To please Clarice I bought the paper and drew red circles around jobs that Apparent-Ed could apply for. I quickly showed her that to rise above subsistence wages I needed to be a qualified engineer or a qualified accountant, or a qualified prison officer or a qualified chicken sexer – qualified either by certificate or by experience. Lowering the bar, I could apply to fill the position of night attendant in a caravan park, or dash about replacing dead car batteries, or polish acres of office floors at two o'clock in the morning. I could shovel sand into a cement mixer for a   bad-tempered brickie, or deliver pizzas, or spend eight hours a day cleaning fish.

'It's obvious that you should look for something in sales,' Clarice concluded. 'If there's nothing in the paper why don't you call up some of your friends at the yacht club or the golf club? And you made so many contacts working for *cafe* – surely somebody there could help. You'd make such a good salesman, Ed.'

I took time off from my household duties to sit in coffee shops and stare into cappuccino froth trying to find an employment message. I went for long walks on the harbour cliff-tops and listened for instructions from seagulls. I sailed *Three Oranges* on languid afternoons and gazed into the teal water for a job solution written in sun reflections. But nothing presented itself.

After some initial amusement, visiting the supermarket began to terrify me. It was full of spectres: retirees who pulled out calculators to see whether the bigger jar of jam represented a better buy. Paying, they milled around me, welcoming me to their world of metered money and pacemakers and piss-stained pants. I shopped as quickly as possible, making a habit of looking only at the shelves.

At last providence took pity on me, outside the supermarket as luck would have it. A roughly-printed sign was taped to the light pole next to my car. I tore it down and stuffed it into one of the white plastic bags I was loading.

I couldn't wait to get my shopping home. My quick perusal of the sign caught the telltale words 'work from home'. When I read it in detail it gave an even stronger clue towards network marketing. It promised no requirement of capital, an ethical product, free training, unlimited income. There was a mobile phone number to call. I rushed into my study to dial.

'This is Murray,' a male voice answered.

'Murray, did you leave a sign on a light pole in Mosman?' I asked, feeling the exhilarating rush of the questioning technique retrieved from storage.

'Yes, one of many. Could I have your name please?'

'Before I give you that, would you answer a question?'

'Yes. Fire away.'

'Is this about network marketing?'

I could feel Murray's sudden reticence through the phone. 'Well, it depends what you mean by network marketing,' he said.

'What do you mean by network marketing?' I countered.

'I don't mean pyramid schemes,' Murray replied, 'they're illegal. This is a legitimate business. Look, the only way you'll understand the opportunity is for me to show it to you, one on one.'

'Now you're doing better,' I couldn't help complimenting him. 'Another question: what's the product?'

'It's new. It's called BBK.'

'Standing for?'

'Look, I appreciate your interest, but if you want to know any more we'll have to meet.'

'Bravo Murray,' I said, 'you've shown some posture. But you've still got a few things to learn. Okay, when and where can we meet?'

**

Chapter Forty

Murray lived in a functional-only block of units which had once been housing commission accommodation but was now forced up-market by inner suburban prices. The lift to the ninth floor had been repainted but the engraved graffiti was still visible beneath the new speckled surface.

Murray answered the door in a navy tracksuit, a towel slung around his neck. His thinning dark hair sprang from his scalp as if trying to get away. As we shook hands I noticed he was sweating.

'I see you do a bit of training,' I said as he led me past an untidy bedroom and another room where a punching bag hung from the ceiling.

'Yeah, I try to keep fit. I used to do some boxing, mostly amateur. I took it up early. See, my surname is Pansy.'

We sat down at a table in the lounge room. Out of habit I went for the first question:

'Could we start with the product, Murray?'

'Before that, Ed, I need to smell your breath.'

I was taken by surprise. Maybe I'd come across a kinky bastard who would suddenly turn an innocent sniff into a crafty kiss. 'I'd rather you didn't,' I replied.

'Look, it's not threatening,' he said, smiling for the first time. 'It's to demonstrate the product. It's called the Better Breath Kit; BBK for short. If you've got perfect breath it is obviously of no use, but only fifteen per cent of people have perfect breath. The rest need BBK. The test analyses and rates your breath using our patent Offendaliser, which puts up the results on a little screen. BBK markets both the Offendaliser and the treatment products.'

'It reminds me of another product, also devised to eliminate unpleasant smells,' I said. 'You might have heard of it. It's pet-food called *cafe.*'

'Good God,' Murray said, 'that networking outfit is a legend. We pinched a lot of what you guys did. We use it in our executive training. The way the company left you high and dry was a shocker.'

'Depends which way you look at it,' I replied. 'But that's all behind me now. I'm after a new challenge.'

He leaned across the table close to my face. 'Come on, just a quick puff,' he murmured seductively. 'Say hurrah.'

I took a deep breath and obeyed with a voluminous cheer.

'Not bad,' he said sitting back in his chair, 'especially for an older bloke. Most oldies rank well down the stale list – in the direction of a sewer rating. Now if you were a prospect, I'd get you to blow into the Offendaliser, take a reading and prescribe a remedy which is always a mixture made up from BBK's six herbal essences. They're harmless, incidentally. There are various ways of taking them too.'

'Clever, but a bit restrictive,' I said.

'Not nearly as much as pet-food,' he replied indignantly. 'Only a certain number of people have a dog or a cat but everybody's got a mouth. Just think, when this thing gets going people will be going around boasting about their rating and breathing into each other's faces. There will be international breath competitions, garlic and onion resistance trophies. It will be huge, and we're in on the ground floor.'

'A familiar story,' I said, 'but you might be right. Tell me, how did you get into this BBK?'

'I'm actually a schoolteacher,' Murray replied, 'senior science and maths. One of my students started turning up at school in a new Mercedes and the story went around that he'd bought it out of network marketing commissions. He started selling BBK in the school and, before long, a lot of the senior students had become his down-line. They'd hold breath assessments at lunchtime. I broke up a meeting one day and while I was hauling this young fellow over the coals for doing business at school he prospected me. I suddenly saw the big picture – although I must say my wife still hasn't. That's why I'm living here.'

'And how are you doing?'

'Started out okay with my warm circle, but now I've hit the wall.'

'You can't cold-call, right?' I said.

'So you know about that.'

'A lot about it. Tell me, do you use marketing by beacons or the questioning technique to uncover the pain in your prospect?'

'I don't know what you're talking about,' he said.

'Right,' I said, feeling an elation that was like meeting an old lover. 'I want you to pretend you've never heard of BBK or me.'

He nodded.

'Mr Pansy, do you enjoy talking to people?'

'Yes. In fact it is the main part of my job.'

'Does this involve intimate conversations?'

'Yes, it does.'

'Do you like to speak in confidential tones, close to somebody's nose?'

'Sometimes.'

'Would foul breath distract the person you are talking to from concentrating on what you are saying?'

'Yes it would, I suppose.'

'If I was to tell you that there was a scientific but safe method of measuring and controlling foul breath, would you want to know about it?'

'Sure I would.'

'And if I was also to tell you that by helping other people to meet the challenge of foul breath you could make a recurring income, would you want to know about that too?'

I held up my hand to signal the end of the exercise. 'I could go on, but you get the idea. See Murray, during your presentation to me you didn't ask one question. Not one. You never got into the driver's seat.'

'But what about knowing the product, presenting the facts, reversing objections and going for the close?'

'That's how they taught your grandfather to sell,' I replied. 'There's a whole new way of selling now, and it applies especially to network marketing. If you're going to get the prospect to look seriously at your product you must get to know him first and then uncover his pain – which the product will then ease or maybe remove.'

'But not everybody is in pain.'

'Yes they are, Murray. Everybody is in pain over time or money;

many over both. If you had enough money you wouldn't be doing network marketing as a second job, and if it results in more money you will be in pain over not having enough time to spend it.'

'There must be books written about this,' Murray said. 'You didn't just think it up, did you?'

'If there are, I've never read them,' I said. 'I was taught by a New Yorker called Nat Cohen and a psychiatrist called Dr Greenstrum and my mate Sid Willis – and I suppose I taught myself some of it too.'

I looked at my watch. 'Hey, Clarice will be home,' I said. 'I must go and heat up my rabbit casserole.'

'No Ed, please don't leave,' Murray implored. 'I need to hear more. Can I at least have your phone number?'

'Let me think about that Murray,' I said as I stood up. 'Tell you what. Give me your phone number instead. I'll let you know if I decide to become a distributor. My wife thinks I ought to be a salesman. There may be some resistance to my taking on BBK.'

As I drove home I struggled with what I would tell Clarice. I could pretend that I'd taken a sales job and then go to work every day in a rented office and do BBK instead. I quickly rejected that idea. It sounded like a bad re-run of what I'd done before. No, network marketing was my profession and I would pursue it for all to see – including Clarice and my daughters.

***

Chapter Forty-One

Rather than having to wait for an opening in the conversation at home to tell Clarice that I was resuming my true vocation, I purpose-booked a table at the Four Winds. I assured her that I would be paying, so that her carefully constructed budget would not be upset.

I arranged for us to be seated by an open window that inhaled the scent of early autumn across the water. Yachts nodded in their sleep just ten metres from our table. They prompted me to talk about sailing *Three Oranges*, and the unexpected delay by the yacht club in accepting my offer to return to the race committee. As we indulged ourselves in locally caught seafood and our favourite Riesling, Clarice told me about some of the new travel packages that had come up at work and the kinds of people who were taking them. If we were better off, she added, we'd cruise the fjords of Norway in July.

With such a calm image before us, I judged this a good time to download my news.

'I've taken a job.'

'How exciting, Ed.' She reached for my hand. 'Sales?'

'No, network marketing. I saw this sign on a power pole and followed it up.'

'On a power pole?' she murmured, withdrawing her hand.

'Yes, but that's not important. I'm not networking power or poles. It's called BBK, a kit to fix people's bad breath.'

I would rather Clarice had hit me over the head with the Riesling bottle and stomped out than just sit there staring at me, her eyes filling with tears. She opened and closed her mouth like a stricken fish, but said nothing.

'Look, I know you hate network marketing,' I continued, 'and I don't blame you. But it's all I've got. I can't get a decent job in anything else. I don't want to be a bloody salesman wearing a clever suit and carrying a briefcase armed with lurking laptop. I've been to hell and back learning to network. That's what I do.'

Clarice stared out at the hulls and their broken reflections in the water.

'It's worse than dealing with a rival lover,' she said huskily. 'First I lost you here, then I lost you to London for a year, and in the meantime we lost our nice standard of living and our financial future, and now, when it looks like beginning to mend, you tell me the nightmare is going to start all over again.'

'What you say is not strictly true,' I said.

'Which part isn't true? Are you going to tell me that it was all worth it, that your wonderful networking made you a fortune?'

I filled my lungs with balmy air. 'Yes,' I said quietly. 'I have made a fortune, and it's sitting in the Mosman Commonwealth Bank

earning interest which has paid for this dinner.'   C l a r i c e
returned to staring through the window. When she looked back at
me she said, 'Let's go home and make love.'

***

Chapter Forty-Two

A lthough I was Murray Pansy's down-line, he treated me like I used to treat Nat Cohen. I was his prize exhibit at the first executive meeting we attended. His up-line, a police sergeant, wanted me to begin presenting at the business opportunity meetings as soon as I could field questions about the products. He offered me an extra commission as well as fees if I would run questioning technique seminars for BBK.

I called Sid out of courtesy to see if he wanted to come back into network marketing and even revive Sharock-Willis, but he said no. He was taken up with his animal hospital plans and, in any case, he told me he never wanted to make another prospecting call in his life.

Murray asked me to set up my office in his spare room, offering to move his punching bag to the lounge room. I was prepared to help him to prospect and teach him what I knew, but my study at home, with the door closed, was like a comfortable sweater, and I wouldn't abandon it.

I set my BBK official starting day for a Monday in the middle of April. As it approached I was both excited and nervous. I remembered the difficult early days of *cafe*, and the mysterious sessions with Greenstrum. I wanted to call him to tell him about Hilda, but then thought better of it. His interest in me probably stopped when his bill was paid.

I cleaned and prepared my study on the Sunday before start day. I bought a new leather-bound prospecting book for BBK and sat it next to the much-travelled one that Nat had given me for *cafe*. I would begin by prospecting my old *cafe* contacts for BBK. After all, they were now my warm circle – or lukewarm circle at least. And even the people who had not been interested in *cafe* may now like BBK. I thought of the Chinese contacts I had made. I seemed to recall that their food could produce toxic breath. And the Japanese with their raw fish; that could do terrible things to their breath once it began to digest. There was so much pain waiting to be uncovered – for BBK to relieve.

***

Chapter Forty-Three

I waited until Clarice had departed for work and the girls for school before sliding behind my desk and opening the old and the new prospecting books together. I ran my finger down the names on an early page, trying to remember how they had responded to my first, faltering, untrained calls. Now they would hear a professional.

'Mr Ling?' I checked the cultured English voice that answered.

'Yes, this is Raymond Ling.'

'Do you remember me, Ed Sharock?'

'In what connection, Mr Sharock?'

'Do you remember us talking about feeding your dog and your cat?'

'No.'

'Would you be interested in talking about another product, much more personal?'

'Not really.'

'How would you rate your breath, Mr Ling?'

'As long as I am breathing I am satisfied.'

'If I told you that you could improve the quality of your breath and build a business by helping others to do the same, would that interest you?'

'Mr Sharock, are you trying to get me involved in network marketing?'

'Is that a problem for you?'

'Yes it is, Mr Sharock. I would normally hang up on a call like this but I've got something to say. At best, people like you just waste the time of people like me who answer the telephone. But if we show interest, you become robbers of time. I know how you work. It is like a cult. My daughter became a network distributor for a series of worthless business seminars. Do you know what we had to do, Mr Sharock? We had to take her to a psychiatric hospital to get cured. Did you know there is one with a network marketing addiction ward?'

'Is this important to improving your breath?' I said feebly.

'It might be important to saving your sanity, Mr Sharock, to say nothing of those you pull into your business.' He hung up.

That wasn't a good start. I copied Raymond Ling's name and phone number into the new book, and in the comments column I wrote 'ref. psych. hospital'.

Whether Raymond Ling was telling the truth about the hospital or not, The Channel took over and created the vision. Patients wandered the hospital grounds addressing imaginary business opportunity meetings under the big trees; they presented the products to each other using hospital whiteboards when hospital staff weren't looking; they cold-called doctors and visitors, or slipped into offices to use telephones. In group therapy sessions they promised each other exponentially-growing incomes. Some of them pretended they were cured so they could be discharged and start prospecting again. And then there was the special section for the criminally addicted. They were networkers who stalked prospects, or broke the law by addressing meetings that they had no right to address, like waiting seminar audiences or church congregations on Sunday mornings ...

I closed the record books and The Channel tiptoed away.

I could tell from the colour of the water on the Harbour that a light northerly had sprung up: the perfect wind to sail *Three Oranges* single-handed.

***

Chapter Forty-Four

Before boarding *Three Oranges*, I called into the clubhouse to satisfy my curiosity. On my way to the manager's office I passed the club noticeboard which still carried the leaflet that a vacancy existed on the race committee for an experienced member.

'Come in and take a seat,' Sandy Harris said, shaking my hand with both of his and grinning up his uneven yellow teeth. I fleetingly wondered whether the yellowing of teeth affected breath quality. He continued: 'Saw you a couple of times going for a sail and I was trying to get down to the jetty for a chat but I didn't make it. You know how it is.'

'Yes Sandy, I know. Anyhow, it's great to be home again and sail on the harbour. You'd be surprised how often I thought of the club and the guys when I was in London.'

'I heard you got out of advertising and into the pet-food business,' Sandy said. 'You still in that, Ed?'

'No, finished with pet-food,' I replied. 'I've just started marketing a new product.' I hoped he didn't want to know what it was. To stop the possible question I said: 'Sandy, did you get my offer to go back on the race committee?'

'Well yes, Ed, we did. And I thought how lucky we were that you were interested. You were very highly thought of before, you know. Anyhow, I put it through to the general committee for what I thought would be a rubber stamp.' He looked down at his desk. 'They decided to keep looking.'

'Can I ask why?'

'Well Ed, you know I can't say too much. We have to be careful of litigation, even in a friendly yacht club like this.'

'Sandy, we've known each other for too long to play games. It won't go any further, I promise. Why was I knocked back?'

'Put it this way Ed, do you remember a fella called Mat Occleshaw? He's not a member any more. He was in that detergent thing. Drove everybody in the club mad. Used the membership list like they were his customers. You probably don't remember him.'

'No, I don't,' I lied. 'Look Sandy, we'll talk about this later. I don't want the wind to pick up too much and blow me out through the heads.'

In actual fact the wind was dropping as I sailed away from the club and out around the point. I'd probably need the motor to get back in. I sailed across to a beach on the other side of the harbour, dropped anchor, put the deckchair up on the cabin roof and stretched out, eyes closed.

I took myself back to Nat Cohen's first *cafe* meeting at the yacht club. From that point, all Sid and I had thought about was how many people we could process. Nat kept reminding us it was a numbers game. If you made the calls, percentages would look after you.

Skilled callers achieved higher hit rates, but all callers got something. We cared only for the people who said yes and proceeded to sell the product. The disinterested and the unsuccessful became our wake. We didn't care who they were or how they felt. If they didn't see the big picture or didn't want the product that was okay for us because it brought us one step closer to the next 'yes'.

The wake contained plenty of what Nat called 'inconsequentials' – people who we'd never see again. But first among our prospects had been our friends, relatives, sports comrades, work mates – all people who were defenceless against allocating some of their life-time to us. A few of them had come on the journey with us – although most had eventually dropped out – but the rest we had used and immediately abandoned.

What I had despised in Mat Occleshaw I now despised in myself. And the money I had made out of it only made me feel worse.

Even though Clarice no longer needed to work for money she continued for the love of the job. And even though I could afford not to be house-husband, the duties lingered simply because I worked from home. I promised myself some domestic help but I was slow to organise it.

Before my sail to The Truth and back, I'd committed to cooking a roast for dinner that night. But by the time I had showered the salt and sun off myself at the club, it was nearly six o'clock. I drove to the Mosman shops and found one of those they'll-swear-you'd-cooked-it-yourself fast food shops. From the dazzling lights of its glass display counters I became a champion cook. I bought the lamb-set multiplied by four, and hurried home before it cooled too much.

I didn't even get as far as tiptoeing to the kitchen before Sybil called from her room that she could smell takeaway. Then Taya rushed in to help me unpack, and remarked how much she hated peas. Clarice finished changing from her work clothes and took over, telling me that we'd need to do some re-heating. I went away to play the more familiar role of drink waiter.

I sat down at the dinner table feeling doubly glum and decided I'd seal myself up behind a wall of silence. Then I became angry because nobody noticed. Sybil was arguing with Clarice over an ankle tattoo which Taya took to be a good opportunity to further her campaign for ear piercing. The conversation led me to thinking about Nat's hand tattoo: 'prospect and prosper' and the fact that my self-esteem had been punctured and all the air had escaped from it.

Suddenly Sibyl turned to me and said: 'I love having you home, Dad.' She showed her beautiful teeth in a laugh and added: 'And you're a pretty good cook too.'

I couldn't help it. I started crying, in big, snotty, shoulder-shaking sobs. The girls had never seen me cry, not even when my father died. They stopped eating and stared at me.

'I've fucked up my life,' I muttered nasally from behind my handkerchief.

'You're not going away again,' Taya said, preparing to join me in the mucous-fest.

'No, never,' I said. 'I just realised today how I've been robbing people of their time, the only thing they couldn't replace. A man called Raymond Ling told me as much on the phone, and then something else happened at the yacht club and the penny dropped. I don't know what to do about it.'

'Not give them their money back,' Clarice advised.

'No, I earned that. In any case, there's nowhere to give it back even if I wanted to.'

'Well, just tell them you're sorry,' Taya suggested.

Chapter Forty-Four

'That's what kids do,' I said unkindly. 'It's not enough.'

'It would be if you were the Prime Minister talking to the Aborigines,' Sybil remarked.

'I'm not talking to the Aborigines,' I replied. 'I'm talking to the people I prospected for *cafe*.'

'Why couldn't you tell them you're sorry on the phone?' Taya persisted.

'Well, for a start, a lot of them are in England. Phoning them would be too expensive.'

'Sent them little cards,' Taya continued. 'Sorry cards.'

'There's no such thing,' Sybil said.

'I'll go to the newsagent tomorrow and settle the argument,' I said as I blew my nose for the final time. 'Thanks everybody for your good ideas and let's drop the subject.'

After dinner I went to my study. The two prospecting books sat on my desk. I threw the new one into the waste paper basket and opened the other. Taya's face seemed to be watermarked on the page, and it looked across at Mr Ling's name. Okay, I'd start with him.

'Raymond Ling,' the familiar voice answered.

'Mr Ling, this is Ed Sharock.'

'Not again, Mr Sharock. What to you want this time?'

'I won't ever call you again, Mr Ling.'

'Is that what you called to tell me? If it is, why bother to call at all?'

'Raymond, I want to apologise.'

'What for?'

'Wasting your time.'

'But you are wasting more time by telling me this.'

'Well, I probably want to thank you as well. I'm done with network marketing and you helped me to see the big picture, the real picture.'

'I'm glad.'

'Can I ask you a final question? Did your daughter really go to a psychiatric hospital to be cured of network marketing?'

'It is a complicated matter,' he said, 'and you don't need to know about it. Stick with your decision. Goodbye Mr Sharock.'

I felt elated as I ruled a red line through Raymond Ling's name in my contact book.

I then called the name above his on the list.

'*Whey*,' a woman's voice answered.

'Is that Mrs Ching?' I said.

'Yes, Mrs Ching speaking here. What you want?'

'This is Ed Sharock. I want to apologise.'

'What you mean?'

'To say I'm sorry.'

'What for?'

'I tried to get you interested in pet-food. I wasted your time.'

'When you waste?'

'Two years ago.'

'I don't remember. You call tomorrow and speak to my son.' She hung up.

I realised that there were two distinct hemispheres to every apology: the maker's and the receiver's. The maker fulfilled most of his need by enunciating his apology. Its value was not dependent upon the receiver accepting it. I didn't give a bugger whether Mrs Ching had fulfilled her hemisphere or not as I ruled the red line through her name.

Starting at some random page in my book was no way to un-prospect. I leafed back to page one and began with my friends. They would be the hardest to apologise to because I'd lose so much face.

But perhaps I'd lost it anyway, and this might win some of it back. For whatever reason, I was determined to do it and I began dialling immediately. <u>By the time I stopped I had marked off twenty</u>.

As I had put the cap back on my red marker pen I noted that I had learned something else about apologising. Irrespective of how angry or how busy they were, everybody would give you a hearing if you said you'd called to apologise. Had I been interested in finding an alternative to the questioning technique, it might have been the apologising technique. People would let you go on and on, as long as you kept saying sorry for this and sorry for that. It had something to do with the play between their power and my pathos.

The next day I cooked my three girls their favourite breakfast of spicy scrambled eggs on muffins. As I clattered around the kitchen there was a warmth growing in my chest. I was becoming dedicated to purification to attain a state of grace. I was a saint in the making.

First I called Murray Pansy to tell him I wouldn't be going on with BBK but I'd buy a kit from him because I genuinely liked the idea. If I liked it, he said, why not network market it? I tried to explain that I'd had an awakening, which I didn't expect him to understand, and please not to contact me again.

***

Chapter Forty-Five

I took a striding walk to the Mosman newsagency to check on sorry cards. With saying sorry now such a national preoccupation, I was disappointed to find only two sorry cards among the hundreds covering every other occasion and human emotion. One showed a picture of a dog looking as though it has just dropped its load in the middle of the white wool carpet, with the inside wording 'oops'. The other featured a purple flower on the front with the caption: 'Please forgive me' followed up inside with 'I'm so sorry …' Neither of these would be suitable for my long list of overseas and interstate *cafe* prospects. The Channel arrived and created the words I needed:

For the hours of yours I wasted
For the dreams I gave you that never came true
For the money I said you'd make but you didn't
For the red faces I made you suffer
For the self-loathing and failure I made you feel –

I am sincerely, profoundly and utterly sorry.

Ed Sharock, former *cafe* King.

I called the once familiar number of Lead Balloon and asked to speak to Andy Hope.

'Ed, good to hear from you,' he said brightly. 'I heard about the *cafe* debacle. I'd love to know what really happened. We should meet up for a drink.'

'I'll certainly fill you in,' I replied, 'but I'm really putting *cafe* behind me. Would you be interested in doing a freelance art job for me?'

'Sure Ed, what is it?'

'Only a greeting card. I've got the wording. I just want a simple layout. How about we meet at that pub in North Sydney where we went the day we got kicked out of Lead Balloon – or thought we did.'

'Okay. I'm free tonight. Say about half after five.'

Andy had filled out since we'd met last. He'd changed from his student look, too. His clothes were now looser fitting and of better quality. He'd let his hair grow and the blonde spikes had gone. His pale blue eyes still sat behind their Holland blinds, though.

I brought our beers to a small table in the roofed garden. We spent the first hour filling in the blank two years. Finally I pulled out the rough fold of the card I wanted, along with the wording pasted inside.

'You can still write pretty well, Ed,' he remarked after he'd read it. 'I dunno what it means exactly but it sure says sorry. What do you want me to do with it?'

'Just design a nice front. I want to send this all over the world, so it has to be classic, if you follow.'

'Yes, I get it,' he said squinting at the card. 'Funny, we've been doing a few single-fold brochures lately. Like cards, really. Okay, I'll work on this one. You got any more sorry messages while I'm about it?'

'No,' I replied, but The Channel squeezed my balls. 'Well, I probably have. I'll email them to you. I don't think I'll use them for *cafe*, but who knows?'

'This is for *cafe*?' he said, raising his Holland blinds.

'Yes. I'm trying to make amends. I feel bad about misleading people and wasting their time.'

'I wouldn't worry,' Andy said. 'I reckon most of everybody's time is wasted. Anyhow, do what you have to do.'

It didn't matter what I had intended to do that night, The Channel wouldn't leave me alone. Fortunately the family had eaten dinner by the time I arrived home and I took my reheated meal into my study and closed the door. I would make my phone calls later, but I had to attend to The Channel and get some writing done first.

Sorry for making a pass at you

Sorry for drinking too much

Sorry for arriving late

Sorry for leaving early

Sorry for behaving badly

Sorry for throwing up/farting/peeing myself/insulting your guests (cross out which ever does not apply)

Sorry for forgetting to pay you the money I owe you

Sorry for losing my temper and ... (fill in)

Sorry for not being sensitive

Sorry for spoiling your night

Sorry for insulting you.

The list went on and on. I could almost hear The Channel cheering. Every time I'd reach for my prospecting book I'd be jolted back to the computer keyboard to write some more sorry card copy. I selected the best twenty sorry card texts and emailed them to Andy. The Channel eventually left me alone and I got back on my phone calls – but now I took particular note of the progress of my apologies. I began to make notes of words and sentences that got the best response.

Andy came to my house at ten o'clock the following Sunday morning – a considerable concession, since he and Hanna usually slept most of Sunday. I made us coffee and took him down to the rumpus room where the table tennis table offered the best work surface.

'We did some good stuff down here,' he said, looking around the room. 'That garden of yours is a good place to smoke and think.' He unzipped his folio case and lifted out a wad of art boards.

'You've been busy,' I remarked.

'Man, you've got something going here,' he said. 'You should take care not blow it.'

'Let's see what you did with the texts before I get carried away,' I said, although I could feel the growing approval of The Channel.

Andy had used a cut-out technique for the special *cafe* card. You could see through the word SORRY on the front so that bits of the text underneath was visible. This was a 'had-to-open' card.

'Perfect!' I said, clapping him on the shoulder. 'Now let's see what else you've got.'

He'd turned all the rest of the texts into cartoons. I'd never seen Andy's cartoons. I was struck by their perception. Even though I knew what was coming inside, I laughed out loud at every one of his drawings on the fronts of the cards.

Chapter Forty-Five

'You're right,' I said. 'These have got possibilities ...'

'That's what I'm saying. You got something. Maybe big.'

The Channel barged in, put a gag on me, and began to speak.

'The company's name is The Apology Factory. It will produce apologies for all occasions, all events. These apologies will be in the form of cards, text messages, faxes, letters, advertisements, scripts to be read on the telephone or in public. The company will make an annual award for the best public apology. Custom apologies by an experienced copywriter might be available.'

'There you go,' Andy said. 'You'd worked it all out before I got here.'

'No,' I replied, 'you threw a spark to The Channel. I'll try to explain how that works one day. I'm sure artists have their channels too.'

'Are you going to make this into a business Ed? Because if you do, I want to be art director.'

'I'll have to think it through,' I said. 'I've got to finish with network marketing first. Then The Apology Factory might be born. And if it is, you won't be art director, Andy. You'll be my partner.'

*****

ABOUT THE AUTHOR
FRASER BEATH MCEWING

A magazine editor for most of his career, Fraser Beath McEwing has written both fiction and non-fiction for leading Australian magazines and newspapers. In 1972 he founded the fashion industry newspaper *Ragtrader* and ran it for 20 years.

His first novel, Feel the Width, was published in 1994. It took a satirical look at the Australian fashion industry of the 60s. His experience, in the early 1990s, with network marketing formed the basis of this satirical novel, cafe.

*****

CONNECT WITH ME ONLINE

https://www.horizonpg.net/author-fraser-b-mcewing

http://www.horizonpg.net

*****

MORE OUTSTANDING TITLES

FROM

Horizon Publishing Group™
Publishing for Generations to Come

The shocking truth about

WOMEN

IN ISLAM

And the rights of women in Islamic law.

F. P. HANNA

WOMEN IN ISLAM

by F. P. Hanna

Non-fiction - Religion - Women's Rights - Islam

ISBN: 9781921369353 (pbk.)

One of the most serious and controversial issues of our time all over the world is the issue of the status of women in Islam and in Islamic law. The issue, for example, of wearing the Burka (the Hijab) by Muslim women in public places, schools, and in courts has recently made it to the front cover of most newspapers and magazines. Some countries have already banned the Burka in public places; others are reluctant for fear of limiting freedom and multiculturalism. But, what happens to a western woman who goes to a Muslim country, such as Saudi Arabia, where Islamic law (the Sharia) is applied? Is she allowed to wear a mini-skirt or a dress of her liking in public places? Or, is she able to wear a bikini on the beach?

Almost all Muslim scholars and writers, including women, have defended the position of women in Islam. While they draw their arguments on a very limited number of verses in the Qur'an and Hadith, however, they take them out of their context in trying to prove that women under Islam are free and have human rights.

This book shows how Islam has always considered women as inferior to men in every aspect: physically, intellectually, morally, and religiously. Their demise and denial of their basic rights are God sanctioned laws that every Muslim follows, not just 'fundamentalists'. Indeed, the Qur'an remains for all Muslims, the uncreated word of God Himself. It is valid for all times and places; its ideas are absolutely true and beyond all criticism. To question it is to question the very word of God, and hence blasphemous. A Muslim's duty is to believe it and obey its divine commands.

This non-fiction book reveals the shocking truth about the real position of women in the Qur'an and Islam, and how Islam is deeply anti-women. It reports the shocking truth of how women are denied their basic human rights in the Islamic law and in real life.

"Women in Islam" by F. P. Hanna (Horizon Publishing Group), RRP A$39.99, will be available (January 2018) from any good bookshop and from Horizon Publishing Group's URL: https://www.horizonpg.net/ OR by emailing: orders@horizonpg.net

Finding Felicity

Love struggles to triumph
over brutal violence

HELEN BRITON WHEELER

Finding Felicity

by HELEN BRITON WHEELER
Fiction

ISBN:978-1-9?????8-4? 9 (pblı)

*F***inding Felicity** is the story of a woman and her step-daughter and tells how love within their family triumphs over serious relationship problems. There are psychological insights into grief and dysfunctional marriage, development of the characters as they deal with these situations and a suspenseful escape from Bangkok to Sydney. The setting is these two cities in 2006.

Chapter One begins in Sydney with Lydia waking to face the funeral of her much-loved husband, Richard. She is supported there by her step-children, Richard's son J.C. and daughter Margaret. At the wake, the question arises: why is Felicity (Fliss), the youngest step-child, not there?

Lydia has a hunch that something is wrong in Felicity's life. When she visits the memorial garden where Richard's ashes are scattered, she feels his presence and talks to him, as she does throughout the book. She vows to Richard to visit Bangkok and look into Felicity's life there.

On the flight to Thailand, Lydia reviews the experiences and characters of her three step-children.

"Finding Felicity" **by Helen Briton Wheeler (Horizon Publishing Group), RRP AU\$24.99, available MOW from any good bookstore and from Horizon Publishing Group's URL: https://www.horizonpg.net/catalog/ OR - by emailing: orders@horizonpg.net**

A CITY GIRL STEPS OUT FROM HER COMFORT ZONE
FOR A CHALLENGING LIFE IN THE OUTBACK

Life
as it is

REBECCA BURGE

Life as it is

by Rebecca Burge

Non-fiction - Biography – Rural women– Mothers – Ranch life – Country life – Northern Queensland

ISBN: 978-1-922238-60-3 (pbk,)

"Life as it is", is what it is-My Life! My name is Rebecca Burge and I haven't always lived on a cattle property in far North Queensland. I was born and bred in Adelaide, South Australia. Growing up in the small country town of Gawler and then spending all my secondary years in Adelaide. The story only touches on my early years and is predominantly about my years on Lamonds Lagoon Station, North Queensland.

I married a "cattle man" and moved from the comforts of city life to the isolation of the bush. It is about all the little stories along the way and some of the different experiences I have had to deal with.

Lamonds Lagoon is four to five hours from the major towns of Charters Towers, Townsville and Cairns. I educated my five boys through Distance Education to the end of year 7. The boys all have their different personalities and this is characterised in this story.

If something is to go wrong, it will. This has only made our life more interesting with many a story to tell. There have been countless snake stories, many animal stories. There have been dramas in the classroom. We have had some interesting Christmas's and a couple of bush christenings. We have experienced all the elements when it comes to disasters. The floods of 2009, Cyclone Yasi, which we are still recovering from and then the bushfires. Droughts are upon us at the moment.

In summary, I moved out of my comfort zone into an unknown "world" away from family, friends and shops. I have experienced so much in these years and it has not always been easy but what stands out beyond all doubt is how important family is, and while we are all healthy and happy, then we are the lucky ones!

"Life as it is" by Rebecca Burge (Horizon Publishing Group), RRP AU$32.99, available NOW from any good bookstore and from Horizon Publishing Group's URL: https://www.horizonpg.net/ - OR - by emailing:

orders@horizonpg.net

F. P. Hanna

BABYLON
THE HARLOT
OF THE SEVEN HILLS

BABYLON
THE HARLOT
OF THE SEVEN HILLS

by F. P. Hanna

Non-fiction - Religion

ISBN: 978-1-922238-08-5 (pbk.)

The author writes:

"I have always been intrigued by the book of 'Revelation'".

The book of *'Revelation'* has been the food for thought for many centuries and predicts the future of humanity. One specific part is chapter 17 in which St John states the following:

"Babylon the Great, the Mother of Prostitutes and Abominations of the Earth."

"...I saw a woman sit upon a scarlet coloured beast, full of names of blasphemy, having seven heads....
And the woman was arrayed in purple and scarlet colour, and decked with gold and precious stones and pearls, having a golden cup in her hand full of abominations and filthiness of her fornication....
And the woman which thou sawest is that great city, which reigneth over the kings of the earth.
And here is the mind which hath wisdom. The seven heads are seven mountains [or hills], on which the woman sitteth."

Revelation: 17:3,4,18,9"

Now, many scholars of different religions attempted over the past two millennia to find out who is *"The Harlot"* and where it sits.

It is very clear from the same chapter that it is a "city", not a country, not a religion. But there is about eighty (80) cities worldwide that sit on seven hills. Religions accuse each other of being the *"Harlot"* as while the Jews say it is "Rome", however, Christians say it is "Jerusalem".

No one has ever found which city it is and who is the *"Beast"*.

You will be amazed to find out in this book who is really the *"Harlot"*, who is really the *"Beast"*, and a detailed explanation of the days we are living in and a glimpse of … the future.

Letters from
THE FRONT

Carte Postale — Postcard

DOROTHY GILDING

LETTERS FROM THE FRONT

by Dorothy Gilding

Non-fiction - World War One - Gallipoli - Australian History

ISBN: 9781921369544 (pbk.)

"There were dead men everywhere, and a good number of our cavalry. We passed Fritz artillery with dead horses attached to their limbers. I come across a wounded Fritz. He was just a young boy and our tanks had run over him. A crew of five had a gun mounted in a shell-hole and the tank had flattened it into the ground, killing the rest. He had both his legs broken and had a very pitiful look. I gave him a drink of water and poked a stick in the ground with a white rag around it so our stretcher bearers would pick him up."

*L*etters From The Front is an authentic account of World War One through the eyes of an ordinary soldier, the story of one man. It seeks to add to our national consciousness of the immeasurable value and sacrifice of all those who have served our country, and our damaged heroes who survived, without in any way glorifying war.

Jim McConnell takes us with him to Gallipoli, Villers-Bretonneux and the Somme Canal to gain another glimpse of the events that symbolise courage, comradeship and sacrifice, and that cost Australia a generation.

As a first-person narrative, it strives to preserve the authenticity of the time and place in which these events occurred; to simply tell the story without twenty-first century judgements, embellishments or condemnations. Much of the story comes directly from this important primary source of actual diary notes. This is a valuable contribution to our World War One literature because so little was passed on in the generations that followed.

It also teaches us how to live well in an imperfect world. Jim McConnell saw people as people, and treated them accordingly, willing to fight and quick to forgive. He then made the most of the life he was left with in postwar Australia.

"Letters from The Front" by Dorothy Gilding (Horizon Publishing Group), RRP A$49.99, available NOW from any good bookshop and from Horizon Publishing Group's URL: https://www.horizonpg.net/ OR by emailing:
orders@horizonpg.net

THE BANK
INSPECTOR

ROGER MONK

THE BANK INSPETOR

by Roger Monk

Fiction - Bank Roberry - Crime/Thriller

ISBN: 978-1-922238-37-5 (ppk.)

One Monday morning, a bank branch is robbed.

No one hurt or threatened.

Not a hold-up.

Not a tunnel into the vault.

A three minutes' robbery and the robber drives away. Not followed. Not caught.

A perfect, flawless crime.

Detective Sergeant Brian Shaw hardly knows where to start, especially as he is distracted by an attempted murder in a nearby street.

A story of greed, treachery and a heart-breaking family feud.

"The Bank Inspector" by Roger Monk (Horizon Publishing Group), RRP AU$24.99, available NOW from any good bookstore and from Horizon Publishing Group's URL: https://www.horizonpg.net/
OR by emailing:

orders@horizonpg.net

THE BANK MANAGER

ROGER MONK

THE BANK MANAGER

by Roger Monk

Fiction - Bank Roberry - Crime/Thriller

ISBN: 9978-1-922238-57-3 (ppk.)

Detective Sergeant Brian Shaw is transferred to a country town. Just an ordinary, average Australian country town where nothing ever happens — except blackmail, fornication, embezzlement, revenge, avarice, brutality, snobbery, rape ... and murder.

Like any other ordinary, average Australian country town.

"The Bank Manager" by Roger Monk (Horizon Publishing Group), RRP AU$24.99, available NOW from any good bookstore and from Horizon Publishing Group's URL: https://www.horizonpg.net/
OR by emailing:

orders@horizonpg.net

THE BANK TELLER

"A thoroughly entertaining yarn"
Fair Dinkum Crime

ROGER MONK

THE BANK TELLER

by Roger Monk
Fiction - Bank Roberry - Crime/Thriller
ISBN. 970-1-022238-74-0 (ppk.)

A top executive dies suddenly.
An accident?
A murder?
An inside job?
Hundreds of suited suspects in one city office
Detective Sergeant Brian Shaw is recalled from Yorke
Peninsula.
From sleepy country town to throbbing city throngs,
clashing personalities, old scores to be settled,
frustrated ambitions, jealousies,
and something new: female tellers.
A hotbed of suspicions from managing director to tea
lady.
And who started the rumour that one of the tellers may
be involved?
Why? Who?
Know why and you may know who!

"The Bank Teller" by Roger Monk (Horizon Publishing
Group), RRP AU$24.99, available NOW from any good
bookstore and from Horizon Publishing Group's URL:
https://www.horizonpg.net/
OR by emailing: orders@horizonpg.net

THE·ANOINTED·ONE

HERB HAMLET

THE ANOINTED ONE

by Herb Hamlet
Fiction - Religion - Christianity
ISBN: 9781922238047 (pbk.)

With the election of a black Pope, *"The Anointed One"* boldly explores a world where the Catholic Church becomes a progressive faith that adapts to the modern world in which it lives. The book gives articulate and well thought out arguments for why the Church should change and these arguments will give readers much to think about.

Prologue

The first black Pope undergoes a near-death experience. He receives a clear message from Christ. Churches must use their vast resources to help the sick and the poor of the Third World. Outdated policies on artificial contraception, celibacy, and women in the Church must go.

"The Anointed One" **by Herb Hamlet (Horizon Publishing Group), RRP AU$32.99, available NOW from any good bookstore and from Horizon Publishing Group's URL: https://www.horizonpg.net/ - OR - by emailing:**

orders@horizonpg.net

A Place of

Light

Jessica Warcon

A Place of Light

Young-Adult fiction
ISBN: 978-1-922238-46-7

John was a forestry worker responsible for looking after protected forests. His job was to make sure people weren't cutting trees down or stealing precious plants and endangering the forest's ecosystems.

But today he was on holiday getting a much deserved rest, and he knew no better place to rest than in the forest which he loved so much. Lisa also loved nature, and they both wanted their baby daughter to love nature as much as they did.

On the drive to their campsite a couple days before, the little family had stopped at a local shop to look at some antiques. There were some beautiful pendant necklaces said to protect whoever wore them. In the spirit of fun, John bought one each for his wife and baby. Although the chain was much too long for one so small, John had immediately fastened one of the pendants around the baby's neck. Instead of wearing hers, Lisa had fastened her necklace to the wrist strap attached to her camera.

They lived only a short drive from this forest, but they wanted to explore parts of it at their leisure—something John couldn't do with his family when he was working. Today they were going to hike to the top of the mountain near their camp. They readied their supplies and put the baby into a backpack on John's back. They put out the fire from the night before and headed off on their hike, leaving some of their gear at the campsite. They knew no one else would be in the forest at this time of year and their campsite would be safe.

"A Place of Light" by **Monica Warcon (Horizon Publishing Group), RRP AU$19.99, available NOW from any good bookstore and from Horizon Publishing Group's URL: https://www.horizonpg. net/ - OR - by emailing:**

orders@horizonpg.net

BUT ONE HEARTBEAT AWAY

A PASSIONATE TALE OF LOVE AND ADVENTURE
IN THE MAGNIFICENT WILDS OF AFRICA

JETTE CHRISTENSEN

BUT ONE HEARTBEAT AWAY

By Jette Christensen

Fiction

ISBN: 9781921369773 (pbk.)

*M*alaika, who's name in Ki-Swahili means guardian angel, is assigned to guide six carefree tourists on a two-weeks safari in Africa. The men sceptical of having a female leader, become even more pessimistic when their compatriots are lost. The group's trip around the country leaves trail of blood. The mystery of what causes their deaths is frighteningly unclear to Malaika when she travels back to headquarters to make her incredible report. Heartbroken, she attempts to unravel the whys and wherefores of the strange circumstances of her clients' disappearances. The taboos and evil spells of Africa are posed against her.

"But One Heartbeat Away" brings the reader into the heart of Africa and gives them a remarkable insight into the natural and cultural landscape of this colourful and fascinating continent. The reader is treated to a host of unique and interesting characters whose adventures through this exotic land are sure to delight and enthral.

"BUT ONE HEARTBEAT AWAY" by Jette Christensen (Horizon Publishing Group), RRP AU$29.99, available NOW from any good bookstore and from Horizon Publishing Group's URL: https://www.horizonpg.net/catalog/ - OR - by emailing:

orders@horizonpg.net

Horizon Publishing Group™
Publishing for Generations to Come

2019